BLOOD
OF
ANCIENTS

SARA C. ROETHLE

CHAPTER ONE

Lyssandra

Daylight woke me. I had been trapped in this wretched carriage for nearly a week. At night, Cael sat with me, though I had nothing to say to him. During the day, it was Xavier or Cerridwen. I had no desire to speak with them either, but I tried. Any information that might help me was worth digging for.

I had no idea who currently drove the horses outside. Probably some poor human possessed by Eiric. I'd caught glimpses of the drivers, but they never looked my way. Eiric himself was yet to make an appearance within the carriage. I suspected he was off somewhere else, implementing other areas of his plan.

Even with him gone, any escape attempt would prove futile. I was defenseless. I knew others rode outside the carriage. I could hear them whispering. I suspected Cerridwen and Xavier were often out there during the

1

night. Or perhaps sleeping in another carriage where I couldn't smother them to death.

Without my sword or my magic, I could not best them. And . . . I wasn't sure I wanted to try. I wanted away from them, yes. And even more I wanted to know if Asher, Tholdri, Steifan . . . *everyone*—I wanted to know if they were still alive.

But escaping Eiric would put me back to the beginning, unable to locate him and unable to divine his plan. No, I was better off playing along, for now. Once we reached Ivangard—

My thoughts halted as the carriage slowed and the door opened. But it was just for Xavier to climb inside. I caught a glimpse of another man on a horse. I didn't recognize him.

The door shut behind Xavier, and I heard the lock outside sliding into place, then we started moving again. I stared at the door. Normally a lock would be found *inside* the carriage, but this one had been prepared especially for me.

On the occasions I was let outside to relieve myself in the dark of night, it felt like I was walking on quicksand. All my body knew was the jolting and rocking of the carriage. Sometimes other members of our small entourage would glance my way, but the glances were never helpful.

Xavier sat back against the cushions across from me. His clothing was different today. Usually he wore simple fabrics in muted tones. Today his tunic was green brocade. His linen pants, a darker green, were fitted to his body. Even his normally shaggy light brown hair had been trimmed.

He watched me from beneath his shortened bangs. "No insults today?"

"I think you enjoy them too much." I had been given fresh clothing as well. Gray woolen breeches, a simple cream shirt, and a pale blue traveling cloak with a deep hood. The outfit was not one I would have chosen, but it was better than Xavier's. I said as much, with a few obscenities sprinkled in.

The corner of his mouth curled. "Ah, there we go. That's better. I was beginning to think all the fight had gone out of you."

"No, I'm just saving it for when I decide to kill you."

"I can't wait."

And he wasn't lying. I knew he still wanted me to kill him, to free him from Eiric. It was a strange relationship we had. We were enemies, but in a way, we were also allies.

I crossed my arms and leaned back against the cushions, resisting the urge to fiddle with the silver bracelet embedded into my skin, cutting me off from my magic. "When will we reach Ivangard?"

"Tonight. I'm surprised you haven't tried to escape."

"I can't kill Eiric if I'm not near him."

He leaned forward, bracing his elbows on his knees. "You know, I feel the same way. And just look at all the good it has done me." His words dripped with sarcasm.

"Women often succeed where men fail."

He laughed. "I will try to maintain my faith, then."

I sighed heavily, tilting my head to look out a narrow

strip of window visible between the curtains. I couldn't see the ocean, but I spotted a gull in the distance. Tonight, we would reach Ivangard. And I wasn't sure where I would go from there.

Silence stretched on. I could feel Xavier watching me, but I kept my attention on that distant gull.

"You know, he was a good man once."

I didn't acknowledge him. If he wanted to speak of Eiric's alleged virtues, I would hear none of it.

"He was my best friend. When we were young, he would have done anything for anyone."

I finally looked at him. "If you think I care, you are mistaken."

He tilted his head. "You are a noble woman for now, Lyssandra. I only hope you can remember yourself once that bracelet is removed." He nodded toward my wrist. "I hope you can remember your purpose after you have experienced undiluted blood magic. It will be different now, without your master to hold your leash."

The carriage went over a few more bumps, then the road smoothed considerably. The city was close. I stared at Xavier, unsure of what to say. "Was Eiric telling the truth when he said he could keep the magic from consuming me?"

He leaned his head back against the cushions, looking up at the wooden roof. "Perhaps he could help you, for a time, but if I were you, I wouldn't trust a single word he says."

"I don't. I just want to know if there is a way."

"Nothing is set in stone. Not life. Not death. You know that better than most."

4

I heard voices outside as the carriage slowed, and distantly, I could hear the city. Xavier's estimation that we would make it there at nightfall was likely correct. It was difficult to tell now that I no longer had the keen hearing of a human servant.

I wondered where I would be taken within the city. Probably a dungeon. I also wondered where Tholdri and the others were, and if they were trying to find me. I knew if Asher was still alive, he wouldn't be far. Even without the bond, he would come for me.

I wished I could tell him to give me time. I could play Eiric's game, for now. All I had to do was somehow outsmart a being so ancient, just thinking about it made my teeth hurt. Simple. I was used to the odds never being in my favor. I had survived this long.

Xavier lifted his head to watch me. "My, that's an unsettling expression. I wonder what thoughts are churning around in that skull of yours."

I answered him with a cold smile.

He replied with a smile of his own, just as cold, and far more . . . unsettling.

"Where will we go once we reach the city?" I asked.

"To the temple. Your new jailers will be the witches of Ivangard."

I considered his words, remembering blue flames sweeping through the streets. The witches of Ivangard had fought beside Eiric.

Xavier's smile broadened. "Well, at least it's not difficult to guess what you're thinking *now*."

"Which is?"

He laughed. "The witches killed many the night you were taken. You want revenge."

My only reply was a blank stare. He was right. There was no reason for me to confirm it.

The carriage halted. Voices murmured outside.

"Have you ever been to Ivangard?" Xavier asked.

"No."

He smirked. "Well then you're in for a treat. Do try to enjoy yourself."

Once again, I only stared. The only joy I would find would come when I chopped off Eiric's head, burned his body, and scattered the ashes across the sea.

THE CARRIAGE AMBLED through the city for a long while as the sky slowly darkened beyond the curtains. Some areas carried the scent of ale, fresh baked bread, and roasted meats, while others reeked of refuse. No one questioned us, though judging by the sound of horses' hooves on the surrounding cobbles, we currently had only a small retinue.

Xavier hadn't spoken again since we entered the city, which was just as well. I did my best to memorize every turn, and stole glances beyond the curtains whenever I could. Knowledge of the city's layout could prove invaluable in the time to come.

The sky turned black by the time we stopped, though lanterns blazed against the darkness. Wherever we had ended up, it was quiet.

Xavier leaned forward as the carriage door opened.

Cael stood outside with two other men I did not recognize. Both wore pale blue livery the color of my cloak, with swords belted at their waists. Judging by the way they held themselves, my guess was that they knew how to use the swords. They were both in their middle years, one with dark hair, and one with silver.

Cael stood out in stark contrast with his crimson hair and black clothing. He was also a good head taller than either of them. I always thought I got my height from my hunter blood, but it wasn't true. My height came from my Blackmire heritage.

Cael watched me from beneath his furrowed brow. The last words we had exchanged had not been pleasant.

When I made no move to exit the carriage, he offered me his hand.

I looked at it like it was a venomous snake. "I don't think so."

Chuckling to himself, Xavier pushed out of the carriage between us. He stepped around the silver-haired guard, then offered me his hand with a mocking smile.

It was petty, and I only did it to hurt Cael, but I took it.

Xavier's hand was warm and dry, gripping my fingers as I walked down the carriage steps, my new boots clicking on the cobbles below. Xavier released my hand, then reached toward my shoulders.

I jerked away.

"Easy now. You need to look the part."

Realizing what he was getting at, I held still as he lifted the hood of my pale blue traveling cloak over my head, covering my hair.

I took a moment to observe the gated courtyard and

7

the temple beyond. The tall walls were white and pristine, with carved buttresses and arched windows. Dozens of lanterns blazed needlessly, lighting up every decorative alcove. The gates were open for our arrival, though we hadn't ridden through. A few other riders surrounded the carriage, none of them looking our way. As far as I could tell, they were human.

I turned as one white door opened beyond the gates, revealing a woman in a similar cloak to my own. Her blonde hair had a reddish hue, but it was nothing like mine. It fell in a shining curtain around her round face. She smiled across the courtyard at us.

Xavier leaned in near my shoulder. "Don't be fooled," he whispered. "She would love to see you dead."

"She can get in line," I muttered.

The two unnamed men fell in behind me while Cael moved to my other side. Everyone watched the approaching *priestess*.

She pressed her palms together as she walked through the open gates, then stopped in front of us, looking me up and down. This close, I realized she was older than I had first thought. Light lines decorated the corners of her slightly uptilted brown eyes.

"Sister Yonvrode, we have anxiously awaited your arrival." Her smile was that of a gracious hostess.

"At least *someone* is excited about it," I muttered.

Her smile faltered, then quickly re-established itself. "Yes, well, you must be exhausted. I can show you to your chamber. Please, come in." She gave the men around me a dismissive look.

Xavier stepped closer. "She does not go anywhere

without an escort. I believe you were already informed of the rules, Gwenvere."

Her smile slipped away, and this time did not return. "*Sister Haith*. And I am more than capable of watching over her."

"We must both do as we are bade, *Sister Haith*." Xavier's smile said that he could stand here forever, waiting for her to back down. I wondered if she knew it was true.

She pursed her lips, then darted her gaze to Cael. "I don't know you."

"He is her uncle," Xavier explained. "Eiric wants him here."

Her expression pinched further, but at the mention of Eiric's name, she didn't argue. Did she know just what he was, or was she simply an unwitting pawn in his game?

"Very well," she said finally. "Welcome to our temple, Cael. This way." She turned and walked back the way she had come.

Xavier gestured for me to follow. Cael was silent at my other side.

If I wanted to escape, this was probably my last chance. Cael had betrayed me, but I didn't think he would hurt me.

I lifted my nose and marched forward. I was here now, and I would see it through to the bitter end. I knew now that the only way to defeat Eiric was to get close to him. I would do what I must.

I followed the woman—Gwenvere—into the temple. The passage was more narrow than I had anticipated. She took up a lantern from the floor against the wall, glancing back at me. "I'm told you're not to be placed with the other acolytes. You will have your own private chamber. It is an honor reserved for very *few*."

When I said nothing in reply, she continued walking, and I followed. She had said *chamber*, not cell. And here I had been quite sure I was to end up in a dungeon.

Cael and Xavier followed, shutting the other two men outside.

I didn't acknowledge either of them. I simply watched Gwenvere from within the shadows of my hood. She walked with a slight limp, almost imperceptible, but it grew more pronounced as she went up a set of stone stairs.

I followed her, my muscles tense and aching from too much time spent sitting. At least with a private chamber, I should have enough room to move around and regain my strength.

I memorized our progress as she led the way down several dimly lit corridors, finally ending at one of many closed doors. I noticed a fresh lock mounted into the stone beside the door. It was the only one I had seen. None of the other doors locked from the outside.

So I wouldn't quite be in a cell, but it was close. Since I no longer possessed the strength of a human servant, I might not be able to break down the heavy oak door.

Gwenvere opened the door, then ushered me inside.

I stepped into the room, then took a moment to stare. It was most certainly not what I had expected.

A large, fourposter bed took up one corner with an ornate woven rug beneath it. Candles lit a bedside table, the polished, cherry-hued wood matching a second larger table with two chairs beneath an arched window. Against the opposite wall, a matching armoire loomed in the shadows. Another door led to a modest bathing chamber.

"I will fetch you in the morning," Gwenvere said tersely, "and we'll have a long . . . *chat.*"

I turned to demand an explanation, but she was already walking out the door, leaving me alone with Xavier and Cael.

"Why am I here?"

"You have much to learn, Lyssandra." Xavier took a step back toward the door.

I looked at Cael, hoping he would offer me something more, but he simply gave me a sad smile, then followed Xavier through the doorway. He turned back for a moment like he might say something, but then he shut the door. I heard the lock sliding into place outside.

More confused than frightened, I quickly searched the room, looking first under the bed then within the armoire. I didn't want to go to sleep when surprises might lurk. There was nothing under the bed, and only more clothes like the ones I was wearing within the armoire, though the cloaks were thinner, more suited to daily wear.

Finally, I took one of the lit candles into the bathing chamber, but found nothing of interest. A bath would have been lovely, but the small wooden tub was empty.

I carried the candle back toward the bed. At least I could lie stretched out—not curled up on a carriage cushion—though sleep would not come easy.

But I needed it now, just as much as any other mortal. I lowered myself to the burgundy blankets, stretching out my stiff limbs. I reeked of blood, sweat, and a week's worth of travel despite my fresh clothing. Perhaps that was the real reason Gwenvere's expression had been so pinched, though I doubted it.

I laid on my back and stared up at the fabric draping the bed posts, wondering where Asher was, and what condition he was in. I wanted to see him more than anything, but if he was still alive, as Cael claimed, I needed him to stay away. If he tried to rescue me now, he would only get himself killed.

I didn't need rescuing. I needed him safe. The rescuing part I could take care of myself.

CHAPTER TWO

I woke feeling no more rested than the night before. Soft sunlight shone through the nearby window, cutting across the small bare table. The door remained locked all night, but I had slid a chair beneath the handle just in case. Even if someone managed to push it out of the way, I would at least have some warning before they came into the room.

I almost wished an ambush *had* occurred. The room was too quiet. Without my bond with Asher, and without my sword, I felt . . . alone. Truly alone for the first time in a long while. I found I didn't care for it.

I climbed out of bed. I had slept in my clothing, leaving my new boots on the floor. Perhaps today I would be offered a bath, but I wasn't betting on it. I froze at the sound of footsteps outside my door. The lock slid out of place.

I was near the window with my back to the wall by the time the door smacked against the chair.

"Oh, *Lyssandra*," I heard Cerridwen sigh.

I stayed where I was. The door slowly scooted the chair out of the way, revealing both Cerridwen and Gwenvere wearing matching blue cloaks. I had already put together that the cloaks were the garb of the Ivangard priestesses. We were all blending in, though Gwenvere was probably an actual priestess.

Or an actual witch. I knew it was a possibility that she had magic, though I had seen no signs of it the prior night. She did feel . . . different. Maybe I should have been able to sense it with ease, but the entire place felt strange to me, like my skin was buzzing even with the bracelet cutting off my magic.

Cerridwen stepped into the room ahead of Gwenvere. Her dark heavy hair hung like a second cloak around her. She was lovely, and ancient. A dangerous combination. I preferred her as Teresa, though she had never reapplied the glamour once her true identity was revealed.

She looked me up and down, wrinkling her nose. "A bath first, I think. We don't want to torture the other acolytes with her stench."

Gwenvere nodded sharply. "And the hair will need to be dyed. We don't want her standing out. Those within the temple are loyal, but some still hold old fears about such red hair."

My heart fluttered. It was silly vanity, but I was attached to the color of my hair. Before I could argue, Cerridwen snapped, "*No*. The hair stays."

I wasn't sure why she was defending me, but I clicked my jaw shut.

Gwenvere's cheeks reddened, but she didn't argue.

Instead, she gave me a sharp look. "Do you need a moment before we head to the baths?"

I was surprised she would even ask. "Yes."

"Very well." She went for the door, glancing back at Cerridwen, who stood with her arms crossed, watching me. Shaking her head, Gwenvere went out into the hall, shutting the door behind her.

Ignoring Cerridwen, I went to the small bathing chamber to make use of the chamber pot. I took my time combing my fingers through my loose dirty hair, then went back into the room and sat on the bed, tugging on each of my boots. I tightened my laces as slow as humanly possible, dutifully ignoring Cerridwen's watchful eyes.

I tied my boot strings into perfect bows, then stood, stretching my arms over my head.

"You're so much like her, I almost feel as if I have gone back in time."

I finally looked at her. "Like who?"

"Lavandriel. It's not just her appearance. You have her demeanor."

"That almost sounds like a compliment."

One corner of her full lips curled. "Merely an observation."

"You miss her." I didn't really care, but information was information. And allies were allies. From our conversations in the carriage I knew there wasn't much hope of turning Cerridwen, but endearing myself could grant me small liberties that might pay off in the end.

"I do."

"And yet, you let her believe you were dead?"

She stalked closer, her movements predatory. She was

smaller than me, fragile even, but I knew it was a mask. "She betrayed me, in the end. She didn't trust me with the key to Eiric's tomb."

"Can you really blame her?"

She lifted a brow. "No, I suppose I cannot. But it doesn't matter now. I am here, and she is nothing more than dust in the wind."

"How did she die?" It was an answer I wanted more than most any other. Lavandriel had blood magic, and as far as I knew, it never twisted her.

"I don't know. She had children, else you would not exist. The blood magic did not consume her as it did Eiric. Lavandriel was stronger than anyone I've ever known." Her dark eyes glinted in the morning light. "Stronger than you, Lyssandra. You won't be able to fight it."

My stomach churned. I lifted my arm, letting my sleeve fall to reveal the bracelet embedded in my skin. "I don't think I have anything to fight." With the bracelet, my magic was gone. And without magic, madness and corruption would not come.

"It will be removed during your lessons, and replaced when you return to your chamber." She stepped even closer until she had to tilt her head to look up at me. "We will hone your magic until you are ready. You will serve your purpose, then you will surely be consumed."

I leaned my head down toward her face. "I wonder if you will be alive to see it." So much for endearing myself to her.

Her lips parted. *Sensual* was the only word to describe her. "I have been alive just as long as Eiric, Lyssandra."

Her hushed words slithered from those full lips. "Do you really think you stand any chance of killing me?"

I wrinkled my nose, leaning close enough to kiss. "Ask me how many *old* things I have killed."

"You reek of blood and sweat," she hissed.

"I hope you choke on it."

The door creaked open behind her, revealing Gwenvere. At Cerridwen's sharp look, she muttered, "We're late already."

Cerridwen shook herself like a bird settling its feathers. "Come, Lyssandra." With a flick of her cloak, she turned and marched toward the door.

Having nowhere else to go, I followed. I might have lost any chance of Cerridwen liking me, but I had also figured out how to get under her skin, and that could prove useful in its own right.

Gwenvere stood stiffly as I walked past her out the door. I still wasn't sure what her role was in everything, but I would make it my next mission to find out.

AFTER SUFFERING the not so tender treatment of Gwenvere brushing out my tangled hair before my bath, I was led to a large atrium where four *acolytes* waited. I fingered the end of my damp braid as a pair of male guards shut the arched doors behind us. Some of my hair had been singed from Charles' fire the night of the battle. Gwenvere had cut off the uneven bits, leaving my braid much shorter than before. Of course, if she had her way, I would probably be bald.

She stepped away from my side and approached the acolytes, leaving Cerridwen back with me. Beautiful trees, the likes of which I had never seen, loomed around us, stretching toward the sunlight provided by massive panes of glass. Manicured plants sprouted from pots all around, some of them blooming with brilliant hues.

I should have been observing the four acolytes, determining who might be a weak link, but I couldn't tear my eyes away from the plants.

"Blooms from Wendshore and beyond," Cerridwen explained, watching me with amusement. "Some medicinal, some poisonous, and some with magical attributes. Which are the most useful depends on the user."

I rolled my eyes toward her. "Let me guess, you prefer the poisonous ones?"

Gwenvere turned toward us, giving her back to the four acolytes. She extended one hand toward me.

I simply stared at her.

Muttering under her breath, she strode across the carved stepping stones between us, her hand still extended. "The bracelet, Lyssandra. We must remove it for you to learn."

Wary, I held out my wrist.

She pushed up my sleeve, chanted a few words I didn't recognize but quickly tried to memorize, then ran her finger along the metal embedded in my skin. The bracelet fell away, dropping into her other hand. I had suspected pain and blood, but my skin was unblemished.

For a moment, nothing happened, then I gasped as magic lit up my veins, as if it was angry to be suppressed for so long. I had felt it briefly after my bond with Asher was severed, but it had been nothing like this. It built up in my chest, hammering against my ribcage to be released. Cael was right. The bond had greatly dampened what had been growing inside me these past years. This was—

Forcing a deep, aching breath, I repeated Gwenvere's words ten times over in my head, but I had a feeling I already had a few of them wrong. My mind seemed to ripple like disturbed water. The magic had startled me, and now it might have lost me the key to removing the bracelet.

"Don't bother," Gwenvere said, reading my expression. "I created the bracelet. You won't be able to remove it yourself."

I deflated slightly, but continued repeating the words in my mind, just in case. The magic settled into my core like it belonged there. Maybe it did. Maybe it should have been there, full force, all along. It hadn't been this way when I was young. My grandfather had been unwilling to wait and see what would become of me.

Cerridwen stepped closer. Until she moved, I had nearly forgotten her. She held a hand toward me, palm out, but didn't touch me. "It really is just like hers— Lavandriel. Eiric was right."

Gwenvere scrutinized me, but her words were for Cerridwen. "If she truly is a blood witch, she'll be difficult to teach."

"You'll figure it out." Cerridwen turned and picked one of the quiet acolytes out of the lineup. They were all young with varying skin tones and hair colors, like they had been plucked from different far off regions. Maybe they had. Though I had met many witches recently, magic overall was rare . . . if they all were actually witches. I still couldn't tell. With my magic restored, everything felt lit up in a different way. I sensed almost as much from the trees as I did from any of the women present.

The girl Cerridwen pointed at smiled. She was of average build, her hair mousy brown, but her eyes . . . I could have sworn oceans roiled within. Watching my expression, her smile broadened. "I've always wanted to see what a blood witch can do."

"Then you are a fool." Cerridwen stepped back as far as the nearest tree would allow. The white trunk stretched up above her, tall enough that the fan-shaped leaves skimmed the glass panes overhead. If it grew much taller, it would need to be cut down.

I tore my gaze away from Cerridwen as the acolyte moved up beside Gwenvere. "Should I give her all I've got?"

Gwenvere pursed her lips. "Yes, but don't kill her."

I tensed. The girl had no weapons, but depending on her magic, she might not need them. "Would someone care to explain what's going on?"

Gwenvere gave me a tired look. "I need to see what you can do. Once I am aware of your skills, I can devise the best way to teach you actual control over your magic. I'm told you'll need it." She glanced at Cerridwen. "Although it would help to know what I'm teaching you *for.*"

Cerridwen wrinkled her nose. "You'll teach her enough control to perform a complex ritual. That's all you need to know."

Gwenvere sighed, then gestured for the mousy-haired acolyte to get on with it.

The next thing I knew, a wave of blue fire was barreling my way, singing the plants just like it would singe my skin. I dove aside, rolling across the stepping stones while reflexively reaching for my sword. But of course, it wasn't there.

I darted behind a tree trunk, annoyed by the laughter of the other three acolytes. "What exactly is the point of this?" I called out, crouching low, ready to spring away again.

I couldn't see Cerridwen from my hiding place, but she spoke loud enough for me to hear her answer. "You weren't simply going to attack her if I ordered you to do so."

"You could have given me the chance!"

"You still have it, Lyssandra. Defend yourself."

Another wave of blue flame emphasized her words, slamming into the tree in front of me. Heat licked my face as I darted away again. The atrium was large, but there were only so many trees to hide behind. I needed enough space from my attacker to come up with a plan. I had my magic now—I might be able to take out Cerridwen too. But . . . she wasn't bleeding. I still didn't know enough.

Another wave of blue flame licked my heels as I ran past the backs of the other three acolytes toward the opposite end of the atrium.

"You can't just keep running, Lyssandra!" Cerridwen called out to me. "You are a witch of Lavandriel's line! *Prove it.*"

I'd gladly prove it if I knew how. Hunkering down

behind another trunk, I focused on my attacker. But I couldn't *feel* her. I needed a blood connection. I could just barely see her face through the dense leaves as she scanned the foliage for my hiding spot. She wasn't even winded. It was as if casting the blue flames cost her nothing at all, which didn't make sense. All magic had a price.

Spotting me, she smiled. Her flames spewed so abruptly that I didn't move quite fast enough. Some of them caught my cloak, burning through the fabric in an instant.

"Don't kill her," Gwenvere hissed.

"Don't worry, I'll just make her *hurt.*"

I barely heard the girl's reply as I ran behind another tree. I needed to act. I might not be at risk of losing my life, but I certainly didn't want to lose my skin either. I had no way to wound the girl, but I might not need to. When I had briefly stolen Ophelia's magic, she hadn't been bleeding. She'd simply gotten my blood on her fingers.

Of course, I had few options for making myself bleed either.

More flames licked my heels. The girl and the other three acolytes were following my movements now, herding me toward one corner of the atrium. Curse it all. What I needed to do next was not going to be pleasant. As I ran, I scooped up a small broken branch. I scraped it against the inside of my palm as hard as I could.

I had no time to look down as I fled to another hiding place—my *last* hiding place—but the sharp sting let me know I'd drawn at least a little bit of blood. From the

24

cover of long, drooping leaves as big as I was, I could see the girl lifting her hands, readying another wave of flame. If she singed my cover, there was nowhere left to run.

I picked up a nearby pot and barreled out of hiding, hurling the pot her way. Thanks to my lack of vampire strength, it didn't quite make it to her, but it did what I needed. She looked down at it long enough for me to tackle her to the ground. The nearest acolyte screeched, staggering back, but I was already on my feet again, running past them before my main attacker could gather more flame.

I heard her cursing behind me. I wasn't sure where Gwenvere had gone, but I caught Cerridwen watching me with a bemused expression as I ran past. I would have liked to smack the smile right off her face, but one thing at a time.

Someone must have helped the girl to her feet, because more blue flame chased me. But something was different now. I could *feel* her. She hadn't noticed the blood I'd wiped across her cheek when I'd tackled her.

I grabbed a slender trunk to spin myself back in the other direction as I willed my blood to chill. The cut on my hand went cold.

"What the—" I heard the girl say.

The other acolytes whispered around her, but I drowned them out, focusing on my blood. The moisture on my palm turned to ice. My teeth chattered. It was always like this, attacking someone else's blood also affected my own, but it was a delayed effect. I had nearly given Ian hypothermia without freezing more than just the blood on my skin.

"That's enough, Lyssandra!" Cerridwen called out.

If I weren't freezing and also out of breath from all the running, I would have laughed. I couldn't reverse the magic, even if I wanted to. I hid behind another trunk, planning my next move.

Suddenly, pain wracked my body. I staggered out of hiding involuntarily, but it wasn't the acolytes who had found me. It was Gwenvere. She held one hand out toward me. "Sorry about this."

She clenched her fist, and it was like my body was being torn apart from the inside. I dropped to my knees, then fell onto my side, writhing on the ground.

Gwenvere and Cerridwen both came to stand over me. The pain lessened, leaving behind a throbbing ache. Gwenvere tilted her head, blocking out some of the harsh sunlight now pouring through the glass panes above. "Impressive power, but the technique is awful."

"Yes," Cerridwen agreed. "It was like this at the fortress as well. She could do nothing without bloodying herself. I had hoped severing her bond with the vampire would be enough."

"She should have been taught from a young age. It will take time to undo her bad habits." Gwenvere pursed her lips. "Not impossible, though."

"Good." Cerridwen smiled. "Teach her, and you won't have to learn what happens when Eiric is . . . disappointed."

Gwenvere's jaw clenched. " . . . Yes. Of course. I will not fail him."

I finally managed to turn from my side onto my back.

The overwhelming pain was still burned into my mind, willing my body to stay still. "What was that?" I croaked.

Gwenvere knelt beside me, seeming almost like she was in pain too. Maybe an old injury had caused the limp I'd noticed the night before. I was too delirious to observe her closely enough to say for sure. A moment later, I realized why she'd knelt as I felt cool metal circling my wrist, stripping away my magic. "True power, Lyssandra. Perhaps someday, you will have it too."

I glared, taking in ragged breaths as she stood. "All power has a price."

Her smile was icy. "Yes, I know that better than most." Her eyes flicked to Cerridwen, but the necromancer still had all her attention on me.

Footsteps preceded two male guards. I had no idea when they'd been summoned.

"Take her back to her chamber," Gwenvere ordered. "Lock her in and guard the door."

The men nodded, and one of them, a younger man with dark brown skin, knelt and wrapped my arm around his shoulder. My body screamed as he lifted me. Maybe I was actually injured. Maybe I *had* nearly been torn apart from the inside, and I no longer had vampire healing to help me recover.

The two men guided me back toward the entrance of the atrium. We passed the acolytes on our way. Two of them looked at me in horror, while the third, her arms wrapped around her blue and shivering friend, merely glared.

I smiled at her through the pain, knowing I'd made yet

another enemy. But if this was how all of my training was to go, I'd surely make many more.

I WOKE to pitch darkness with panic crushing my chest. I stifled my gasp, going still as I remembered where I was. After what Gwenvere had done to me, I was escorted back to my room where I had fallen into a fitful sleep. I must have slept the entire day away without obtaining a single meal.

Not that I thought I could eat. My stomach growled painfully, but it was a dull echo compared to the rest of my body. There was nothing *temporary* about Gwenvere's magic. She had actually damaged my body. Though how bad the damage was, only time would tell.

I blinked up at the near-darkness, trying to recall what had woken me. I could smell rain, hence the lack of moonlight through the windows. Maybe the rain had woken me. The smell of moisture on the stones outside would have been pleasant under any other circumstance.

But the smell . . . there was something else. Like turned earth. My pulse sped. There was a vampire in the room with me.

I didn't sit up, but whoever it was would have already noticed the difference in my heartbeat and breathing.

"What do you want?" I asked, willing the fear out of my voice. It might just be Cael.

"You talk in your sleep."

I inhaled sharply at the voice. "I was wondering when I would see you again." I sat up, squinting in the darkness. My superior night vision was yet another thing stolen from me when the bond was broken. I could barely make out Eiric sitting in one of the chairs beneath the window.

His face was turned away from me. It was difficult to tell, but I thought he might be peering out at the night sky. "Cerridwen told me what happened. You are weak, and you lack control."

"It's difficult to focus with flames licking at one's heels."

He laughed softly. "Yes, a crude plan at best, but Cerridwen suspected you would not attack someone who had shown you no aggression. Was she mistaken?"

There was no reason to lie. They already knew enough about me. "No. She was right. So I need control for your ritual?"

"Yes, it is imperative."

"Why?"

He laughed. "No, Lyssandra. I will tell you only what you need to be told."

I considered my next words. He truly was mad if he thought I would simply go along with everything he wanted. I had only cooperated thus far to get close to him. And now, here he was, and I had no way to kill him. If the bracelet wasn't around my wrist, I would boil his blood. I would kill us both if that's what it took. But the bracelet was there, and I could only vaguely recall the words Gwenvere had spoken to remove it.

"No more questions?"

My mind raced. He could disappear in an instant. I needed to learn all I could from him while I had him, as much as it disgusted me to converse so casually with him. "Why were you watching me sleep?"

"I've not much else to do. My plan is almost in place. Only one loose end remains."

"Which is?"

He tsked at me. "As I've already said, you'll only know what is necessary until the time comes for you to know more."

"Afraid I'll use your plans against you?" I bit my tongue. Eiric was ancient and arrogant. I would gain more from him by remaining civil.

His laughter let me know he would not take my threats seriously regardless. "Though I have done you a great service, you are not my ally, Lyssandra. You have made that clear."

"Does Cerridwen know your plan?"

"She knows what I want her to know."

Arrogant bastard. I had no pity for Cerridwen, but she had spent countless centuries trying to free him. She was loyal to an absolute fault. Or perhaps it was no fault. We were all loyal to the wrong people at some point in our lives. Most of us learned better. I had a feeling she ultimately would too.

I blinked, and suddenly he was standing right next to my bed, close enough to touch. Close enough to shove a dagger through his heart, if I had one.

I swallowed the lump in my throat. "Where is my sword?"

"You will have it again when it is time. I don't want it giving you any funny ideas."

"If you give it to me, I may feel more inclined to cooperate."

He leaned close, making me regret my words. "My dear," he hissed. "I do not need your cooperation. Your heart is far too large for your own good. I could use almost anyone against you."

My breath trembled from my lips. He was right. All he had to do was capture Asher, Tholdri, or anyone else I might be inclined to save, and he had me.

"And what about you?" I whispered. "Is there anything left of *your* heart?"

He leaned even closer. His breath was hot on my cheek. He'd fed recently, or it would have been cold. "I lost my heart the day my sister betrayed me. And here you are, looking so much like her. It speaks volumes about my restraint that you are still alive."

"I'm alive because you need me."

"For now, Lyssandra. For now."

I turned toward him, but there was no one there. The windows were shut, and I hadn't heard the door. I flinched as a scream echoed somewhere in the distance. Hopefully it was only someone screaming at a fleeting glimpse of a mad vampire flitting past.

Once I stuffed my heart back down my throat, I checked the rest of the room to make sure I was actually alone. Then I put the chair back beneath the door handle, for what good it would do.

Once that was done, I paced the room, willing my aching limbs to work normally. Much of the pain was in my chest and abdomen, like the inner tissues were stretched and torn.

Eiric wanted me to learn control. And once I did, he would capture someone I loved to use against me. He would force me to perform his ritual, then he would kill us all.

I had to act *before* I learned full control. Which meant I needed a weapon. I either needed to remove the bracelet or find my sword. Preferably both.

But one thing at a time. I sat back upon my bed. Judging by how my body felt, I needed more rest. But sleep would not come easy now that I knew Eiric might appear again at my bedside. That thought alone was far worse than any nightmare my feeble mind could possibly conjure.

CHAPTER THREE

I was awake and fully dressed in a fresh blue cloak from the armoire by the time someone came to knock on my door. When the sound of the lock sliding out of place didn't follow the knock, I stood. Whoever was out there was simply feigning politeness. I obviously couldn't answer the door with it locked from the outside.

I stepped lightly, but the new boots would never be as silent as my old ones. "Yes?"

"Are you decent?"

I sighed at the sound of Xavier's voice. I was hoping for someone more interesting, but perhaps he was just the person I needed. Someone who might actually tell me what the scream I'd heard the previous night was about.

"I'm dressed, if that's what you mean."

The lock slid, and the door opened. Xavier stood alone in the hall. It was odd, with me being a prisoner, that there were no guards outside my door. Perhaps Eiric thought I stood no chance of breaking the lock. He was probably right, but still. It seemed careless. Xavier still wore the green brocade I'd last seen him in. His shaggy hair appeared freshly washed, his face clean-shaven.

I looked him up and down. "And here I'd thought we all had to wear pale blue in this place." I gestured to my cloak.

He smirked. "Only the guards, priestesses, and acolytes."

"So everyone but you."

He stepped past me into the room, leaving the door open. I could easily run . . . though he was far faster than me now. I turned to follow him with my gaze.

"Don't forget Eiric and your beloved great uncle." He looked around my room with his back to me. "Cerridwen doesn't have to wear the robes, but she is more comfortable blending in." He turned and gave me a wide grin. "Though you know all about *that*, don't you?"

I did. With her glamour, she had blended in perfectly at the fortress, tricking even Drucida. There was no saying what information she had gathered while she was there. "What do you want, Xavier?"

The grin remained plastered on his face. "Your teacher is not feeling well this morning. I'm to see you fed."

I ignored the second part of his statement, though I was painfully hungry. "Gwenvere?"

"Yes. One of her acolytes was torn to shreds last night, and now she is unwell."

I stared at him, but his expression never shifted. "You're serious?"

"I believe you met the girl before Gwenvere was forced to drop you like a sack of manure."

36

I tried to be irritated and failed. Xavier could insult me all he pleased. I did the same to him just as often. "The girl who attacked me? She's dead?"

He nodded, still smiling. "Only bloody ribbons left behind. Quite a gory sight. I might think to blame you—" He spun a slow circle. "But of course, I don't see how you could have, locked in here as you were."

I pursed my lips. I had seen deaths like he described. The shadow creatures Matthias summoned killed in such a way. Perhaps a summoner was their culprit.

Xavier watched my face. "You know something."

It was funny to think that in such a long life he had never encountered the creatures, but perhaps I was just *lucky*. And he was *lucky* that he hadn't encountered the summoner Merri had brought with her to the battle. If anything could kill Eiric or Xavier, it would be the shadow creatures.

I paused at my own thoughts. Now *that* was an idea.

He tilted his head as he continued watching me. "Oh yes, you have thought of something quite wicked, haven't you?"

"See me fed and perhaps I'll tell you." Though I wouldn't. All I would do for now was wish I had stayed near the summoner that night.

Xavier offered me his arm.

I rolled my eyes, but took it.

He led me toward the door. "You know, it surprised me when you took my hand and not your uncle's."

I stiffened at his words, but kept walking. "Cael betrayed me."

"And that makes him worse than an enemy?"

"Yes. An enemy would be justified in his actions. At least you make it clear just what and who you are."

He swung the door shut behind us, then we continued down the hall. "And yet, you do not make it clear who *you* are. You claim to be my enemy, but you do not treat me as such."

"I insult you at every turn."

"Friends may do that just as much as enemies."

I considered my next words. I wasn't sure why I had been trying to turn Cerridwen. I had a far better chance with Xavier. We both essentially wanted the same thing. "We're in the same position." I tilted my head. "Well, perhaps not the same, but similar enough. We may be enemies, but in a way, we are also allies."

"Or just partners in misery."

"Is that not the same thing?" I asked.

He laughed, leading me down wide stone steps. Sconces lit the walls, though there was enough light from the open rooms we occasionally passed to see by. "I will say one thing. Life is at least a bit less dull with you around."

"What a fine compliment."

He glanced at me as we reached the landing. "From someone who has lived as long as I have, it is a compliment of the highest order." He dropped my arm, then turned to face me. "But don't let it go to your head. You know I can't help you, Lyssandra."

Yes, I knew for a fact he couldn't. But that didn't mean he didn't *want* to. "Why were there no guards outside my door? Yesterday, two guards were ordered to be my jailers. Now, they are nowhere to be seen."

He studied me with hooded eyes. "You think yourself still capable of breaking down that heavy door?"

"All it would take is someone unlocking it by mistake, and I could escape. Eiric would have no one to perform his ritual."

"He could simply take you again."

"Perhaps, but why risk it?"

His face grew a little pinched.

I recognized the expression. "There's something you're not supposed to tell me."

His nose wrinkled. He looked like he'd been sucking on a lemon.

I smiled. "Interesting. So there's something about there being no guards at my door." I took a moment to consider the implications. "Could it be that he *wants* me to escape?"

Xavier said nothing. He just stood there watching me with that irritated, mildly pinched expression.

"Alright." My smile widened. "I'll stop before you're forced to swallow your own tongue. But thanks for the hint."

"I gave you no hint," he grumbled, then took my arm again and led me down another hall. "How are you, by the way? I've heard Gwenvere's magic can be difficult to recover from."

"I feel like I've been hit by a horse, but it's nothing compared to how I felt last night." Between the visit from Eiric and the lingering pain, more sleep had been out of the question. I'd spent most of the night staring out my window at the dark clouds.

We reached the dining hall, and my mouth watered. I couldn't recall the last time I'd had a proper meal.

I also couldn't recall the last time I had wanted one, but I did now. After the shock of losing the bond, I had slowly regained my resolve. I would be strong. I would defeat Eiric. And if I survived, I would find Asher again.

Xavier led us to an empty table while women of every age, shape, and color watched us. Despite their differences, the blue robes gave them an eerie air of sameness. I could sense some magic in the room, but not enough to lead me to believe that all the priestesses were witches. I was a poor judge of such things, but I guessed that maybe only a handful had actual magic.

Xavier gestured for me to sit. "I'll fix you a plate."

I sat, then smiled up at him. "Not worried I'll try to escape?"

His face pinched again, and he spun away.

I watched him go, then turned my attention to my thoughts. For some reason, Eiric wanted me to attempt escape. But why? Perhaps I could find some other clues when I next saw Cerridwen.

I glanced across the tables, casually observing the women who had mostly returned their attention to their meals. I was barely paying attention, but my eyes snagged on a familiar face. And she was staring at me openly.

Eyes wide, I stared back. What in the light was Isolde, a hunter of the Helius Order, doing dressed in the clothing of an acolyte?

She gave me a look that said, *Don't you dare give me away,* then she turned her attention back to the young woman beside her.

Xavier returned with our meals before I could gain her attention again. He slid one plate before me, then sat beside me on the bench. "You look like you've seen a ghost."

"Yes," I said distantly. "It's a sensation I've come to know quite well."

He didn't comment again after that, and Isolde never looked my way.

I truly hadn't thought I could be any *more* in the dark, but as always, I had been wrong.

XAVIER left me in my room with the excuse of having other tasks to attend. I was yet to see Cerridwen or Gwenvere, and I wasn't sure if I would. I had caught a few whispers in the dining hall about the dead girl, but nothing to let me know what had killed her. All I knew was that one of the other acolytes had found her body. That had been the source of the scream.

I paced my room, glancing from time to time at the door. Xavier had locked it on his way out, but no guards. The wood and lock were both solid, and I only had human strength, but I was still physically fit. I might be able to kick the door hard enough to break the lock.

But would I be doing exactly what Eiric wanted?

I had already played into his plans far too much. In staying put, was I in some way thwarting him?

I stopped pacing to glare at the door. Even if I broke it down, that didn't mean I had to escape. I could simply investigate the rest of the temple. Maybe I could even find my sword.

I stretched my sore limbs, mentally preparing myself. I

was just about to run at the door when I heard footsteps coming down the hall outside.

I huffed, then relaxed, listening to the footsteps. They stopped right outside my door, then *silence*.

"Lyssandra?" a voice whispered.

I rushed toward the door, pushing my ear against it. "Isolde?"

"Keep your voice down. I don't have much time."

"What are you doing here?"

"Where is Markus?"

I frowned. "Answer my question, and I'll answer yours"

"Gregor Syvise wants your head. He believes you're here in Ivangard, though how his suspicions proved correct is anyone's guess. I arrived here long before you did."

I deflated with her words. I had already known the Helius Order would hunt me, believing I had killed their Potentate. And Gregor would know exactly where I would be taken—even before I knew. Because he knew whatever Eiric put into his mind. I had hoped with us so far from the Order, Eiric could no longer control him.

"Lyssandra?"

"Still here." I let out a long exhale, then said my previous thoughts out loud.

"Yes, Markus told me his suspicions about that before he left. I don't think he's controlling Gregor any longer though. I'm not sure if he ever was. I think he simply gave him some ideas about you."

I thought it over. Perhaps Eiric hadn't needed to control Gregor. All he needed to do was plant evidence against me, and send anonymous word that I was, or would be, in Ivangard. "None of this answers why you're here, and dressed as an acolyte."

"Because I am an acolyte as far as anyone here is concerned. I pledged myself, and that was that. When I heard hunters would be sent here to find you, I rode ahead believing Markus would be at your side."

"You rode by yourself all the way here?" It would have taken her at least two weeks. She must have left only days after Markus and Steifan. Eiric's plan had been in place all that time. If they had waited just a few days longer, they might have learned in advance where Eiric planned to take me.

"I'm not some defenseless damsel," she snapped. "Now where is Markus?"

"I left him a week's ride to the southwest. He may have tracked me here, or he may not have. The last time I saw him, he was toppling from a rooftop with Asher."

"Well can't you, you know, *communicate* somehow with your master?"

Her words made me feel sick to my stomach. I told her what had happened in the briefest way possible.

She was silent for a long moment as she digested my words. When she finally spoke, it was to say, "Light, Lyssandra. You've made a complete mess of things."

I scowled, though she couldn't see it. "It's not like I did it on purpose."

"I know, I know." She was quiet for a moment. "I have to go. Do you want me to slide the lock before I leave?"

Of course she hadn't offered to do that until now. "No," I decided on gut instinct alone, even though I had just been debating it before her arrival. "I'm not ready to escape just yet."

"Suit yourself."

"What will you do now?"

"I didn't pledge myself just to find you and Markus. If Eiric wants hunters to come here, it can be for no good reason. I plan to find out what that reason is before they arrive. When I heard someone matching his description had been seen entering the temple, I decided to investigate further." She was quiet for a moment again, then, "I have to go. I'll try to come back another day."

I listened as her footsteps retreated down the hall. She was right. As much as I wanted to break down the door, I needed to find out what Eiric was planning, and what it had to do with the witches of Ivangard.

CHAPTER FOUR

I t was late afternoon by the time I heard another knock on my door. I had been stretching my stiff limbs, trying to rid myself of the lingering pain of Gwenvere's magic. I did *not* want to make her angry again, though I undoubtedly would at some point. I wasn't even sure if her tension had anything to do with me. Looking back at my arrival, she had already seemed on edge.

The lock slid before I could reach the door and I stepped back as it opened, revealing Cerridwen and two male guards.

Her brow deeply furrowed, she stepped into the room. "My apologies for taking so long to come for you. We've encountered some . . . complications."

By *complications*, did she mean the dead girl?

She looked around the room, seeming distracted. "Was Xavier here?"

My eyes widened, but fortunately she wasn't looking at me and didn't seem to notice. "No," I lied automatically.

He'd claimed he'd been sent to feed me, so why wouldn't Cerridwen know about it?

She pursed her lips, glancing around the room one last time before shaking her head. "Let's go."

"Where?" I looked at the guards now waiting out in the hall with their backs turned.

"We'll get you something to eat. Then, magic practice. I do hope you'll do better today." Seeming to dismiss her suspicions about Xavier, she glided toward the doorway.

I followed her. "You know, maybe things would go better if someone actually *taught* me something."

She stepped between the two guards, then turned to face me. Her dark eyes were dull. She was clearly tired of the whole affair. "You've had ample teaching, Lyssandra. That is not the issue."

"Then what is?"

"*You.* For Lavandriel, magic was like breathing. She hardly even needed to think. She could simply will things to happen, and her will was stronger than anything I've seen in my long life. I had hoped by attacking you, I could lure out the full force of your magic. But you are weak, and time is short."

I crossed my arms, trying and failing to not be insulted. "Are we on a schedule?"

She pursed her lips again, considering her words, then shook her head. "I don't know why I speak to you at all. Let us go."

She turned down the hall and started walking, leaving both me and the guards behind. Once again, I was stricken by how easy it would be for me to escape. Both men were armed, but I had been training in combat my entire life. If I caught them off guard . . .

But no. By now, I was entirely sure that's what Eiric wanted. Or maybe it was Cerridwen who wanted it. Who knew? Maybe she just wanted me to believe time was short so I would panic and act.

Just as one of the guards turned to eye me expectantly, I marched past them, walking fast enough that the hem of my cloak trailed behind me. With my longer legs, I caught up with Cerridwen before she could reach the stairs.

"So what's the plan then? Will I have more fireballs hurled at me today?"

Cerridwen continued down the stairs as the guards hurried after us. "Unless you'd simply like to cooperate and use your magic willingly."

The stairs were wide enough for me to walk at her side. "You mean, unless I willingly try to kill one of those girls instead?"

"You don't have to kill them, Lyssandra. You need only learn control. Control will allow you *not* to kill them."

I lifted my wrist with the bracelet as we reached the landing. "You know, I'd have more practice if I wasn't forced to wear this all the time."

She gestured for me to continue down the nearest hall. Once we were both walking, she said, "It's for your own good. You went many years without your magic, but it doesn't mean it wasn't there, blossoming inside of you. Witches grow more powerful as they age, no matter what constraints are placed upon them. Feeling the full force of it day and night could easily drive you mad. We need you at least relatively sane, for now."

SARA C. ROETHLE

I glanced at her, but I couldn't tell if she was lying. "It wasn't overwhelming yesterday. I felt it, yes, but I was still able to think and function. The only issues were the fire-balls and Gwenvere's horrible magic." Thinking of the experience in the impressive atrium brought another question to mind. "Is there a reason we *practiced* in such a lovely, *easily destroyed* place?"

We neared the dining hall, the guards still following us silently. "True witches draw power from nature. We thought it might be helpful to you, though it seems it was a useless thought. And the damage is nothing to worry about. Healing magic can mend the plants."

"True witches?"

She turned to face me as we reached the heavy doors. "That will be enough questions, Lyssandra. Will you prac-tice willingly, or is it simply in your nature to do things the hard way?"

"I will not attack an innocent." I leaned close to her face. "But I would gladly try my magic on *you*."

She smiled sweetly. "I could drop you just as easily as Gwenvere did." She stepped back, nodding for one of the guards to open the door to the dining hall.

She probably thought I was starving after being alone all morning, so I would pretend to be so. Xavier had come to me without her knowing, and I wasn't about to out him.

And Cerridwen could boast all she pleased. She might be able to cloud my mind with glamours, but unless she had something hidden up her sleeve, my magic was more dangerous than hers.

That was, if I could actually learn to control it.

IT SEEMED I wouldn't have fireballs thrown at me after all. The remaining three acolytes stood in the shade of a slightly charred tree, hands laced behind their backs.

Gwenvere looked about one hundred years old as she glared at them, and I didn't think it was just irritation. Her coloring was off—a bit ashen. "You *will* do what I say."

The girl with short black hair and small eyes shook her head.

"You'll be fine," Gwenvere pressed.

The girl looked at the one beside her, then they both lowered their chins and shook their heads.

Sighing loudly, Gwenvere pinched her brow and turned toward Cerridwen. "They won't do it. After the *incident*, they are frightened."

"Incident?" I asked, once again covering for Xavier. If he hadn't come for me that morning, I would have no way of knowing about the death.

Cerridwen watched me with an air of suspicion. "The girl who attacked you yesterday was murdered. I have already assured Gwenvere that you are not the culprit."

Gwenvere's eyes flared, but she quickly composed herself. "The girls believe Nona died because she used her magic for harm. I don't know where they came up with such a silly notion, but they are holding fast."

The girls in question lowered their heads.

"Can you think of any other reason she might have been killed?" I asked, then regretted it. I was a prisoner—I owed these women nothing—but old habits died hard, and I was curious to know what had torn the girl to shreds.

"She wasn't feeling well," the dark-haired girl blurted. "She retired early last night. We think the killer saw her leaving the dining hall and stalked her then." Her eyes filled with hope. Hope that someone might actually listen to her and figure out what happened to her friend.

"Did she have any enemies?" I asked.

"*Enough*," Gwenvere snapped. "This is none of your concern." She glanced back at the three acolytes. "Leave us. I'll think of a punishment for each of you later."

With their eyes on their feet, the three girls hurried toward the doors. Only the one who'd spoken dared a pleading look back at me as the doors opened, then they went out into the hall. I met her gaze until one of the guards shut the door behind them.

Gwenvere was giving me a look that should have physically burned. "I'll just have to teach you myself."

I crossed my arms. "While that sounds like a *wonderful* time, aren't you worried about there being a murderer in your midst?"

Her gaze shifted. "I'm sure they have already fled."

"And it's so easy to enter and leave this temple?"

I expected Cerridwen to cut in at some point, but she simply watched the conversation with mild amusement.

Gwenvere lifted her nose. "No one can enter this temple without a direct invitation from either myself, or a handful of our most devout sisters."

I almost had to smile at the information. It was just too easy. They must have warded the temple, which could prove valuable information for me once I actually came up with a plan. I remembered Gwenvere inviting us in upon our arrival. Now I knew there was a reason for it.

"Exactly," I said, as if I already knew as much. "So that means the murderer was someone invited inside, likely someone already living here."

Gwenvere's cheeks reddened. "Why do you care? Why are we even speaking of this?"

Cerridwen lifted a hand to hide her silent laughter, and I realized Gwenvere didn't realize what I was—at least, what I had been in a previous life.

"Why are you laughing?" Gwenvere huffed at Cerridwen.

Cerridwen lowered her hand, her eyes still sparkling with amusement. "Our dear Lyssandra was once a hunter of the Helius Order. Someone dies, and her first instinct is to ask questions."

Gwenvere's jaw dropped. She looked me up and down for a long moment. Finally, she cleared her throat, laced her hands in front of her, and straightened her spine. "Well, I must say, that explains a lot."

I wondered what else Cerridwen had or hadn't told her about me. She knew about the ritual, at least. She knew I needed to learn control over my magic. "I can help you find the killer."

Cerridwen's laughter wiped away. "There is no time for that, Lyssandra. And you have no way of finding a killer when you cannot roam the temple freely."

Gwenvere seemed more stunned than ever. Ignoring Cerridwen, she asked, "Why? Why would you want to help? Yesterday, Nona and I both caused you injury."

I glanced around at the lovely trees and plants, many

now damaged from the previous day, before turning my attention back to Gwenvere. I didn't really have an answer she would understand. "Because it's what I do. Who I am. I hunt monsters." I glanced at Cerridwen. *"All of them."*

Gwenvere didn't seem to know what to say to that.

Fortunately, or unfortunately, Cerridwen stepped in. "It's out of the question. Lyssandra has her purpose, and your dead acolyte is your problem, not ours. Now, seeing as we have no other participants today, perhaps we can focus on the fundamentals of casting rituals. Perhaps new knowledge can help Lyssandra learn control." She gave me a dark look. "Even controlling her *tongue* would be a nice place to start."

I stuck the mentioned appendage out at her. She might have prevented me from looking into the murder for now, but I would find a way. I wished my motivations were as noble as I'd claimed, but really, my primary need was selfish. If a summoner killed Nona, I needed to find that summoner. They might be a killer, but that didn't mean I wouldn't use them if I could. Desperate times, and all that.

Cerridwen watched me like she knew my thoughts, or she at least suspected. It would do me good to remember that she was just as old as Eiric, and not half as mad. Trying to outwit her might be a fool's game, but it was still one I intended to play.

MY EYES BLURRED as I squinted at the faded text. Gwenvere stood at my shoulder. Her irritation had waned into exhaustion. We'd spent all afternoon and evening studying what she swore were the most simplistic rituals she could think of. And it *had* worked, to an extent. The words helped focus my mind far better than the panic of having fireballs thrown at me. But my magic—

It was a yawning abyss inside of me. I could not fathom its depths, nor could I control what might come out of them. The longer the bracelet was off, the more that cavern beckoned.

I shook my head, trying to focus on the words before me, but my mind wandered.

Cerridwen had retired when night fell, I assumed to find Eiric. The thought of them in bed together—the thought of *anyone* in bed with such a psychotic monster— gave me chills.

"That's enough for this evening," Gwenvere sighed, drawing me out of my thoughts. "I do believe Cerridwen might actually be pleased with our progress."

I turned away from the tome atop a tall wooden table to face her. "Why do you answer to Cerridwen? What bargain could she have possibly offered you?"

Her expression turned guarded. "That's none of your concern, Lyssandra."

I crossed my arms and leaned my butt against the table. "Just how much do you know?" I didn't have hope that I would learn anything useful from Gwenvere— Cerridwen would not have left me alone with her if there was a chance—but it still bothered me. Why were the priestesses working with Eiric?

The stern line of her mouth softened. "If you were to investigate Nona's death, where would you start?"

I considered my answer. I knew nothing of the temple or Ivangard, but that didn't matter. I always started in the same place. "I would start with the body to identify what type of monster killed her. I would examine the scene, looking for anything that might have been left behind. Then I would study Nona herself. I would read her journals, question those close to her, and try to determine why someone would want her dead."

She glanced around the room. We had moved to a small, candlelit study, and we were quite alone. It wasn't the first time I'd considered how odd that was. "You would really help me just because it's the right thing to do? Even though we hold you prisoner here?"

"Nona was not my jailer. She may have had a foul temperament, but she was young. She could have grown out of it. I would like to see her death avenged." *And I would like you to tell me everything you know.*

Her breath shuddered out of her. "Nona was not the first. Two weeks ago, there was another."

That didn't rule out Eiric. It was before I had arrived, but I hadn't seen him during the journey. It did, however, rule *me* out. Had Xavier merely been teasing when he suggested me as a culprit, or did he not know about the previous death? With Gwenvere suddenly opening up, I figured I may as well ask.

"Do Cerridwen and Xavier know of the previous death?"

"I did not tell them directly, but they may have heard whispers. Either way, they do not seem to care."

"So why help them?" I asked.

She wrinkled her nose. "No, Lyssandra, you need not

know the terms of our bargain. I appreciate your advice regarding Nona, but I should return you to your chamber."

I pulled my shoulder back before she could grab my arm. "I can find her killer, Gwenvere. I swear it."

"You can do nothing from behind a locked door. And even less if you make me put you there by force."

My confidence wilted at the memory of her magic. It had felt like she was literally tearing me apart. Like what happened to Nona . . . but I didn't think Gwenvere was the culprit. She wanted the murder solved. It did, however, mean that a summoner wasn't necessarily involved. Someone else with magic similar to Gwenvere's could be the killer.

She watched my shifting expression. "I see you're much more reasonable than Cerridwen believes. Let us go." She motioned toward the door.

Not wanting to press my luck—or her temper—I walked ahead of her. There were two guards waiting for us outside the door. Gwenvere could lock me back in my room tonight, but tomorrow, I would try again. She had already warmed to me considerably, which was something new. Perhaps Tholdri had finally rubbed off on me. Just the thought made me wonder where he was, and if he was alright. I hoped he was far away, but knowing Tholdri, he was somewhere in the city, planning my escape.

CHAPTER FIVE

Asher

The man stared at me blankly. It was fortunate the hunters were gathering information in other parts of the city, because they might have been conflicted had they witnessed me bespelling the foolish man before me, even knowing I had trailed him leaving a den of thieves.

There were no moral implications in my choice of prey. My reasoning was simple. Thieves and other scoundrels would know more city secrets than any others.

He blinked slowly, the lantern light making him look ghoulish, though I likely looked far worse. Had I not bespelled him, surely he would have run.

"Tell me what you know of the priestesses," I ordered.

Again, that slow blink. His short dark hair was oily, the skin beneath his eyes puffy and pink from too much wine. "The priestesses?"

This was the other issue with bespellment. One was forced to lead their prey carefully to obtain worthwhile answers. Rather than clarify, I tried a new question. "Why can no one but the priestesses enter the temple at the center of the city?"

Another blink. "No one can step foot on the temple grounds. My boys have tried. We just . . . can't."

The information was not new. Others had said as much to the hunters during the day. They had arrived earlier, leaving those of us unable to walk in the light to trail after them. It had been like that for roughly a week. Markus would follow his bond with Lyssandra, leading Tholdri and Steifan across the countryside, then Geist and I would track their scent in the night. Each night when we found them, I held hope that we would reach Lyssandra with her captors—and every night I was disappointed. The hunters and their horses could only travel so far without rest. And Eiric, with any number of servants and stolen horses at his disposal, had easily remained ahead. I could have attempted to follow the tracks, but many of the roads were well traveled. Too many scents, and too many tracks. It was too big of a risk that I might choose the wrong path.

I eyed the man before me. He likely knew nothing else of value. He did not know the priestesses' secrets. The temple had walls and guards, but neither could keep *everyone* out. It simply wasn't possible. There was something else going on—likely a ward.

"I heard once that you have to be *invited*," the man continued.

I had been ready to dismiss him, but his words regained my attention. "Invited?"

"By one of the priestesses in charge. That's how the new acolytes get in. One of my boys saw it."

I frowned. Of course they would have kept an eye on the temple, trying to figure out the best way in, if only to rob the priestesses blind. Normally, I would have detested the notion, but these particular priestesses would be deserving. For they were the Ivangard witches, according to Geist.

"What did the priestess look like?" I asked.

Another blink. His eyes were growing cloudy. If I didn't release him soon, his mind might break.

"The priestess who invited the acolytes into the temple," I clarified. "What does she look like?"

He shook his head slightly like he didn't quite understand, and I knew I had lost him.

So be it. There was still one last thing to do.

I stepped closer. The smell of sweat and wine on him wrinkled my nose. The very thought of drinking from him turned my stomach, but I could not waste more time. I needed to be strong. *Lyssandra* needed me to be strong.

"Don't move," I ordered.

The man watched me blankly, not a hint of fear in his eyes. Even if his mind fully survived the bespellment, he would not remember a thing. He would hide the bite from his *boys*, lest he become a target himself.

And if he did not, it wouldn't matter. They would never find me unless I wished to be found.

GEIST WAS WAITING for me outside of the small home. I had wiped the blood from my mouth, but he would still smell it on me. Not that he would pass judgement. He would feed this night too.

His dark eyes searched my face. "Anything?"

"Much of the same. Except a claim that one must be *invited* to enter the temple."

He arched a dark brow. "Invited by whom?"

"A priestess. That is all he could tell me."

He turned to lean his back against the wall. He'd tied his long black hair away from his face, most of it blending in with his black coat. "Well, it's more than we knew starting out. But it's unfortunate we brought no witches with us. One *might* have managed an invitation."

I had thought the same. If the priestesses recruited young witches to their order, one of the witches from the fortress—Ophelia or someone similar—could have proven a valuable asset.

I stood stiffly beside him. My body ached, and I wasn't sure why. It had started just the previous night, when I awoke from my resting place far outside the city walls.

"We'll find another way. Keep searching."

Geist bowed his head slightly. "Of course."

"And if you see Cael, leave him to me."

His lip curled. "You believe you can best him?"

"I believe there is no other option."

With that, I turned away. The night was young. I would ask more questions, then I would watch the temple. She was so close. So close I could almost feel her, and yet, she was out of reach.

62

The dull ache thrummed in my chest as I started walking. I might have thought it was my heart, but that was already damaged. Despite the blood I consumed, I hadn't felt its beat a single time since I lost her.

CHAPTER SIX

Lyssandra

It seemed somehow wrong that the sun should rise happily every morning despite Eiric's existence. I had half-expected him to visit me again in the night, but I had remained blissfully undisturbed. I readied for another day of casting minor rituals. I might have been excited about the possibilities if I weren't hesitant to learn too much. I wasn't sure if Eiric had a particular timeline, or if he would force me to perform *his* ritual as soon as he thought me ready.

I stretched near the window, wishing I could do more to work my body. The pain from Gwenvere's magic had finally faded, leaving behind only its terrible memory. I wished I could speak to Drucida about it, though I was sure she had never seen anything like it. There was something very strange about the witches of Ivangard. Drucida would be horrified to learn of the bracelet around my wrist. I had spent the early morning hours repeating

Gwenvere's chant—what I could remember of it—while stroking the cool metal, but the bracelet stayed put.

A knock on the door drew my attention, but the lock slid and the door opened before I could acknowledge it. Cerridwen stood outside.

I hardly looked at her. "Do you have nothing better to do than to pester me?"

She didn't react at all to my taunt. In fact, she seemed in an entirely foul mood as she glided into the room.

I looked her up and down, from her gleaming hair falling across her blue cloak, down to her soft brown boots. "I'd think you would be happier being reunited with the man you love after so many centuries." I lifted a brow at her tense shoulders. "Or at least a little more relaxed."

"Enough, Lyssandra. I have no patience for your antics today." A leather-bound tome suddenly appeared in her hand.

My eyes widened briefly, then I scowled. "Wasting your glamour on simple parlour tricks?"

She held the book out to me. "When it's as easy as breathing, then why not?"

I ignored the book. "Where is Eiric?"

"It's daylight, Lyssandra."

She was right, but I really hadn't expected to sleep through the night. "Did he go somewhere far away?"

Her lips twisted. Maybe that was the reason for her foul mood, though Eiric being far away seemed to me like a good thing. A *very* good thing. Of course, it was an awful thing for whoever he was terrorizing.

She shook the book at me until I took it. The leather felt ancient in my hand. "What is it?"

"Something to help you pass the time. Gwenvere is unwell today, and I am otherwise preoccupied."

I finally observed the book. The leather was etched with ancient symbols. I opened it, wrinkling my nose at the scent of old ink and parchment. I scanned a few hand-written lines. The writing was neat, with well-practiced flourish.

I looked up at her, a question written on my face.

"Lavandriel's grimoire," she explained.

I was so shocked, I nearly dropped the book. "Why would you give this to me?"

"You are her descendent. She would want you to have it."

"Don't pretend to care."

Her expression darkened. "Believe what you choose. Despite her betrayal, she was still my friend. And you are the last of her line, Lyssandra."

"Eiric was her half-brother. I am certainly not the last." I thought of Alexander, my grandfather's cousin, but kept quiet. I didn't know if he was alive, but if he was, I had no desire to meet him.

She rolled her eyes. "You know what I mean, Lyssan-dra. If she was alive right now, you are the person she would choose to have it."

I held the book to my chest. "I still don't understand your motivation." There had to be more to it. Cerridwen had lived amongst the witches and had set them up to die. There was no kindness left in her heart.

Her dark eyes gave me nothing. "You don't have to understand. Just take the book, Lyssandra."

I watched her for a moment longer, then nodded. "I will."

With that, she dismissed me, then walked toward the door. I opened my mouth to ask when I would next be fed, but she shut the door before I could. The lock slid a moment later.

Scowling, I carried the book to my bed. I sat, cradling it in my lap as I smoothed a hand across the aged leather. There was something in the book Eiric wanted me to learn. There was no other reason for Cerridwen to give it to me. They could have forced me to learn it, but why try when my curiosity would do the job for them?

I settled back and prepared to read. Eiric could win this one. I would not pass up a glimpse into Lavandriel's mind, even if the glimpse could only be stolen through her rituals. Thinking of rituals, I closed the grimoire and looked once more at the cover, but the runes were different. It was not a match for the tome I'd found at the fortress, the same tome that matched another I'd seen in my grandfather's study.

I hoped Drucida had hidden the other well, for if Eiric knew she had it, I may have unintentionally set her up to die.

IT WAS hours before the door opened again, revealing only a pair of guards delivering my first meal of the day. They avoided eye contact and kept their hands close to their swords. I might have tested them, but there were better ways to escape. Instead I watched them with Lavandriel's grimoire held against my chest. Once they left the food, I ignored it. Not that I wasn't hungry, but I had no idea who had sent them. I felt more comfortable being fed directly in the dining hall, where it would be more difficult to poison me.

Perhaps none of the witches meant me harm, but one could never be too careful. With a heavy sigh, I turned back to my reading. Most of it made little sense to me, and I wasn't sure what Eiric hoped I would learn, but I would bite off my own tongue before I believed Cerridwen had done something selfless for me. There was still something within the pages I needed to find.

And so, as the sky grew dark, I continued to read. The sun lowering, which had once signaled danger, now left me with a sense of melancholy. Had Asher awoken for the night? And if so, where was he? For all I knew, he could be in the city below. He could be anywhere, for I could no longer feel him.

I could no longer feel much of anything at all.

CHAPTER SEVEN

Asher

"Are you sure this is wise?" Tholdri leaned in near my shoulder as we watched the temple across the street.

Markus had witnessed a priestess leaving the temple the night before with a basket of food to be delivered to a nearby family. Probably *her* family, and since she went at night, it was likely not a sanctioned use of the temple's food stores. I did not relish the thought of frightening a kind soul, but I would do what I must. If she was leaving the temple in relative secrecy, she would not be immediately missed.

"You remember the blue flames, don't you?" Tholdri whispered when I did not reply.

I did, but they were not a concern at present. I could snap the girl's neck before she could do much harm, though I hoped it would not come to that. I needed information, not blood. If we could not enter the temple without invitation—and I *had* tried—then we would acquire an invitation.

I heard her soft footsteps long before I saw her. The guards at the gate saw her first, and let her by without question. Was her delivery sanctioned after all, or did the guards simply not care? Perhaps she had arranged a deal with them.

My thoughts quieted as I watched her hurrying down the street, blue cloak swirling around her ankles. Once she was far enough, I followed. I heard Tholdri's soft curse back in the alcove, but what had he expected? I was better off tracking the girl alone.

I followed her from street to street, already knowing her destination thanks to Markus. I would take her just as she was close, when her defenses would be down.

She neared the door, clutching her basket. I could smell bread, cheese, and fruit. Simple supplies. Judging by the rickety door she approached, her family would likely starve without her. If I was forced to kill her, would they too die as a result?

I pushed away my thoughts. It didn't matter. Just as she reached for the door, I struck. I had her lifted from the ground with a hand over her mouth before she could scream.

"Drop the basket," I whispered.

She instantly obeyed. At least her family would not go hungry, for tonight.

I carried her away from her home toward an agreed upon location where Geist, Markus, and Steifan would be waiting. Her only chance of survival now was complete cooperation. I hoped she chose it.

Tholdri caught up just as I reached the location. Panting lightly, he held open the door for me. "You didn't have to rush off like that."

"Yes, I did." I entered the abandoned home. It was filthy and stank of excrement, but it would serve its purpose.

Markus held a lantern partially shielded by his body. Geist stood beside him with that ever-present infuriating smile on his face.

Steifan looked at the girl with open sympathy. The deep slice across his face from temple to chin, a wound incurred during the battle at the fortress, seemed out of place with his kind expression. He was the kindest of them all. I knew it was why Lyssandra cared for him deeply, even though he'd only been in her life a relatively short time. Genuine kindness appealed to her, though she would never admit it.

I kept the girl clutched against my chest with her mouth covered. From what I'd seen, the witches needed use of their hands to cast the blue flame.

"Do not struggle, and you will live. Scream, or fight, and you will be dead in an instant."

She nodded as much as she could, wiping the moisture of her mouth across the inside of my palm.

I set her down, but stayed close. Despite my threats, if she struggled, I would simply grab her again. We needed her alive, for now.

As soon as she was down, she turned to face me, stumbling, but not falling. She ignored the others, deeming me the greatest threat. "W-what do you want?" Tears shone in her pale eyes. She was so very young, and likely innocent.

"A way into the temple," Geist said behind her, "nothing more."

She whipped around, as if just noticing him. Perhaps she'd been too panicked to take everything in. "No one goes in without invitation from a priestess."

"Precisely," I said behind her. "And you are a priestess."

She backed toward the corner of the small room, trying to place all of us in her sights. "I'm only an acolyte. I cannot invite anyone in." Her eyes whipped back and forth. "Please. I only pledged so that I might feed my family. I have nothing to do with whatever you are plotting."

"There must be another way in," Markus said, his attention on the girl.

She gnawed her lip, her tears finally falling. "Are you the ones killing acolytes? Is this what happened to Nona?"

I lifted a brow. "Nona?"

Her gaze shifted back toward me. "Please, just don't kill me."

"We are not murderers," Markus said blandly, though the statement wasn't entirely true for any of us. "We just need to enter the temple to rescue a . . . friend."

Friend. What a bland statement for what Lyssandra was to him.

"You mean you're not the killers?" she asked.

It might be a mistake, but I shook my head slightly. Perhaps less panicked, she could think of a way to help us.

She gnawed her lip again, mulling things over. "Help me get my family out of the city, and I'll tell you the way in. I had no idea what I was getting myself into when I pledged. I would have been better off starving."

Geist stepped closer. "You are in no position to be making demands, girl."

She moved away from him, then stood a little straighter, rapidly regaining her composure. "Oh, but I am. I don't want to end up torn to shreds, but I cannot abandon my vows unless I want my family to pay for my offenses. The priestesses . . . they're not what I thought. There are things keeping me from saying exactly what they are, but they don't know *everything*. Get us out of the city, and I'll tell you the way in."

"What do you mean, they are not what you thought?" Geist asked, likely the only one truly interested. We already knew the priestesses were witches, and not devout followers of the light.

The girl gnawed her lip again, hesitating. "They are not *normal* women. I cannot say more."

So she knew about their magic. She was wise to be frightened. "Fine," I agreed before anyone else could speak. "We will help you out of the city." Perhaps once she was free, she would be more inclined to speak. And . . . she was trapped. It was clear for all to see.

Geist gave me a tired look. "This will only delay Lyssandra's rescue."

"It will not take long, and it is what she would want."

We stared at each other until finally, Geist nodded.

The girl gave me a hesitant smile, obviously not realizing what I was despite how quickly I had brought her here.

"We'll get you out tonight," I said to her. "Now tell us everything you know."

She shook her head. "Once we're out, I'll tell you. You

can kill me if I'm lying, but I will have no way of forcing you to uphold your half of the bargain if I tell you now."

She was right, so I nodded. "Let us go."

"DO YOU BELIEVE HER?" I was alone with Tholdri again, this time monitoring a crypt instead of a woman.

"Her fear was genuine."

While there was a chance she was cunning enough to lie to a vampire, I believed the acolyte's claims. She wanted out of the city, despite her family's chances of survival being so slim. She had been more afraid of the priestesses than a room full of strange men. She had found her friend's body torn to bits within a temple where only the invited could enter. Someone had invited in a monster, and Lyssandra was in there with it. Eiric wanted her alive, for now, but the monster might not.

Tholdri leaned against a crumbling wall circling an expanse of newer graves. The citizens of Ivangard were brave to continue burying their dead. Most places in the Ebon Province used fire, but the *priestesses* believed in the old ways, and all dead were interred.

"But she doesn't know anything," Tholdri argued. "Why would the priestesses go to such lengths to enforce loyalty?"

I was surprised he felt the need to ask. Perhaps I had given his normally quick mind too much credit. "Whatever the priestesses' secrets, they are enough to bury them. They do not care about one acolyte, or she would not be able to sneak about as she has been. But it is easier to keep a flock loyal if all are bound by the same fear."

The girl had started talking once she was out, with a promise from Markus, Steifan, and Geist that her family would soon follow. She quite literally couldn't say that the priestesses had magic, which meant they had bound her words in some way. There were few things she was actually able to tell us, but she had gotten the most important bit out. We now knew of a way into the temple.

Tholdri looked at the entry to the crypt. It was barred by iron, but that would hardly slow me, not with the blood I had consumed. He shook his head slowly. "I'm afraid to consider what secrets they would deem so important."

"Shall we find out?"

He glanced at me. "What about the others?"

"They will get the girl's family out. Once they have gathered their things, Markus and Steifan can transport them with their horses, and Geist can see to the humans."

The acolyte herself had been easy to carry over the wall. She believed the city guards would stop her if she tried to leave through the gates, so they were obviously part of whatever the priestesses were hiding. The girl hadn't wanted to risk being discovered while her family packed their things.

Geist could carry her kin out of the city himself. It would not be an issue.

Glancing around, Tholdri pushed away from the wall and approached the crypt.

There was no need for his caution. The night was silent enough that I would have heard anyone watching us, but no one had come near this part of the city since our arrival. The acolyte had made no suggestion of why that might be. She had only heard rumor of the path through the crypt. She had never gone through it herself. According to her, others had tried, and had not returned.

I studied the iron bars as we reached them. They were bound with hinges on one side and a lock on the other, like a slatted, circular door. But why lock a crypt that no one ever visited?

Why, indeed. I gripped the bars, then yanked the door hard enough to break the lock. The shriek of metal was sharp and sudden, echoing through the quiet night. Birds startled from withered trees, flapping up toward the moon.

Beyond the bars was a circular wooden door, unlocked. Tholdri pushed it open, then peered inside. "Perhaps we should have brought a torch."

Stale air wafted out, the musty odor lingering in the back of my throat. "The moonlight will be enough, for a time."

"For you, perhaps, but not for me."

"You're waiting here regardless."

He leaned away from the door to look at me. "You can't be serious."

"If this truly is a way into the temple, it will be easier for me to remain unseen alone. I will find Lyssandra on my own."

He seemed irritated, but didn't argue. Perhaps he was clever after all. "Just don't get yourself killed. Lyssandra will have my head."

I hoped his sentiment was correct. I hoped the

severing of the bond had not changed her feelings toward me, but I could not be sure. Not until I saw her. The moment I saw her, I would know.

I walked past him without another word.

"Oh, goodbye then," Tholdri muttered caustically behind me.

I ignored him. Despite my claims, it was difficult to see within the strange crypt. Even the dead needed at least a hint of light to see. I traced my fingertips along the carved wall to my right, remembering every crevice. If I found Lyssandra, I would need to lead her back this way. I could not risk the slightest stumble in the darkness.

The smell of old death grew stronger the deeper I went. I passed multiple alcoves where the *honored* dead were tucked away. I did not envy their final resting place. Had I died when I was meant to, I would have likely ended up in a shallow grave. I would be nothing more by now than a bit of bone. Perhaps that was how it should have been. Without Eiric, all of us would have died when we were meant to, and I would have never known Lyssandra.

By the time I reached another door, the darkness was absolute. I ran my fingers across the dried out wood. No one had deigned to maintain this place in a good long while. I felt my way toward the handle, giving it a slight turn. *Locked.* And this time, were I to break it, someone on the other side might hear.

I pressed my ear against the door, hearing nothing, but the touch sent a feeling like lightning through my bones. Odd, since touching it with my hand had not produced the same effect. My best guess was a hidden ward. Someone did not want this door opened.

Thinking of Drucida's enchantments, I withdrew, retracing my steps until I found another hall. I traveled down it, searching blindly with my hands. Many of the bodies were walled behind stone, but some rested in open alcoves. They would have been embalmed to limit the odor, but it was not an issue now. All that was left of them were ancient bones. *Brittle* bones, but perhaps they would do.

I wrapped my hand around some ancient human's leg and pulled, wanting the thickest bone I could find. The crack and clatter was not as loud as I'd feared. I waited a moment in absolute silence, and when the silence continued, I shook away bits of cloth and dust, then returned to the door with my newfound . . . tool.

Growing impatient, I used my free hand to feel for the handle, then with its location in my mind, I hit it with the bone hard enough to damage both. The brittle bone snapped, but not before it knocked one side of the handle off the door. Before it could clatter to the stones at my feet, the entire door froze solid with a sudden burst of cold.

I stepped back. Even just gripping the bone, my fingers were partially frozen.

I listened as I waited for them to thaw. Triggering the ward might have alerted the witch who had created it. It was so with Drucida's enchantments.

Moments ticked by until I could finally move my fingers. The trap would have been far more effective against a human. Any of the undead could simply thaw out and heal, as long as they didn't break a finger off in the process.

I set the bone aside, flexing my fingers a few more times, then knelt to observe what remained of the interior lock and handle. They were easy enough to slide aside, and no further traps triggered.

I opened the door and stepped inside. I smelled grain and aging cheese. The crypt led directly into a cellar. How . . . distasteful. But no matter, I was now somewhere below the temple. According to the acolyte, the wards were in the walls. One could not go through or over them, but one could go *under*. At least, that was the theory. I would soon discover whether it would prove correct.

CHAPTER EIGHT

Lyssandra

I sat in a chair beneath the window in my chamber, staring out at the darkness. I was so tired I could hardly string together a coherent thought. I had read through over half the grimoire, looking for anything useful. It had taken time to understand the composition of the rituals, but once I did, I was able to determine what many of them were for. I had hoped for something useful. Finding nothing had settled my mind into a dull buzz. There were rituals for healing, and rituals for light. Rituals to create enchantments like Drucida's, and rituals to read energy like Ophelia. Then there were others that I couldn't comprehend at all. I suspected one of those was what Eiric desired.

I rubbed the bracelet around my wrist, irritated that with it, I couldn't actually attempt the rituals regardless. And I *wanted* to try. It felt *right*, those moments when I was whole again. But I didn't feel like I was going mad.

Quite the opposite, really. Cerridwen had made it seem like my mind would warp further by the day. Of course, I had only been granted access to my magic for hours, not days.

I inhaled sharply at a soft knock on the door. When the lock didn't slide, I crept toward it, already suspecting who it was.

"I imagine you heard about the dead girl. Do you know anything more about it?" Isolde whispered, having heard my footsteps.

I leaned my back against the door. I hated to admit the incident had not been heavy on my mind since receiving the grimoire. "Just that the girl who died was not the first. I haven't seen the body, but from what I've been told, I suspect a summoner. Or more specifically, the creatures a summoner can call from other realms."

"Well that's comforting."

I stretched my neck from side to side. It was stiff from looking down at the tome for so long. "It's only a theory, but you should be careful. If these creatures are within the temple, they can kill in an instant. But they fear light. Keep a lantern handy." I thought again of the ritual for light. It seemed complicated, but if I could learn it, it might save my life if I faced the shadows once more.

"They are hardly terrifying if they fear light."

"Trust me, I'd rather face anything afraid of a sword."

She was silent for a moment, then, "Are you ready for me to let you out of there now?"

"No." Though it grated—I hated waiting almost as much as I hated being trapped—but there was a reason

Eiric was making it so easy. *Too* easy. "Are you able to go out into the city?"

"Not yet. Newer acolytes cannot leave until we swear our official vows. I'm told there is a *binding ceremony*, whatever that is."

"Whatever it is, don't go through with it. Some women here are true witches. If they bind you magically, you may not be able to leave."

Silence again, then, "You really have magic?"

My breath left me. I had grown more comfortable with the idea, and Tholdri had been more than accepting, but Isolde was a devout hunter. "Yes."

"Then I expect you to use it to protect Markus, and to ultimately free him."

"His life technically ended. He may not survive without a master." I wasn't sure about that, but it had been Drucida's theory.

"*You* now survive without a master. So it is possible."

I couldn't argue with her. I should have died the night Cael's ghouls attacked me. And yet here I was, surviving on my own. "I will do everything I can."

"Good. One last thing. I don't think you're the only prisoner here."

"What?" I gasped, my mind racing with thoughts of who else might have been taken. Did Eiric already have someone to use against me?

"There are a few other locked doors at the northern end of the temple, far from you. Last night, I heard someone crying. I haven't risked investigating further."

That explained why she hadn't visited. "How have you

managed to investigate at all?" There were guards everywhere, and she seemed to walk about as she pleased.

She snorted softly. "I've been training my entire life, Lyssandra. This is nothing." And with that, she was gone.

I stayed leaning against the door for a long while. I was tired and hungry, but I couldn't seem to make myself lie down. I stretched my neck again, and had just straightened when I sensed a new presence outside the door, though I'd heard no footsteps.

I went still, waiting for a knock, or for the lock to slide. Only Eiric, Xavier, or Cerridwen could sneak up so silently. Since it was the middle of the night, I was betting on Eiric. It could also be Cael, but I doubted it. My eyes darted around the room, futilely searching for a weapon. I knew I needed to keep him in my sights, but being near him made me feel physically ill.

The wood creaked behind me, ever so slightly, like someone was leaning against it, but I heard nothing else.

"It's you."

My heart stopped. This was a dream. I had actually fallen asleep, and I was dreaming. "Asher?"

The lock slid. I moved out of the way as the handle turned, then the door opened, and there he stood. I realized in that moment that I really hadn't expected to see him again. I had expected to either die by Eiric's hand, or to have Asher die trying to reach me.

We stood facing each other for the first time without the bond between us. The first time, other than the night we met.

He moved too fast for me to follow, then his hands were in my hair, his mouth pressed against mine.

My body melted against him. Safe. I was safe. But it was a lie. Even so, my shields crashed down. But he couldn't feel me. The bond was gone. I tore my mouth away from his. "You can't be here!" I gasped.

The door was still open behind us. We weren't safe. Not in the slightest.

"I know a way out. I can take you there."

I pulled back, even though my body ached to be held. "I cannot leave. Eiric must be stopped."

His silver eyes glinted. I was no longer a human servant—he could possibly bespell me and make me leave if he wanted—but I knew he would never betray me in that way. "We can figure it out together, somewhere safe."

"He will only find me again. And if you are near, he will use you against me." My heart pounded in my ears as I glanced past him out into the hall.

In the blink of an eye, he had the door closed, but it wouldn't do any good. It wouldn't keep Eiric out. We wouldn't even see him coming.

He closed the space between us, but didn't touch me again. His hands flexed, then relaxed, and I knew the effort had cost him. "I cannot leave you here. Markus, Tholdri, Steifan, and Geist are out in the city. We can come up with a plan."

I shook my head, fighting the trembling in my body. If Eiric found us—if he found *any* of them. "They need to leave. Gregor is sending hunters to Ivangard to kill me. Eiric wants them here for some reason. Isolde came ahead of them."

"I smelled her outside your door. Why didn't she let you out?"

He sounded so affronted, I almost had to laugh. Only if I tried, my throat was so tight I might cry instead. "I asked her not to. I don't know why, not for sure, but Eiric *wants* me to escape. I have been provided with too many opportunities for it to be otherwise." I winced, hating my next words. "Please, Asher, you need to go. Eiric has already threatened to use those I love. We cannot make it so easy for him to find you. He can track me through our shared blood, but not you. You must stay away from him."

He didn't budge. He was so still, he could have easily passed for a statue. "Those you love?"

I sighed. Maybe he hadn't heard me on the rooftop. Part of me was relieved, but I couldn't let it stand. I needed him to leave. "Yes, I love you, you idiot. Now you need to leave before you can be used against me. The thought of you, Steifan, and Tholdri all remaining safe is the only thing that has kept me moving forward. I *will* protect you all, but you need to let me."

He stepped close again, his fingers tracing the edge of my jaw. He looked down into my eyes. "Even without the bond, you would love a vampire? You would not choose freedom from me?"

I had never seen him so unsure. I had assumed that even without the bond, he would know exactly how I felt.

I stepped into his arms, then hugged him tightly. "It was never the bond. You should know that by now."

One of his hands lifted to the back of my hair, pressing me against him. "What would you have me do?"

"Leave, now. Stay alive. Eiric is mine to finish, and mine alone."

I knew he heard my words, but he didn't let me go.

"We helped an acolyte escape the city in exchange for knowledge on entering the temple. She was afraid for her life."

"At least two girls have died." I went on to tell him my theory about a summoner within the temple.

"This is all the more reason for you to leave with me now."

"You know I cannot."

He finally released me, then stepped back. "Just promise me one thing."

"I will try."

"Don't die."

I managed a small smile. "That is a hefty demand."

"Promise me."

He knew I could not, and neither could he, so we were just left staring at each other.

"At least let me tell you the way out," he said finally.

I nodded. "If I need to escape, Isolde will unlock the door."

He detailed the way he'd come in. It was simple enough. I could find the cellar and he'd broken the ward. I'd just have to hope no one else noticed that the way out was no longer barred.

We were left staring at each other again.

There was so much more I wanted to tell him. The bracelet, my magic, Lavandriel's grimoire. But there just wasn't time. It wasn't worth the risk. "Asher, you need to leave." I reached for him.

A pained expression crossed his face. "Someone is coming."

He was gone before I could say a word, and I was left

holding my breath with my heart hammering against my throat. If it was Eiric, he would smell Asher's scent on me. He would know he was in the temple and he would try to catch him. I would have to delay him by any means necessary.

I stood still, conflicted. Asher had shut the door on his way out, but had he locked it? I waited with my heart pounding in my throat as the lock slid, then the door opened.

Cael strode into the room, his features contorted with rage. "You fools." The door swung shut behind him.

I remained still, wishing I had a weapon.

His face was drawn, thinning out with that other-worldly energy always just beneath the surface. I caught glimpses of shadows around him, reaching out, then being withdrawn, as if he was forcing them into hiding.

I backed away until my thighs hit the bed.

His jaw twitched, caught halfway between his human form and the more monstrous one. He took several deep breaths, letting me know he was barely maintaining control. He didn't need to breathe, he was simply trying to calm himself.

Tense moments ticked by, until finally, he spoke. "I can smell Asher all over you."

I lifted my chin defiantly.

"If Eiric realizes he's in Ivangard, he will try to capture him."

I instantly deflated. "You mean he doesn't know?"

"He can't track Asher like he can you. They share no blood. As long as Asher's scent is mingled with the stronger smells of the city, he is invisible. Or he *was* invisible. Now his scent is here. I don't know where Eiric is, but if he returns tonight, he will notice. We cannot risk it."

I remained still, though in my head, I was screaming. Why had Asher risked so much to come here? Just to see if I was alive? Cael was right. We were *fools*.

His jaw twitched again. Almost too fast for the eye to follow, Cael lifted the nearest chair.

I flinched, thinking he meant to hit me.

If I didn't already hate him, the look in his eyes would have struck sympathy. It hurt him that I was afraid of him.

He extended the chair my way. "Hit me as hard as you can, and do not stop until you draw blood."

I stared at the chair. " . . . *what?*"

"Do it, Lyssandra. The blood will overpower Asher's scent. It is the only way. Eiric rested somewhere other than the temple last night, but I fear he will soon return. I can't say how much time we'll have."

I still didn't take the chair. "Why are you helping me? You sided with Eiric. You are my enemy."

He lowered the chair, stepping closer. There was a wild look in his eyes, sending a shiver down my spine. "How can you still not get it? He murdered my brother. And it may not have been by his own hand, but he murdered my sister too. He would have broken your bond with Asher, and Asher would have died. There was no other option. He offered me a bargain to save myself, but I didn't do it to live. My existence is cursed, and I deserve to die. But not before he pays for what he has done."

"But why did he even offer you the bargain?" Our conversations since that night had been so short and filled with venom, I had never gained clarity on the matter.

His face was slowly returning to human. To the kind features of the uncle I'd thought I had finally gained. "I believe he wants me for the ritual. It is the only explanation. There is no other reason for him to keep me alive. After what I did, he cannot use me against you. You would not care if he harmed me."

The chair was still in his hands, waiting for me to make my decision. Waiting for me to harm him. Just a few hours ago, it would have been an easier choice.

"You would still see him dead?" I asked.

"Even if it endangers both our lives."

I took the chair from his grip. "And you care if Asher lives?"

"He must remain out of Eiric's sight. Eiric knows if he captures him, he can make you do *anything*."

He was right. He was absolutely right. And now Asher's scent was all over me.

I lifted the chair. "The blood will be enough to cover the scent?"

He didn't so much as flinch. "You will need to get enough of it on you. And I will cover his path upon my departure."

"I still don't trust you. Not fully."

"You do not have to. Now hit me, Lyssandra. Time is short."

Before, I could have hit him hard enough with a single swing. Now, with only human strength, the process would be more difficult. But he was right. Eiric could not catch wind of Asher's scent.

Fighting the nausea building in my stomach, I lifted the chair, and swung.

CHAPTER NINE

I used cold water to wash the blood from my skin and clothing, but not thoroughly. Cael was right. Blood would overwhelm Eiric's other senses. Even blood that was anything but human.

I left just enough of the blood on me that it was clear I had at least made an effort.

Eiric sometimes seemed to read my mind, but I didn't think he actually could. Centuries of manipulating vampires from his tomb had simply made him highly perceptive. Perceptive enough to see that I had attacked Cael in a fit of rage. Cael had taken the punishment, and had left my chamber bleeding heavily. Heavily enough that the wounds would not heal immediately.

I shivered at the recent memory as I sat back on my bed. I was a fighter, yes, but my brand of violence did not come from rage. Not usually, at least. Even pretending it was so had shaken me.

Cael's fierce resolve as I beat him bloody had shaken me even more.

I lifted my head as the lock slid and the door creaked open. It was still the middle of the night. Cerridwen stood in the dark hall alone, the whites of her eyes catching the scant moonlight.

"I spoke with Cael."

I turned my head away, realizing Cerridwen might be more difficult to fool than Eiric. Eiric's arrogance and madness overshadowed much. Someone with no humanity left could never comprehend human nature. Cerridwen understood me far better than he ever would.

I turned my gaze out the window. "What of it?"

She stepped into the room, gently shutting the door behind her. "I know he betrayed you, but we need him alive."

"*You* need him alive."

"You would truly kill your own uncle?"

No. Yes. I just wasn't sure anymore. "He is no uncle of mine."

She reached the side of my bed. "Were you injured?"

I didn't answer.

She sighed heavily. "Another girl died tonight."

I whipped my gaze to her without thinking.

"I thought that might get your attention." She crossed her arms and jutted out her hip beneath her blue cloak. "Upon Gwenvere's request, I have agreed to let you look at the body."

"Why?"

"Because we need her cooperation. I am no witch, and Eiric lacks the patience to properly teach you the ritual. We will only have one attempt, and you must be ready."

"So you'll have me solve these murders to keep Gwenvere on your side? Why doesn't Eiric simply force her? He's not above threatening those she loves."

She smirked. "Gwenvere would let *everyone* around her die before she'd let us force her into anything."

"So threaten *her* life instead."

"She knows if we kill her, we'll have to find someone else, and few have her knowledge of the darker arts. You've seen her magic. It is not a gift granted by nature, or by the *light*."

Now she finally had my attention. "What do you mean? If it's not a natural gift, how did she obtain it?"

Arms still crossed, she considered me for a long moment. "I suppose there's no harm in telling you. The flames wielded by the acolytes are just as unnatural as Gwenvere's magic. I believe had you faced one of them directly the night of the battle, your sword would have glowed."

"You're saying their magic is demonic?" I thought again of the possibility of a summoner in the temple.

She hesitated, then nodded, as if still debating how much she should tell me. "Some practitioners can summon beings from other realms, *demons*, for lack of a better term. Most use these demons externally, but some take the demons within. And *some* can put the demons in other people."

I stared at her. "You're telling me Gwenvere and the witches with blue fire have demons inside of them?"

She answered with a single nod.

"But why? Why would they do it?"

She shrugged one shoulder. "Why else? Power. As

you've seen, the witches here are a force to be reckoned with."

I wondered if that was the real reason Eiric wasn't forcing Gwenvere into anything. Could it be that he feared the witches of Ivangard? It was a possibility. He had feared Drucida's witches enough to kill them before they could seal him away again. He wanted all witches and vampires dead. Anyone who could pose a threat. After centuries of imprisonment, he had grown paranoid.

Cerridwen tilted her head. "What are you thinking?"

"I'm thinking that anyone who would take a demon inside of them is mad. I've seen creatures from other realms. I've seen them kill in an instant. It is not worth the risk."

She shrugged again. "The witches hold this city. The Archduke and all the guard have been charmed into protecting them. The little magic they had before was weak. They saw their families hunted and destroyed. To them, the power and protection is well worth the risk."

I understood the sentiment, but I thought Drucida's tactics were superior. "But if they already have power, what did Eiric offer them in exchange for attacking the fortress?"

She shook her head. "No, Lyssandra. You've asked enough questions. Now, will you observe the girl's body? Tell us what is hunting them?"

I didn't miss her saying *what* instead of *who*. The remains must be grisly, though probably no worse than the other deaths I'd seen recently.

I stood, and her gaze lowered to my stained clothing.

"You will change first, I think."

I nodded, even though I might get more blood on me when observing the body. I hated to think it, but the girl's death might have been a blessing. With so much blood on the ground, Eiric would be able to smell nothing else.

"One last question," I said as I walked past her toward the armoire.

"Go on."

I opened one door, not looking back at her. "Would you ever take a demon inside of you?"

"I have survived for centuries, Lyssandra. What do you think?"

I shook my head as I pulled out a fresh cloak. Her meaning was loud and clear. Anyone with even a hint of survival instinct would not take such a creature inside of them. Even if there was powerful magic to be had . . .

Such power was never free.

THE GIRL WAS FOUND in her chamber. As far as I could tell, she had been sleeping peacefully when the attack happened. I had been almost sure upon simply hearing details of the deaths that something like the shadow creatures Matthias could summon were the killers, but now, all sense of surety had left me.

This death was different. Just as gruesome, but different. Instead of her entire body being minced into a puddle, the bulk of the damage had occurred in her chest and abdomen. The ribs were cracked open, the flesh shredded. I would have thought the heart might be gone—

SARA C. ROETHLE

many monsters liked to steal hearts—but it was still partially intact within the cavity.

I stepped back, breathing shallowly against the smell. The death was fresh. There was no rot, but the damage was enough to perforate the internal organs and intestines. Death doesn't just smell like blood.

Gwenvere, Cerridwen, and two guards stood within the small chamber, the latter two holding lanterns near their bodies. They were yet to speak, but everyone was looking pale and ghoulish in the warm light.

"Have you seen anything like this?" Gwenvere asked.

I didn't want to simply say no. She had put enough faith in me to convince Cerridwen I should be involved. I didn't want those privileges revoked. "It could be any number of things at this stage. It would help if I could investigate the rest of the temple, and to learn a little more about how people get in and out." I wondered if she knew about the route Asher had taken. If she knew *anything* could come in without invitation, as long as it knew the way. They might not be able to go over the wards, but they could go under them.

She looked at Cerridwen, who nodded.

"The wards on the temple are simple," Gwenvere explained. "Ten priestesses, including myself, created them. An invitation by any one of us is needed to enter the temple."

"That's why you met me at the gates?" I asked.

She nodded.

I turned my back on the body, fully facing her. "And what if all ten priestesses are killed?"

She frowned. "The ward would cease to exist. We put it in place for safety, nothing more."

I doubted that. The priestesses may have taken in demons to increase their magic as a means of protection, but many of them had attacked Drucida's fortress. They weren't innocent. They were using their power to make enemies. Enemies who might want to see any one of them dead.

"And what about leaving?" I asked.

Another glance at Cerridwen, who shrugged. "Any can leave, though the acolytes must ask for permission if they are to leave before they fully pledge themselves."

"Why?"

Her cheeks reddened at my tone. "We are not villains, Lyssandra. If any of the acolytes learn we have magic and are not bound to keep our secrets, it could spell disaster for us all."

Once again, I doubted it. I had been at the fortress when the witches attacked. These women could take care of themselves. There must be *other* secrets they were guarding. Maybe it was the demons, but if that information got out, what could anyone really do about it?

"Well, if only those you invite can come in, the killer is one of your own."

Her brow furrowed. The guards had backed further away, averting their gazes from the body.

"And someone with magic, or at least beyond human strength," I continued. "The damage wasn't done with a blade. Someone ripped her apart." I motioned toward the body behind me.

"I do not possess such capabilities," she hissed, misinterpreting my meaning.

"I'm not accusing you," I sighed. "But if anyone else has similar magic . . . It did feel like you tore my insides apart."

She glanced back at the guards. "Leave us."

The two men hesitated, but at her glare, quickly shuffled out of the room.

"Are they bound to keep your secrets as well?" I asked as the door shut behind them.

She turned her attention back to me. "They are, but they don't need to know more than they must. My magic is not physical, Lyssandra. The pain you felt was only in your mind."

My brows lifted. "But the pain lingered. I felt awful the next day."

"Your mind believed without any doubt that your body had been damaged. Belief is a powerful thing."

I wondered if she knew she'd just given me the upper hand. If her magic couldn't actually damage me, I had nothing to fear but pain. Pain, I was used to.

"Does anyone else have similar magic of a more physical nature?" I asked.

She shook her head, not even considering the option. "None of the priestesses or acolytes are capable of this." She looked past me toward the body for a moment, then quickly averted her gaze.

It was nice that she had the luxury, but if magic wasn't involved, there was something I was missing. I turned back toward the body, then knelt beside the bed. Her expression was peaceful. She hadn't seen her death coming, which led me back to the idea of summoned demons. Maybe one had gotten loose. Or maybe . . . my mouth went dry at the thought. Maybe one had gotten *out*.

There was no delicate way to ask what I needed to know. "Did all the girls who've died have demons inside of them?"

Gwenvere gasped. "How did you—"

"I told her," Cerridwen said simply.

"But—"

"You know her secrets, Gwenvere. It's only fair."

I knew fair play had nothing to do with why Cerridwen told me, but now wasn't the time to argue. I stood, stepping away from the body again. The mutilation lined up with my thoughts. It looked exactly like something had exploded out of her.

I looked at Gwenvere expectantly.

Her mouth gaped. Her eyes were wide, stunned. "They did, but that isn't how things work. The demons are not corporeal. It's just magical energy. They don't have claws and teeth."

"I've seen demons kill before."

She shook her head. "No, this is different. And even if it was the case, it would have happened to more of us by now."

I stepped toward her. I was right. The more she spoke against it, the more I knew I was correct. "I'll need to know more about what you do with the demons, and I'll need to know more about the three girls. Perhaps there was something about them that made things work differently."

Gwenvere's expression shut down. "Your help is no longer needed, Lyssandra."

"But—"

"No," she cut me off. "I'll see to this on my own." She didn't look back at Cerridwen as she spoke. "Return her to her chamber, or do whatever you want with her. Just get her out of my sight."

Cerridwen looked ready to laugh, but she contained herself. Ancient beings found the strangest things amusing. She gestured for me to join her near the door.

I stole a final glance at the body. If I was right, more girls were going to die.

The only question was, where did the demons go once they escaped?

CHAPTER TEN

Asher

"Isolde is there? Are you certain?" This was the first emotion I had seen from Markus since Lyssandra had been taken.

I had left the fortress the way I'd come, meeting with Tholdri before rejoining the others. They had successfully smuggled the girl's family out of the city. Whether they would survive going forward was up to them.

I leaned lightly against the wall. My skin ached where I had touched Lyssandra. She was alive. I had seen it with my own eyes. So why did she feel like little more than a fantasy? "I recognized her scent. Lyssandra confirmed it."

Tholdri's expression was dark. "You should have made her leave with you. It's insanity for her to stay."

I would have liked to agree with him, but Lyssandra was right. Eiric would find her again. She would never be safe until he was dead—truly dead. "Isolde is here because the Helius Order is coming. We thought Eiric made

Lyssandra a target simply to isolate her, but there is more to his plan. He wanted to lure them here."

Geist tilted his head. "But why? What are the hunters to him? Targeting witches and vampires, I understand. We are true threats to him. But the hunters will die as easily as insects beneath his boots."

Tholdri frowned at his words. At first I thought he might be offended, but then he shook his head. "It must have something to do with our bloodlines. When we faced the Nattmara, they claimed our blood was more powerful than mortal blood. We could sustain them for far longer."

Geist raised a brow at him. "You truly faced a Nattmara?" When Tholdri nodded, Geist smiled. "My, you are just full of surprises."

"Tholdri is right," Steifan interjected. "There is no other explanation."

"Eiric is mad." Markus glowered at everyone. "Pondering his motives is a waste of time. We must focus on the facts." He looked at me. "Can you scout outside the city? Determine when the hunters will arrive?"

Though I hated the idea of such a mundane task, I nodded. "It will have to wait until tomorrow. The sun will rise soon." We wouldn't see the sunrise in the boarded up hovel, but I could feel it drawing near.

"But what good will that do us?" Steifan asked.

Markus' jaw twitched. He was always on the edge of irritation. I would have blamed the bond with Lyssandra, but he had never seemed terribly patient. "Eiric has implemented the legs of his plan all in perfect time. He will have done the same with the hunters' arrival. They will be here as soon as he needs them, which means another part of his plan will soon be revealed. Perhaps the *final* part of his plan."

"The ritual," Tholdri agreed. "But he doesn't have the other half of the grimoire."

I shook my head slightly. *Fools*. Eiric had proven us to be fools time and time again. "Unless he knows we have it, and that it's already here with us, in Ivangard."

"But how can he know?" Steifan asked.

I shook my head again. I couldn't be sure, but— "Lyssandra believes Eiric wants her to attempt escape. Perhaps so that she can be followed. She worries that he will use any one of us against her, but he may instead seek the grimoire. He may know that we have it, but he has not yet located us."

Tholdri let out a long breath. "I suppose hiding it wasn't such a bad idea after all. He may find us eventually, but it is not with us."

There was that, at least. Eiric might find us eventually, but he would not easily find the grimoire. It was cold comfort, at best. I would not know any real comfort as long as the woman I loved was in the hands of a madman. My instincts urged me to attack Eiric myself, but I knew my capabilities. While I would gladly die for Lyssandra, I would not die needlessly, not while she might still have use of me in the future.

And so, I would find the hunters. They would let us know how much time we had left. Time until what, was anyone's guess.

CHAPTER ELEVEN

Lyssandra

Something was on top of me, pinning the blankets on either side of my body. I hadn't even remembered going to sleep. Now, hot breath smelling of rot steamed the side of my cheek.

I remained perfectly still, trying to gauge the situation. Whatever was pinning me . . . it wasn't human. Not even close. Its mere presence raised all the tiny hairs across my body. A feeling akin to nearly stepping on a venomous snake set into my bones.

Moments ticked by, then a low growl trickled out of the thing's throat. I wanted desperately to open my eyes, but any movement might set it off. It lowered itself near my face again, huffing across my skin. *Scenting* me.

I heard a sound on the other side of the room. The lock sliding out of place? The door creaked open and the thing lunged off of me. I sat up, catching just a glimpse of long, black limbs, a too large head, and a protruding maw as it rushed toward Gwenvere and Cerridwen standing in the doorway.

Gwenvere shrieked and fell back out of sight. Cerridwen lifted her arm as the creature slashed at her with long talons. Her breath hissed out of her, then it was gone. It had all happened in the blink of an eye.

I was on my feet rushing toward them before Gwenvere could stand. Sprawled on the stone floor, she appeared unharmed. Cerridwen, however, cradled her arm. Blood soaked her blue sleeve.

My heart was thundering so loud in my ears, I couldn't make out her words until she cleared her throat and tried again.

"*Lyssandra.* What was that thing doing in your room?"

I took a few deep breaths. "It was straddling me in my sleep. *Scenting* me." I wasn't worried about her arm. She could heal quickly, and even if she couldn't, she deserved far worse.

Gwenvere finally stood, visibly trembling. "What was that thing?"

Anger tickled my throat. "You should know. You have one inside of you." The long talons were perfect for tearing through any young girl's chest.

Gwenvere inhaled sharply. "That's not what they look like. They don't look like anything. They are simply concentrated energy."

I gave her my best bland look. "I've seen shadow creatures slither under doors in a pool of black mist, only to reform into monsters able to kill in a heartbeat. The thing inside you may not have form currently, but I'm guessing that creature is what it will turn into as soon as it figures out how to remedy its situation."

I couldn't be sure about my claims, but it would be too big of a coincidence otherwise. A demon, several demons, had torn their way out of the acolytes, and now they were roaming the temple. Although, I wasn't sure what had happened to the demon that had escaped before my arrival. Perhaps it had returned to its own realm, or perhaps it was simply hiding.

Gwenvere's breath came too fast. If she didn't calm herself, she was going to faint. "It's just not possible," she said again.

"Lyssandra is right," Cerridwen said behind me. "Demons must be summoned to this realm. They do not simply arrive. You have dabbled in magics you do not truly understand. I can only hope you'll remain alive long enough to fulfill your purpose."

Gwenvere's breath came faster, her skin turning ashen.

"Not helpful," I said to Cerridwen, turning to give Gwenvere my full attention. I hesitantly gripped her arms, looking into her eyes. "You need to remain calm. If the demons can be put into people, there must be a way to take them out."

Her eyes still showed too much white, but she managed a few deep, ragged breaths. "It's not—" Her breath whooshed out of her, deflating her chest. She shook her head. "It's not possible. There's no way to undo it."

"You cannot be sure of that."

"I am." She tried to laugh, but her voice cracked. "I am

sure. I'm the one who summoned the demons to begin with."

I dropped her arms like she'd burned me. "*You* put the demons in those girls? In yourself?" I had expected someone like Matthias. Someone ancient and twisted.

She nodded. "I—" she cut herself off, licking her dry lips. "You don't understand the things I've seen. It's a miracle I'm still alive. The rest of my family is not." She shook her head. "I only wanted to be strong enough to protect myself. I wanted the others able to protect them-selves too."

"Your followers were not protecting themselves when they attacked the witches' fortress." I bit my tongue too late. I hadn't wanted to throw accusations until I'd learned all I could from her.

Her expression crumbled as she looked past me to Cerridwen. "The ones who left us?"

I glanced back to see Cerridwen's cold smile. "They volunteered. It was their choice. You know what Eiric promised them."

"Then why haven't they returned?" Gwenvere asked.

Cerridwen continued smiling, and I realized some-thing. The witches here were not my enemies. I didn't have to hunt the witches who'd attacked the fortress. Eiric had already killed them.

Cerridwen's dull eyes let me know I was right. They would have been difficult opponents, but they had trusted him. He'd probably had them killed in their sleep.

"What did he promise them?" I asked.

She tilted her head. "What do any so consumed by power seek?"

I frowned. Of course. Of course that had been the price. "He told them he would make them immortal, like him."

She nodded.

Gwenvere seemed ready to pass out again. Her shallow breaths were too loud. "Those fools. Those utter fools."

Cerridwen watched her until she'd regained control of her breathing. "Those who left the temple chose their own fates, and you have chosen yours. Do not forget the bargain you have made."

Gwenvere swallowed loudly, then went still. "Very well, but if you want me to finish my task, we must take care of the demons."

Cerridwen looked at me. "I believe this is your specialty, is it not?"

It wasn't, but it might pay off for me in the end. "I'll need my sword."

She nodded slightly. "Sword, but no magic."

"Fine." I turned back toward Gwenvere. "Just what did Eiric offer you? Why are you working with such a monster?"

Her lips formed a grim line.

"Fine. Then tell me this at least. Was it worth it?"

She was still for a moment, so still I couldn't even tell if she was breathing. Finally, she answered me with a single nod.

I watched her, waiting for more, but she averted her gaze. I would ponder what she deemed a greater boon than immortality later. For now, I had demons to hunt. And I was finally going to be reunited with my sword.

It almost made the demonic encounter worth it.

Almost.

CERRIDWEN LED me through a maze of hallways and staircases, finally ending somewhere on the top floor, near the eastern edge, if I had correctly kept track. If this was where my sword would be kept going forward, I needed to remember it.

Gwenvere had reluctantly joined us on our journey. The demons were her problem, after all. I could hardly believe she'd been so foolish. It was mad to summon such beings to begin with, let alone take them inside of you. She had to be sweating now, wondering when her own demon would break free. *If* it would. Perhaps the girls had met their untimely ends because they weren't strong enough to contain the creatures. Thus far, only acolytes had died, and Gwenvere had admitted that many priestesses also carried demons within.

Cerridwen stopped in front of a closed door. I didn't see a lock, but when she held her palm against the surface of the door, something clicked within. She opened the door, then stepped inside.

I followed, observing the unremarkable room. Dusty crates, furniture draped with white sheets, rolled up rugs and curtains . . . nothing seemed special about the room. The perfect place to hide an ancient relic.

She walked toward one large crate and pushed it aside. Behind it, leaned against the wall, was my sword, quiet in its sheath.

"Not hidden very well," I commented.

Cerridwen brushed the dust from her palms and stepped back. "No one here could get past the lock I placed."

I glanced back at the open door, still not seeing a lock. I'd just have to take her word for it. What was important now, was that I had my sword.

I approached the blade, feeling oddly apprehensive. I wasn't sure it would work for me when I couldn't access my magic.

Gwenvere remained near the open doorway, watching us warily.

I lifted the sword by its hilt. It felt different now without my added strength, the long blade almost too heavy for my build. I held it before me, and the eye snapped open. Its lid fluttered, giving me a sense of panic.

"Good," Cerridwen said, observing the sword over my shoulder. "I was worried it wouldn't sense you without your magic, but it seems your blood is enough. Whether it glows for you . . . I suppose we'll find out soon."

I glared at her. "Well if the demon rips my heart out instead, I suppose I won't be around to worry about it."

"Do you lack faith in your skills?"

"Against a creature from another realm? Most certainly."

"You are far too honest," she laughed.

We both turned just as Xavier appeared in the doorway. "What exactly do you three think you're doing?" His cheeks were flushed, and he was out of breath. Since I knew he could run long distances without tiring, he must have been searching the entire temple for us.

Cerridwen waved him off. "We have a demon problem. Lyssandra will take care of it."

Irritation pinched his features. "Eiric needs her *alive*."

Cerridwen stepped in front of me. "Obviously. That is why she must kill the demon we found crouching over her in her bed. Why did it go to her chamber of all places?"

His expression softened—barely. "The demon was in her chamber?"

"Crouching over her in her bed. Whether it wanted to taste a blood witch or a hunter is anyone's guess."

He stepped past Gwenvere, not acknowledging her. "Then you should find it and get rid of it. Lyssandra needs to work on the ritual."

His sense of urgency over the ritual made me suspect that Eiric was listening in. He might be trapped by sunlight, but his connection to Xavier meant he could *visit* whenever he pleased. This was Eiric's order, not his. Xavier didn't care about the ritual.

But that also meant Eiric was willing to send the woman he *loved* to face a demon, rather than risk me dying and thwarting his plans. Cerridwen was a fool to continue helping him. It would be her undoing sooner or later. Perhaps even today.

Feeling something akin to sympathy, I stepped around her, still gripping my sword. "I've faced demons before. My sword was made to defeat them."

Xavier rolled his eyes. "Yes, I'm well aware. Eiric banished many demons before he was sealed away. He will do so again when he arriv—." His face puckered. "When he awakes," he corrected.

118

So he wasn't here, as I had thought. Which meant I had bloodied Cael for nothing. Unless Cerridwen or Xavier might have noticed Asher's scent . . . Regardless, it was too late to take it back.

While I didn't particularly want to face the demon, I also didn't want to lose my sword so soon. "Eiric said himself the sword rejects him now. It has chosen me. I am the only one who can wield it until it chooses another. If I don't find the demon, it may attack me when I'm vulnerable."

His nose wrinkled, and I knew he wanted to say something Eiric wouldn't like. Or maybe Eiric was trying to make Xavier say something *he* didn't like. Either way, the result was an awkward silence.

I started fastening my sword across my back, over my blue cloak. "Well now that that's settled—"

"I will come to protect you," Xavier said through gritted teeth.

"Maybe the demon will kill you and end your misery." I smiled sweetly at him.

Something flickered in his eyes. Something different. He wanted to die. More than anything else, he wanted to die. So what was his hesitation? Would Cerridwen simply bring him back in a form far worse than the one he currently possessed?

He turned away before I could study him further. "Let us go. If the demon is still in the temple, the sword will track it."

He left the room and started down the hall before anyone could argue.

I watched Cerridwen for her reaction, but she simply

lifted her nose and followed him, leaving me alone with Gwenvere.

She met my waiting gaze. I had my sword, and if I tried to escape, Gwenvere might not try to stop me. Now more than ever, I was sure that was what Eiric wanted. At some point, I might just give in to his wishes. But for now, I marched dutifully into the hall, unsheathed my sword, and asked it to find a demon.

CHAPTER TWELVE

I eventually took the lead. Well, my sword took the lead. I held it in front of me, waiting for any sign that a demon was near.

Xavier came next, walking too close to my shoulder. If we were attacked, I wouldn't have enough room to move properly. Of course, he was now far faster than me. Maybe having him near, and forced to protect me, wasn't the worst thing.

"Why are you doing this? Why do you care?" His words were almost too low to hear.

I kept my attention trained on the hall. An acolyte emerged from a room ahead, gasped when she saw us, then hurried away. News of another death had already spread. The temple was eerily silent.

"What do you mean?"

"Why are you hunting this demon?"

I shook my head. I'd thought Xavier had come to understand me to a degree, but perhaps I'd been mistaken. "It will kill innocents if we don't stop it."

"But why is it up to you to stop it? You are a prisoner here."

"Do you see anyone else volunteering?"

His laugh was little more than a frustrated huff of breath. "No, I do not, but I'm beginning to think you're just as mad as Eiric."

His words made my gut squirm. I had seen no signs of my own madness, but . . .

Sensing my shift in mood, he sighed. "You know what I mean."

We turned down another hall. My instincts told me to venture lower. Somewhere dark.

"Was the demon really crouched over your bed?"

I nodded. "It was on top of me. Scenting me, I think."

"I wonder why."

"I take it you don't know much about demons?"

He glanced at the two women trailing us, speaking to each other in hushed tones. "No. The demons that haunted Cerridwen after she brought Eiric back were shadows. They weren't fully in this realm. Still dangerous, yes, but not like things fully summoned. Gwenvere is a fool."

I was glad Gwenvere's human hearing would not be keen enough to overhear, though I completely agreed with the sentiment. "What did Eiric offer her in exchange for her help? It wasn't immortality. I know he offered that to the others."

He shook his head. "I cannot tell you, Lyssandra. Just know that she is a pitiful, fearful human, just like the rest of you."

I let it go. We reached a set of stairs and ventured

BLOOD OF ANCIENTS

down. Following my instincts, I went straight for the next landing, continuing down until we were on the temple's base level. I didn't want to take the path Asher had detailed to me, lest Cerridwen and Gwenvere discover the unwarded way into the temple, but we might have to if I didn't find the demon elsewhere. I would check *everywhere* else first, and hope for the best.

Another young woman in blue robes caught sight of us. Instead of running, she stood to one side of the hall and watched us pass, her eyes mainly on my outstretched sword. I heard Gwenvere speaking softly to her, and she retreated into the nearest room and shut the door.

"Where exactly are you leading us?" Xavier asked. "Has the sword spoken to you?"

"Demons like darkness," I explained. "I think." I shook my head. "It at least seems a good place to start."

"I heard about the summoner, Matthias, from Amarithe. Is that where all of your *impressive* demon knowledge comes from?"

"Some of it. The shadows he could summon feared light." I thought about it. "But there was another . . . being. His name was Renault. Or at least, that was the stolen name he went by. He seemed like a mortal man—he even fell in love with a mortal woman—but he wasn't from here. It was strange though. He didn't seem . . . evil. Far from it."

"Intriguing." He waited while I chose a random door and opened it.

Just a bedroom. My sword responded to nothing within. We moved on.

We had checked several more rooms by the time Xavier spoke again. "What happened to him?"

With my mind on our task, I didn't immediately catch his meaning. "What happened to who?"

"The man who was actually a demon."

"When the summoner died, he was forced to go back to his own realm, leaving behind the woman he loved."

"A fate worse than death, some might say. Though I would know nothing of it."

I glanced at him. "You mean, you know nothing of love? Didn't you love your *master* once?"

"Like a brother. But I was a young man when he made me his servant. Since then, my life has not been my own."

I considered his words as we checked another room. Gwenvere and Cerridwen had fallen further behind. "Then I pity you. No wonder you wish to die."

"And yet, I am probably the only one who will survive, along with Eiric. How ironic."

We reached a door at the end of a long hall, finally finding a way down. I could have simply asked Gwenvere for directions, but I preferred her out of earshot. Xavier only seemed to speak candidly when no one else was close enough to hear—and when Eiric was not in his mind.

I started down the dark stairs. We had no lantern, but if the demon was hiding below, my sword would glow. Or, I *hoped* it would glow. I wasn't sure without access to my magic.

Xavier walked down at my side, going silent.

I heard something scurrying across the floor, but it

was too small to be the demon. Perhaps a rat. I wondered if the demon could lose its form at will like the shadows. It had seemed pretty solid perched over me in my bed.

We reached the foot of the stairs, and still my sword did not glow. I was about to dismiss the space when I caught a whiff of something rotten.

"What is that?"

Xavier kept his voice low. "Not something I care to observe."

"It's a good thing you're used to acting against your will. We need to find a light."

I heard footsteps behind us a moment before Gwenvere reached us, holding a lantern. "Here. I thought we might need this."

I took the lantern gratefully. It must have been why she and Cerridwen had fallen so far behind. Wanting to see the source of the smell just as little as Xavier, I followed my nose, winding my way around apple barrels and various crates. At the far end of the cellar, I found what was rotting. It was the corpse of a male guard.

I wished I had a free hand to hold over my nose, but one was occupied by my sword, and the other with the lantern. The guard had been disemboweled, and his face slashed by long claws.

I looked over at Gwenvere as she joined us. "I think we can all guess what happened to him."

She pressed her hand firmly over her nose and mouth, then mumbled, "The first demon to escape, judging by the smell."

At least she had come to fully accept my theory, which

was well beyond a theory by now. The demon we'd encountered proved it. "I wonder how many more bodies we'll find. Has anyone else gone missing?"

"We monitor those coming and going, not everyone within the temple. Though the guards' barracks should let us know if anyone has been neglecting their duties."

Xavier knelt beside the body, observing the wounds. "I believe the more important question is, where did *this* demon go? If there are three, what are they all doing?"

The bracelet around my wrist suddenly felt heavier than before. "I could track it if I had access to my magic."

"How can—" Gwenvere began.

"That's not an option," Cerridwen cut her off, then looked at me. "If you cannot use the sword to track it, you will return to your chamber."

I frowned. "I didn't say I couldn't use the sword to find it, just that I could also use my blood. I would know right away if this particular demon was still in the castle." Of course, the body was old. The connection between victim and killer might have long since faded, but Cerridwen didn't need to know that.

"It's not happening, Lyssandra." She gave me a knowing look, her dark eyes unwavering. "You will save your magic and strength for performing rituals." She encompassed Gwenvere in her gaze. "You will teach her more this evening. Eiric was pleased with her progress the last session."

I shifted uncomfortably at the mention of Eiric. Had Cerridwen told him I'd come farther along than I actually had? Yes, I'd learned to cast a few rituals, but whatever he had in mind was something much, *much* more.

"But what of the demons?" Gwenvere asked. "What if one comes for her again?"

I didn't like being talked about like I wasn't there, but it was a good question.

Xavier and Cerridwen exchanged a look, and I realized Eiric was likely communicating with them both, hence Cerridwen's sudden shift in demeanor.

"I will take the sword and remain nearby while Lyssandra trains," Xavier said. "If the demon comes, Gwenvere can return the bracelet to Lyssandra's wrist, and I will return the sword so that she might use it to banish the demon."

Interesting. Eiric would allow me access to my magic, *or* to the sword, but not both at once. Did he fear me becoming too much of a threat, or was it something else?

Gwenvere seemed just as confused as I was, but she reluctantly nodded. "Very well, give me until this afternoon to prepare, then I will teach her. I can only hope we're all still alive by then."

I wanted to ask what would become of the other acolytes who had taken in demons, but perhaps it was a question best saved for when Cerridwen was not around. Xavier, however, it seemed I was stuck with.

I took one last look at the body, wondering if he'd happened upon the demon down here, or if he'd been dragged away from his post. I turned my attention to Gwenvere. "You should warn everyone to not venture into dark places alone. Perhaps caution will spare a few lives."

Her jaw tense, she nodded. Maybe she was expecting me to tell her it was all her fault. It was, but I wouldn't rub it in. Having to live with a demon inside of her until her dying day—which might come sooner rather than later—was punishment enough.

IT SEEMED XAVIER and I were having a contest. A contest to see who could go the longest without speaking. Since he was immortal, it was probably him, but I'd at least give him a run for the title.

We had spent most of the day in my room, with a few short trips to the dining hall. The hall had been mostly empty, but the few present had stared more openly than ever. It was a relief each time to be back in my isolated chamber. I had stored Lavandriel's grimoire beneath my bed the previous night, and had left it there thus far. Perhaps Xavier could tell me why Cerridwen had given it to me, but . . . maybe Eiric didn't actually know about it. If I showed Xavier, that might change. On the other hand, I wanted to see if Gwenvere could make sense of some of the more confusing rituals within, and I wasn't likely to be alone with her. Not while Xavier had my sword . . .

My eyes lowered to where my sword leaned against the wall near his knee. He had positioned his chair beneath the window, tilting his head back to catch a ray of sunlight on his cheeks. I wondered how long he'd gone without sunlight, trapped in Eiric's crypt. And I wondered what Cerridwen had done alone for so many centuries.

"Why didn't Cerridwen free you sooner?" I asked abruptly before realizing I'd just lost my imaginary contest.

His eyes remained closed. For a moment I thought he was asleep, but then he answered, "For a time, she sought a cure for Eiric's vampirism on her own. She had no use of me. Then, when he learned to speak into the minds of young vampires to set his own plans in motion, she worked against him."

I sat up a little straighter. "She did?"

He finally opened his eyes and sat up. "I told you that Eiric was a good man, once. A good friend. That being said, Cerridwen was always his better half."

"And yet, she now plays a part in his schemes."

Xavier nodded. "I was surprised at first too. Though she loved him and wanted to save him, she also fought against him. She was devastated by the deaths of all those innocents."

"But she chose to be a necromancer," I countered. "She chose to embrace death."

"Only to bring him back to life. One of the few truths he told her in the end was that he had mistakenly corrupted his own blood. He had a slow, painful death ahead. He wanted her to save him. When she could not, she settled for bringing him back."

Shaking my head, I leaned back against my pillows. It was almost sad, or at least terribly tragic. I thought about Elanore. When Alexander went mad, she took her children and fled. Had Cerridwen and Eiric produced any children, would she have done the same?

"So eventually Cerridwen gave in to Eiric's demands," I thought out loud, then tilted my head toward him, "but it was not Cerridwen who released you. It was Amarithe."

His chin bobbed slightly before he leaned his face back

into the ray of sunlight. "That is correct. I think Cerridwen blamed me for Eiric's descent. I was his best friend. I should have saved him."

"Surely she understands that no one could have saved him."

One corner of his mouth curled. "Of course, but that doesn't stop her from wanting someone to blame."

"Just as she blamed Lavandriel."

"Yes, just as she blamed Lavandriel, her dearest friend." His smile broadened. "You know, Cerridwen has strong emotions toward you because of her."

I lifted a brow, though he couldn't see it with his eyes drifting closed again. "She is my ancestor, and I share her resemblance, but I'm not *her*."

"But Lavandriel is dead, and Cerridwen misses her friend. She also hates her friend. And loves her. Thus, she's not quite sure how to feel about you. She is probably trying to not get attached since you'll likely die before all of this is through."

"Why are you being so forthcoming with me?" I asked.

His smile wilted. "Perhaps I see a bit of Lavandriel in you as well. Or perhaps my time with you is the first real conversation I've experienced in centuries."

"What does Eiric's ritual entail?"

He sighed dramatically, slumping further in his seat. "Great power, and great sacrifice. The first, you may not have enough of. The second, you will make regardless."

"Comforting."

He lifted his head. "Honest." He looked toward the door. "I believe Gwenvere approaches for your lesson." He reached for my sword as he stood. "Are you ready?"

I nodded. I would soon have my bracelet removed, and my sword would be near me. I wasn't sure what Eiric feared, but I would certainly do my best to find out.

CHAPTER THIRTEEN

Tholdri

I watched the moon lifting slowly into the sky, stars glittering peacefully. I had started riding a few hours prior. Geist and Asher would search for the hunters, and the rest of us would be ready. We needed to speak with them before they could reach the city. Hopefully we could make them understand they were walking into a trap.

While they might not listen to Steifan, many of them had known me my entire life. They had known Markus too, but he was . . . less agreeable. They had to know Lyss would never have killed the Potentate. It was madness that they believed it at all.

Well, not quite madness, I admitted, if only to myself. After the blame she received from her uncle's death, and the judgment she had endured over her red hair, and even to just the fact that she was a woman . . . she had never been well-liked. Few had taken the time to truly get to know her.

"No sign of them yet."

I turned at Geist's words. I had sensed him only moments before he spoke. He stood just a few paces away, opposite my horse so as not to startle the beast. He was always observant of such things.

"How far did you travel?"

He lifted one black-clad shoulder, barely perceptible in the night. "They will not arrive tonight, nor tomorrow night, unless they come from another direction. Asher will see them if they do."

Markus and Steifan waited near the other city entrance, where Asher would report back once his scouting was through.

"Good. So we have time."

He moved closer at a human pace. "If we were wise, we would venture farther, stop them from arriving at all."

My spine stiffened. "You mean kill them."

He shrugged again. "Convince them. Kill them. Whatever it takes to prevent Eiric from using them. They will surely die in Ivangard regardless."

He was probably right, but I would never attack my fellow hunters, no matter what was at stake.

Unless they were trying to kill me. Since I'd fled with Lyss, that might be their aim.

"We will not kill them."

"Very well."

I turned to observe him, but his dark eyes were on the distant moon, just a sliver of light left to it. He was lovely to look at, similar to Asher, though not similar at all. His bronze skin would be deep brown with any sunlight, and his hair was pure black. "You would refrain from attacking them simply because I asked?"

He turned enough to give me a small, knowing smile. "Are you so shocked?"

I angled my head away as my cheeks burned. *Light*, I was the one who was supposed to make others blush, not the other way around. "You're an ancient vampire. I imagine you are used to doing as you please."

"Yes, I am. And it would not please me to kill the hunters. It would please me even less to do so against your will."

I kept my gaze on the dark, distant mountains. "Did you know Cedrik before he joined the Order?" It still felt odd referring to the Potentate by his given name. Even odder to think of him as Lyssandra's grandfather, a man of witch blood.

He sidled a little closer, sending a nervous thrill through my gut. "No. He was already a hunter when I met him. He had killed many vampires, even without true hunter blood running through his veins. Not like our Lyssandra."

That was right. Her hunter bloodline came from her father. The Potentate had forged his own records, and those of his daughter. "If he was hunting vampires, how did you come to be friends?"

"I have long had friends amongst the witches, across several generations. He knew of me. When I heard about two blood witch brothers hunting vampires, I had to see for myself."

I finally looked at him to find him already watching

me, but I was too curious to look away. This was a part of the Potentate's history that even Lyssandra knew little about. Cael had shared some, but it seemed memories of the past hurt him to speak of. "Was Cael . . . "

He sighed. "He had committed himself to necromancy at that point, to grant himself an upper hand against the vampires. Both he and Cedrick were relatively weak magically."

"A necromancer, but not a vampire?"

Now it was his turn to look away. "I am reluctant to share the next piece of this tale."

"You turned him into a vampire, didn't you?"

He sighed again. "Cedrik and I spoke at length on what had happened to his sister. I believed his cause noble, and I did not want him to get himself killed before he could fulfill his purpose. I thought—" He glanced back to find me still watching him. "I thought in creating such a creature, we might stand a chance against Eiric."

"And that's why he meant for you to claim Lyssandra," I concluded. "He knew he could trust you."

"He did. And I would have done as he asked. Although, I do not mind not being Eiric's primary target currently."

"And what of Markus' master?"

He lifted one shoulder and let it fall. "I spoke of Cedrik's tale to other ancients when I came across them. Some had noticed the younglings of their flocks acting strangely, and went to hear Cedrik's tale themselves. I believe he convinced one of them to claim Markus. And then, someone killed her," he finished. "Quite possibly, the death was arranged by Eiric."

I nodded along with his words. "He'll use Asher if he

can. He'll use any of us, but he's arrogant. He'll want to hurt Lyssandra as much as he can just to feel like he has won."

"I agree."

"Do you think we can kill him? If we simply stormed the temple and attacked, do you think we would stand a chance? I trust Lyss, I really do, but she is only one woman."

He reached around my back and I tensed, but he only patted my horse's neck. My horse let out a huff a breath. Usually she was on alert around vampires, but not Geist. "He bested Asher easily, and we do not know how devoted Cael is to his cause. I believe it would be foolish to rush in unless we were truly running out of time."

My shoulders slumped with defeat. He was right, but — "I just hate leaving her there."

He stopped petting my horse, then ever so lightly, placed his hand along my shoulder. When I did not step away, his fingers curled downward, gripping me through my cloak. "I believe if Asher can wait, so can we."

I laughed and shook my head. I could tell Asher was barely containing himself. His rage lurked just beneath the surface. "You're right. You're absolutely right."

His hand remained on my shoulder, and I was glad we were alone. I wasn't sure Markus could stand another hunter cozying up to a vampire. He might rush toward Lyssandra himself, if only to end his torture once and for all.

CHAPTER FOURTEEN

Lyssandra

The first thing I took note of as I woke the next morning, was that there wasn't a demon on top of me. That alone was a great relief. I had trained the previous evening with Gwenvere, bracelet off, and sword just out of reach across Xavier's knee. He had watched it like a hawk the entire time. That Eiric would not let me possess my sword and magic at the same time, made me all the more determined to do so.

I got out of bed, then quickly readied myself for the day. Xavier was supposed to wait outside my door during the night, ready to rush in should a demon arrive. His other purpose was to take me for my morning meal once I was ready. It seemed he was now my personal guard, a task that irked him, though I knew he didn't hate my company.

He just didn't like it either.

The door opened before I could knock from the inside. The sight of my sword strapped across his back made my teeth clamp together. It made more sense than him carrying the scabbard around, but it still bothered me. It was *my* sword, after all.

"Do you always wear such a charming expression in the morning?" he asked.

I walked past him into the hall, blue cloak flowing behind me. "I take it there were no more demonic encounters during the night?"

He followed behind me as I headed for the nearest stairs. "None that I know of. Of course, I was trapped in a cold, barren hallway."

"Would you have rather slept at the foot of my bed like a dog?"

"A chair in your room would have sufficed."

I kept walking. I actually had considered offering him a place in my room. It wouldn't have been the first time he saw me sleep—but I preferred sleeping unobserved.

"Where is Eiric?"

He caught up to my side. "What makes you think he has gone somewhere?"

I hadn't seen Cael since I'd bloodied him. He'd thought there was a chance of Eiric scenting Asher that night, so he couldn't be far, but . . . judging how everyone was acting, he was not often around. Seeing no reason not to, I said as much.

Xavier walked beside me down the stairs. "He comes and goes. There is much to prepare for the ritual."

"Like what?"

"You're better off not knowing."

I shook my head as we reached the landing, then headed toward the dining hall. I was quickly acclimating to temple life. Sometimes it felt as if doom wasn't impending for everyone I loved. "Fine, at least tell me why he doesn't want me to have my sword and magic at the same time. Is he afraid of me?"

He chuckled. "No, Lyssandra, he is most certainly *not* afraid of you."

"Are *you* afraid of me?"

"With access to both an enchanted sword and your magic?" He shrugged. "I would be a fool if I weren't cautious."

"And yet, Eiric often leaves you alone with me. He leaves me trapped in a room with just a single lock. It's almost like he wants me to escape."

He gave me a close-lipped smile as he opened the dining hall door for me. "And yet, you have not made an attempt."

I didn't walk through the door. I had been keeping my suspicions to myself, but Gwenvere and I had made progress on practicing smaller rituals. I had no idea how much time I had left. "Why does he want me to escape?"

His pinched face was answer enough. I was right. Eiric wanted me to escape, and there could only be few reasons. For one, he wanted me to lead him to Asher and the others so that he might use them against me. And there was only one other reason I could think of for his absences. The other half of the grimoire. Did Drucida still possess it?

I hoped not. I hoped Eiric never darkened the streets of her fortress again.

"Are we going to eat, or would you have us both starve in the hallway?"

I rolled my eyes and walked past him. He wouldn't starve. Eiric was powerful enough to keep him alive.

The dining hall was even emptier than before. Everyone who was able to hide behind a locked door was likely doing so. The few women present sat close together with plenty of guards nearby.

The guards watched us with cold expressions, likely blaming us for whatever evil had infiltrated their temple. Or likely blaming *me*. I was the only true newcomer, along with Cael, but they saw far more of me.

I spotted Isolde amongst one cluster of women, but didn't attempt to catch her eye, not with Xavier standing right next to me. I might feel I could speak candidly around him, but if he knew of Isolde's presence, he would hand her to Eiric in a heartbeat.

I sat at an empty table, and Xavier went to fetch our food. I watched as Isolde noticed my sword across his back. Her gaze whipped to mine for just a moment, then quickly averted. I wanted to speak with her again about what I'd learned so far, but with Xavier *protecting* me, I would not have an opportunity.

I turned as the dining hall door opened, and Cerridwen entered. Spotting me, she glided across the space and sat.

I squirmed, uncomfortable with her nearness. "Cael and I searched all night for the demons," she muttered, her voice low enough that only I would hear it. "I believe they have either fled, or they faded back to their own realms. If they were weak enough to be ensnared to begin with, it stands to reason that they may not be able to maintain themselves on their own for long."

"And yet, they were strong enough to *tear* their way to freedom. Do you truly believe they are gone?"

"It doesn't matter. They are not our problem, and Xavier can keep you safe until the ritual."

My pulse quickened. "And just when will that be?"

"Soon." She stood as Xavier reached us, giving him a nod before walking away.

His expression sour, he slid a plate in front of me. Toasted rye bread, eggs with runny yolks, and a boiled potato. His own plate in hand, he took Cerridwen's vacated seat.

A few times as I ate, I caught Isolde stealing glances my way. She wouldn't look suspicious in the least, as the others were stealing glances too. But . . . there was something different in her expression. Something felt off about the entire day.

Soon, Cerridwen had said. Soon Eiric would have me perform the ritual. I'd been hoping to get closer to him, to figure out his weakness, and yet, I had barely seen him. I had accomplished nothing, and I was running out of time.

I could change my mind and attempt escape, but once I was in the city, Asher might not know to stay away.

I was left with only one option. I needed to remove the cursed bracelet from my wrist, and I needed to steal my sword from Xavier. Even if I had to kill both him and Gwenvere to do it.

WHEN THE TIME CAME, Xavier escorted me to Gwenvere's study. Gwenvere awaited us in her blue robes with her reddish blonde hair neatly combed away from her face, which had recently been scrubbed clean. She probably hoped a fresh wash would decrease the swelling around her eyes, but it was still noticeable. Had she cared for the girls who'd died, or was she simply fearing for herself?

I had decided to leave Lavandriel's grimoire hidden under my bed. As much as I wanted Gwenvere to take a look at it, Eiric seemed to visit Xavier's mind frequently. If there was a chance that Cerridwen gave it to me without Eiric knowing, I wanted to keep it secret.

I approached Gwenvere, sending a few candles flickering as I held out my wrist. She looked down at the bracelet, then opened her mouth to speak the words. I'd finally memorized them, but they didn't work for me.

Before she could mutter the full chant, something screeched through the room.

I staggered back, knowing it was the demon from the previous day without needing to see it. And once I spotted it, I wished I hadn't. Its long black limbs seemed wrong, but it moved too quickly for me to figure out why. Its open maw was aimed not at me, but at Gwenvere.

I darted out of the way. If I'd had my sword or my magic, perhaps I could have saved her, but I had neither. My back slammed against a nearby shelf as the demon's claws sliced across Gwenvere's chest. Its maw dove into her throat.

"Here!" Xavier shouted.

I turned just as he tossed my unsheathed sword my way. At the risk of my own limbs, I lunged away from the shelf to catch it, fumbling with the now unfamiliar weight.

Panting, I wrapped my other hand around the hilt, then turned toward the demon, lifting the sword in front of me. I caught a glimpse of the creature pinning Gwenvere to the floor, then my sword glowed bright white, forcing me to turn my head.

Hissing words snaked not through the room, but through my mind. *You will free me.*

Beyond the sword's glow, I could see the demon approaching, its bloody talons extended toward me. A reptilian tongue slithered across teeth as sharp as daggers. I could not tell if it was covered in glistening skin, or impossibly fine scales. It was horrifying either way.

"Free you?" I rasped.

Free me now, witch.

It reached me, and I swung my sword, my weaker muscles at least having enough memory to complete the movement. The blade swung in an arc, lopping off the demon's head. I expected hot blood to spray, but instead the head toppled to the floor, then dissipated in a cloud of black smoke. Moments later, the body followed.

I stared at the space the demon had occupied for a heartbeat, trying to catch my breath, then rushed toward Gwenvere, sword in hand.

Her blue robes were soaked crimson. She looked like she had been mauled by a bear. Her chest was just so much meat, but she was still alive.

She rasped, choking on her own blood. A vampire

might have been able to save her, but it was the middle of the day.

Her panicked eyes found mine. Her mouth moved, forming silent words I could not hear, then her fingers brushed across my wrist where I braced myself near her body.

The bracelet fell away from my wrist.

She tried to say something else that I couldn't quite understand, then her eyes went wide and still with death.

I stayed still too, sensing Xavier approaching my back.

"Interesting. It seems the demon was after its summoner, not you. It probably came to your chamber because her scent was there." He laughed. "And here she was doing all of this so that you would save her."

I kept my back to him, snaking the fingers of my free hand toward the fallen bracelet. "Me? Why?"

"I suppose there is no harm in telling you now. She had a blood disease—you probably noticed the limp. She wasn't improving your magic just to help Eiric. He promised her you could save her. It wasn't death itself she feared, but a slow, painful withering that would take years." He laughed again. "In a way, she got what she wanted. Eiric didn't want you to know because you might have healed her in secret, gaining an unlikely ally."

I still didn't move. I had my sword, and my magic was thrumming in my body. Any moment now, Xavier would realize the bracelet had been removed, and was now hiding in the palm of my hand.

Eiric wanted me to escape. I didn't want to play into his plan, but I was running out of time, and I didn't even know if he was within the temple.

"Lyssandra? Are you injured?"

I took a deep breath, realizing I was going to feel bad about this later. With my back shielding my actions, I looped the bracelet around my fingers, then slowly sliced my palm across my sword.

I felt the blade sensing my purpose, and a single word entered my mind. *Wait.* The word was loud and clear now that I had my magic back.

And so I waited.

Xavier came closer. I sensed him reaching for my shoulder.

Now.

I gripped my sword and spun to my feet, slashing at Xavier before he could react. I only managed a small slice across his thigh, but it was enough. I could feel his blood.

He was *mine*—a stronger connection than just wiping my blood on his skin.

I thought of ice. I willed the blood across my palm to freeze, and ice instantly stung my skin, more intensely than I had ever experienced. The bracelet might have been suppressing my magic, but it was still growing within me. It hadn't stopped the rapid progression which had begun as soon as I was separated from Asher.

Xavier staggered back. Ice formed around his leg, then moved up his body.

There was no fear in his eyes. No surprise. "Kill me if you can," he rasped, then his jaw slammed shut. In a moment of desperation, he had disobeyed Eiric's orders.

I knew I should kill him. I knew I should lift my sword now while he was frozen in place. He *wanted* me to do it.

I had killed so many, but staring at him . . . I couldn't do it.

A mixture of anger and desperation pinched his eyes, but Eiric would not allow him to speak. My hand was numb with cold. I couldn't freeze him more or I'd risk injuring myself.

"I'm sorry." Shaking my head, I ran.

CHAPTER FIFTEEN

I slammed into a wall down another hallway, almost dropping my sword, then hurled myself down the stairs, praying to the light that I wouldn't impale myself. I had slipped the bracelet into my pocket, but I didn't have the sheath for my sword. I reached another hall where an older priestess caught sight of me.

"Wait!"

I lifted my sword, and she scurried down the nearest hall.

With my limbs burning, I ran faster, trying to remember the directions Asher had given me. The wards shouldn't be an issue for someone leaving a main entrance, but I couldn't risk being stopped by the guards.

I reached the lower level of the temple. I was close. The storeroom should be just around the bend.

"Lyssandra!"

I recognized Cerridwen's voice and kept running. I couldn't let her catch me. But didn't Eiric want me to escape? Perhaps not now that I had both my magic and my sword.

I reached the door of the storeroom and threw it open.

Cerridwen rushed in right behind me. "Stop right there!"

The space went pitch black. I couldn't see my own nose, and it wasn't just darkness, it was *thick*. Like I was pushing through something solid.

"Touch me and I'll boil the blood in your veins," I warned. I kept walking despite my instincts. Occasionally I bumped into something that was actually solid, a crate or barrel. Everything was crowded, forming a maze, just as Asher had described.

I was pretty sure Cerridwen didn't have offensive magic, but she was still quick and practically immortal, with glamour the likes of which no one in the current century had ever seen. Her power was that of the old blood. I couldn't let her catch me.

I pushed through the darkness, one hand trembling around my too-heavy sword, while the other groped for the way out.

"Lyssandra, you don't know what you're doing. Without the bracelet, your magic will soon overwhelm you. You must let me replace it." Her voice was closer now, though I couldn't quite pinpoint her direction. It was almost as if the darkness itself was speaking to me.

"I think I'll manage on my own, thanks." Although I wasn't sure. It was starting to feel different. *Stronger*. My fingers pressed against stone. The far wall. Now where was the door? I hadn't been able to see it before everything went dark.

The darkness shifted, and suddenly I could see again, but everything around me was solid stone. My hands were empty. Another illusion. I hadn't reached the far wall after all.

I closed my eyes. I had been taught by Ryllae how to overcome glamours, but I had never faced someone like Cerridwen. I had never tried to overpower an ancient mind before, and I didn't think I could.

"I can keep you trapped in this little stone box until you beg me for release." Cerridwen's voice surrounded me, though I knew in reality she must still be standing near the door of the cellar.

At least she hadn't tried to touch me. Maybe she feared what I might do if I could draw her blood.

Ignoring her, I squeezed my hands shut. Glamours could affect sight, smell, *touch*, everything. But touch was the hardest. I squeezed my uninjured hand until I could feel my sword's hilt pressing against my flesh. It was amazing that in such a short span of time my callouses could grow so soft, the grip was almost painful. I opened my eyes and could see my sword, but my surroundings were still glamoured.

Forward, my sword said into my mind. Once again, the words were startlingly clear. My sword had struggled to communicate past my bond with Asher, and the bracelet had cut off that communication altogether. Maybe this was why Eiric didn't want me to have both my magic and my sword.

I stepped forward, toward the nearest stone wall. I walked until it seemed like I would run right into it, then stopped.

155

"You cannot escape, foolish girl."

"Then why don't you come in here and get me?" I snarled, casting a glare back in her general direction—I thought.

Forward, my sword said again.

I looked down to find its eye open, rolled ahead of us. Could it see through the glamour? I obeyed, wincing as I felt like I would run into a stone wall, but instead I stepped through it.

Cerridwen cursed, and instinct alone told me to turn as the walls around me winked out of existence. I lifted my sword just in time to hold it to Cerridwen's throat as she reached for me. The sharp tip pierced her skin, drawing a bead of blood to trickle down to her collarbone.

Her dark eyes were alight with irritation, visible even in the now-dim space. Her blood continued to well around my blade's tip, but she did not step away.

"Tell Eiric not to worry. I will find him soon enough."

"He's not here," she snarled.

"I know."

I reached behind me until my wounded hand hit a door handle. It was loose—broken from the other side. Asher must have replaced it to make it appear normal, though few would even notice the door in the far back corner of the large but crowded space.

Cerridwen watched as I opened the door and stepped back, keeping my blade between us. "I can move faster than you can follow, Lyssandra."

I glanced down at her bloody throat, then lifted my still-bleeding hand. I never thought I'd be grateful for healing human slow, though Cerridwen's wound would heal much more quickly. "And I can boil the blood in your veins. Would you like to test me?"

She scowled, her eyes flickering with internal debate until finally, her hands lifted in temporary surrender. She was a coward—she always had been. It was the reason she let Lavandriel believe she was dead, rather than facing her. And it was the reason she let Eiric seduce Amarithe into helping him escape, rather than risk her own life. Now, with both my magic and my sword, she feared me, and she could not contain me with glamours.

I stepped further back into the dark space, then slammed the door in her face.

All of my bluster faded with sudden panic as I fumbled to move a heavy table in front of the door. Something clattered from its surface, and I realized it was old bones. I'd found the crypt Asher had come through, but my luck wouldn't last for long. I needed to escape before Cerridwen could figure out how to catch me without risking her own neck. That would likely entail her summoning the temple guards. If none of them were bleeding, they would easily overwhelm me.

I thought of needing a light, and suddenly my sword was glowing for me. I could see which way to go. Saying a silent prayer, I ran with my sword creating a blinding beacon through the dark.

I COULDN'T BELIEVE I'd made it out into the city, and now I needed to hide before nightfall. I couldn't let Asher find me, and Eiric . . . I hoped he was far away. Even the very first vampire required travel time, though it would only be a fraction of what someone on horseback would need.

Which meant I must act quickly. I had my sword and my magic. I had nearly killed Eiric once, and now he couldn't use my bond with Asher against me. Not if he couldn't find him. I had to kill Eiric before that could happen, but first, I needed to catch my breath.

I darted down an alleyway, glad for the deep hood on my blue cloak. The fabric had incurred a few bloodstains, but I could bunch up the stained area and hopefully hide it well enough if anyone saw me.

Once I was sure I was alone, I pressed my back against the nearest wall, hiding my sword within my cloak. The dry wood scraped against the soft fabric covering my back. I took several deep breaths.

Gwenvere was dead. She had hoped I would save her, and instead she had saved me. It was all her fault—she had summoned the demons—but maybe the demon was her first attempt to cure herself. Maybe she thought that with its strength, she could live.

It hadn't worked, and now I was left wondering what happened to the demon inside of her when she died. I also wondered what Cerridwen was doing now. She might have been afraid of me, but she had still made the choice to let me go. She hadn't given chase—yet.

I had run far from the graveyard I'd found surrounding the old crypt into the more densely popu-lated city, but I would soon need to find a way out. Or perhaps I was better off hiding amongst so many scents. I just wasn't sure. The scents wouldn't keep Eiric from finding me, but they would throw Asher off.

I palmed my face with my free hand. *Markus.* Markus could track me. He might even be doing so now. I needed to keep moving. Glancing both ways down the alley, I ran.

Tholdri

"YOU HAVE TO BE WRONG. We can't risk returning to check." I scanned the horizon for the hundredth time, looking for signs of the hunters.

Asher had finally located them, around two days away. We had ridden through much of the night, hoping to cut them off far from the city.

"Her location has changed. I'm sure of it." Markus' eyes squinted against the sunlight. "And she feels . . . different."

"Different how?" Steifan asked. He stood with his horse's reins in hand, both he and the animal looking horribly unhappy to be there.

Markus shook his head. "I don't know." He swiped a palm angrily across his face. "I just—we need to go. I must go back to the city. She needs help."

I glanced back toward the city, the tall walls now out of sight. We needed to reach the hunters, but if Lyss was alone . . . "She told Asher we must stay away. Eiric can track her."

"All the more reason to help her," Markus growled. His eyes were too wide, panicked. "I *must* go to her."

"Eiric will use you against her," Steifan said softly.

159

"I don't care!" Markus spun toward him. "I don't care. You don't understand. I must go."

I took a steadying breath, hoping I wouldn't regret this. "Then go. Try to find her without being seen. But if she tells you to leave, then leave."

He turned toward me, surprise cutting through his anger. "You will not come?"

"I trust Lyss and will obey her wishes. But, if you must go to her, I would at least like to know what she plans. If you can escape again before Eiric finds her, if she is really even free from him, then we may better know how to help her."

He nodded once. "I will find her."

He turned away to ready his horse. He wouldn't reach the city until well after nightfall, and by then it might be too late. But it was good that he was going. If he wasn't with us, Asher could not use him to find Lyssandra.

Something told me that having them together was exactly what Eiric wanted.

CHAPTER SIXTEEN

Lyssandra

I crouched on a rooftop as night closed in. I had opted for staying within the city. As far as I knew, Cerridwen had no way to track me. Xavier might track me through Eiric, but what would he do when he found me? I might no longer be a human servant, but with my magic . . . in some ways I was stronger. Easier to kill, but also far more dangerous.

Eiric could find me no matter where I was. When he came, there would be no escape. But I could hope that he was not near—not yet.

I watched the people milling in the streets, oblivious to what was happening in the temple. I hoped that with Gwenvere dead, the remaining demons would be forced back to their realm just like Renault had been, but I wasn't sure. They were *inside* those poor girls. They might no longer need Gwenvere to anchor them.

The bracelet was a heavy weight in my pocket. It was

fortunate I had managed to keep it away from Cerridwen and Xavier, but what I intended to do with it, I wasn't sure. If I was wise, I'd toss it into a well so it could no longer be used against me. Gwenvere had not been present at my capture, which meant someone else had put it around my wrist. She was not needed for it to be used against me again. But had she been lying about its removal? If she had died without releasing me, would it have remained around my wrist forever?

I wasn't sure, but I doubted Eiric would have risked it. No, I thought its removal was something more simple. The words, and magic. I couldn't remove it myself because it cut off my magic. Now, I might even be able to put it on someone else, like Cerridwen. Not that she'd let me get close enough to try.

And that wasn't the real reason I had kept it. I knew that. I had kept it because I wanted the option of wearing it again myself. This was the longest I had gone now with access to my full magic, and I found it disturbing how easily it settled into my core, coiled like a snake. If I didn't use it, it might build. It might become unbearable.

It might drive me utterly mad.

Shaking my head, I watched the darkening city. As the moon lifted high, I sensed a familiar presence at my back.

"Are you trying to lead Cerridwen right to me?"

"She could not follow me if she tried." Cael stepped up beside me, then crouched down. The roof was tall enough, and the streets still loud enough, that no one would notice us.

"And you would leave the temple so easily after the bargain you struck?"

"I only came to stay near you. And you are here now. What do you plan?"

I glanced at him. His cheeks were hollow, his bones protruding. He wasn't quite in his ghoulish form, but he was close. All signs of the injuries I'd inflicted were healed. "I don't know. I saw an opportunity, and I took it."

"Xavier will be punished for letting you go."

"He didn't have much of a choice." Not that it mattered. I knew that my great uncle's claim would prove correct. My guilt made me squirm, but I shook it off. Guilt, I could live with. For now.

"You know this is what Eiric wanted. He wanted you to escape to lead Cerridwen to Asher. I believe she intends to weaken him with the ring so he can be captured."

I had almost forgotten about the ancient ring, and the fact that Cerridwen still had it. "I know, but I think we're running out of time. I had hoped to find an opportunity to kill Eiric, but I've hardly seen him. He is elsewhere."

Cael turned his head toward the distant temple. "I imagine that will change soon. Xavier will have communicated what happened."

"I know. And I will be ready with my sword and my magic. It is the best I can do. I almost killed him before, at the fortress."

He let out a harsh huff of breath, almost a laugh, then turned his attention back toward the people below us. "You caused him pain, which he healed in mere minutes. It will take more than boiling his blood, Lyssandra."

"I have access to my full magic now."

He finally solidly looked at me, his eyes scanning my

SARA C. ROETHLE

body like he could see the magic coiled within. "And will you die to kill him too?"

"If I must."

"Let me help you."

I stared at him. I couldn't bring myself to fully trust him—not after what he'd done—but I was out of better options. He was powerful and frightening, and perhaps almost as hard to kill as Eiric. "Isn't this what you wanted? For me to be strong enough to face him?"

His expression crumbled, just for a moment before returning to its usual grim lines. "Yes, I wanted you to be strong. And I wanted to be around long enough to help you. So let me."

I didn't like it, but Eiric had to die. And I would do everything needed to accomplish that end. "I accept your help, and must ask more of you."

He nodded for me to continue, his skin stretching too tight over his bones.

"I need you to make sure Asher stays away. Eiric can find me anywhere. I can't have Asher near me when he does."

He glanced down at the people in the streets again. "You chose this place to hide your scent."

"I did. I—" I blinked at him. "But how did *you* find me?"

"You and I share far more blood than Eiric does with either of us."

Of course. I should have considered it sooner. Cael had been watching over me long before I knew of his existence. I might have even been able to use the connection from my end to track him when he disappeared from

166

the fortress. So many mistakes I had made . . . I hoped they wouldn't bury us.

He turned his attention downward once more. "I will keep Asher away if I am able, but Eiric can track me just as easily as he tracks you. It will be better if we both elude him entirely."

I nodded. "That is our plan, then, and Eiric will know it. He'll know we intend to kill him when he comes for us. He will be ready, so we must be ready too."

"Together, we will do all we can." He looked at me again. "And if me dying will save your life, you will make that choice. If me dying will enable you to kill him, you must do whatever it takes."

I met his gaze, no tears, no flinching. "You know, we could have done this from the start. At the fortress."

"You were weaker then. Now, without the bond, and without the bracelet, your magic crawls across my skin."

And here I'd thought I was containing it admirably. "We still could have tried."

"And Asher would be dead. And you and I . . . we would still be here. Only your heart would be ruined."

I studied his face. Even in his withered form, he still looked so much like the Potentate, my grandfather. I had never felt his love for me, nor had I felt love from my great uncle. After my parents had died, without Tholdri, I would have been alone. They had chosen to leave me alone.

"I wish he would have told me the truth from the start. I wish you both had. Things might have been different now."

His chin lowered. "It was Cedrik's choice. I could not go against him."

"You speak little of your past with him."

He turned away again. "Some things, Lyssandra, are simply too painful to relive."

I followed his gaze, watching the people below. It would be some time yet before the crowd thinned, but their movements should have fully obscured my trail. I would remain aloft for the night, in hopes that Asher—if he was still in the city—would not catch my scent.

I stood, then took a step away from the edge of the roof. "Some of us have never been given such a choice."

I turned away. I wasn't sure just what my magic could do now, but I needed to figure it out. I needed to be ready. I would not be cut off from it again.

CHAPTER SEVENTEEN

Asher

The hunters kept close watch around their camp. If I crept too near, some might sense me, but there was no reason now for me to move any closer. In the short time I'd been watching them, they had already told me everything I needed to know.

They were here to hunt Lyssandra. They had been ordered by Gregor Syvise on the grounds that she had murdered their Potentate. That these men—and there were only men, no rare female hunters—would so easily believe such claims boiled my blood. She was a better person than any of them could ever hope to be. They would not believe the claims if they were leveled at one of their own. They *wanted* to believe Lyssandra was a murderer. They wanted to believe they were right about her all along. What sort of woman would become a hunter, and why did she have such vibrant red hair? Certainly such things meant she could not be trusted.

Though their muttered conversation vexed me, it also granted me greater respect for Isolde—and for Markus, remaining by her side all these years.

And Tholdri . . . I felt compelled to thank him once I found him, which would be soon. He needed to know where he could find the hunters so that he might reason with them. Though I was beginning to see what a terribly foolish plan that was.

I crept back across the rocky landscape, thinking once again of Lyssandra, and the life she had endured.

Parents killed when she was young. As much as she blamed herself, she was not to blame. She should have been taught to control her magic. She should have been raised as a witch—

My thoughts halted. If she had been raised as a witch, would she have already been mad by the time I met her? Would I have met her at all?

My mind avoided the idea, moving on to the next stage of her life, training as a hunter with men who hoped to see her fail. Her grandfather, watching it all from a distance. Her uncle Isaac had been the brother of her father. Knowing nothing of her magic nor of her true past, he had taken her under his wing, teaching her what he could. He was a rare light in her life, like Tholdri. And Karpov had killed him right before her eyes.

And she had been blamed. Just like she was now being blamed.

I flexed my hands as I walked. I could reach Tholdri more quickly, but I wanted time to calm myself.

Next came her encounter with me. That night . . . I still remembered it fondly, up until the point where I found her bloody and broken. I still remembered the look in her eyes as she spotted me in the common room. She had known what I was, though she initially pretended otherwise.

She had accepted my company because part of her sought death, and I had done the same. If I was finally to die, why shouldn't it be at the hand of a lovely young huntress? Such a strange girl, with her fiery red hair.

But then, there was no violence. We simply talked. Influenced by a mixture of wine and grief, she told me more that night than she had at any time after that. I had watched her speak, every emotion—joy, sadness, anger—playing openly across her face. I had seen, for the first time in so many years, something good in the world.

It had given me hope in a time when all hope had been lost to me.

Our goodbyes were bittersweet. I knew I could not keep her. In the morning, when the wine wore off, she would want nothing to do with me. I left knowing the memory of that night was all I would have.

I wasn't really sure why I went back. Perhaps I just wanted one last glimpse of her before the sun rose. But then, before I could reach the inn, I heard the animalistic sounds of the ghouls, and the frightened shriek of her horse. I smelled her blood. So much blood.

I ran. There was never any memory of killing the ghouls. I knew I had done so, but the actions were not in my mind. All I could remember was kneeling beside her body. At first, I'd thought she was already dead. Then I heard her weak breath. Her thready heartbeat. I opened a vein and dripped blood in her mouth, but I could not coax her to swallow.

I lifted her gently in my arms and carried her to my lair at the time, a small ramshackle home deep in the mires. I laid her on the floor, for I had long since lost interest in human comforts. She was still on the verge of death. The small amount of blood I'd dripped down her throat had not been enough. I gave her more, and it pooled in her mouth once again.

Fearing for her weak breath, I moved her onto her side, pouring out the blood. But her breath did not return. It had not been enough. She had been too close to death.

I resorted to my only remaining option. I sliced open my inner arm from wrist to elbow, took her own badly mangled arm in my grip, then I pressed the wounds together. I pulled her against me, willing the magic to work.

It wasn't like when I took other servants—men and women desperate for a taste of eternity. It wasn't like the times early in my undead life when I was so lost and filled with need for companionship that I would do almost anything.

It was simply . . . an unwillingness to let her die. But death had already come for her, and she could never be fully living again. I willed my blood into her veins. I willed my *life* into her veins.

She woke several times after that, crying out in pain. Her body was changing, and it was never a pleasant process. I was grateful that for the majority, she remained unconscious.

That night, she became mine.

Even though later she railed against me—she hated me, despised me even—I was glad for it. I was so glad that once I found her again, she wanted nothing to do with me. Something different had happened. She was not a true servant. I had never considered myself a believer in the light, but I believed in it then. I had been blessed. For once in my long life, I had been blessed. She wasn't a devout servant. She was still herself.

I let her live as she pleased. I stayed away. And I had never been more content, simply knowing that she was alive, and it was because of me.

And then . . . she decided she wanted to kill me.

I stopped walking, looking up at the small sliver of moon. In another night or two, it would be completely dark.

I smiled. When I realized Lyssandra was looking for me, that she wanted to kill me, I started watching her again. Not always, but I checked on her, telling myself I simply wanted to see how she was progressing.

Then, when the Nattmara nearly killed her, everything changed. There was no going back.

And even if she had not become truly mine, I would not have wanted to.

With a heavy sigh, I continued walking, intent now on locating Tholdri. She was still mine. Mine to love and mine to protect. She had asked for time, but I was not sure how much of it I could give. I could not risk it being a mistake.

We would stop the hunters, and then, Eiric had to die.

I caught Tholdri's scent before I reached the hilltop where I knew he would be waiting. We had agreed upon the location the previous night. If he started riding as soon as I reached him, he would find the hunters by the following evening, before they could reach the city.

I ignored the sharp stab of rage at the thought of the hunters. I rarely struggled with bloodlust, but for those men . . .

I pushed the thoughts away as Tholdri noticed me. There was something odd about his expression. Not quite worry, but *something*.

I crested the hill and stood before him. "What is it?"

"What makes you think there is something?" He shifted his stance.

I watched him, though my senses were trained on the night around us for any hint at what he was hiding.

"Before I tell you, you must swear you won't run off."

I tilted my head, stepping closer. No ill had befallen Lyssandra. His demeanor would have been different if it had. Markus and Steifan were likely both well by that same logic. But I could smell them faintly. They had spoken with Tholdri before moving to the other agreed-upon location to wait for Geist. He had gone toward the mountains to search for the hunters in case they had taken an alternate, but less likely route.

"I can promise you nothing. What has happened?"

Tholdri stood a little straighter. "Promise me, or I cannot tell you."

My eyes narrowed. As a hunter, he was difficult to bespell, but perhaps not impossible. It might have been worth trying, except for the fact that Lyssandra would never forgive me when she heard. "I can agree to grant you time to fully explain why I should not *run off*."

He swiped a palm across his brow and shook his head. "I suppose that is the best I can hope for." He lowered his hand. "Markus sensed that Lyssandra's location has changed. He believes her to be out in the city, away from the temple, though whether she moved there under her own power is unknown. He went to investigate."

My heart, which rarely beat these days, leapt into my throat. "How long ago?"

"Early. He should have reached the city by now, though it may take him time to locate her if she sticks to the crowds." He stepped toward me. "But you cannot go. You know you cannot."

I could. I very well could. But . . . she had asked me not to. I knew she did not want me to. "What will Markus do once he finds her?"

He studied my face, careful to avoid direct eye contact. "I believe he'll have no choice but to do exactly what she *wants* him to do."

My heart settled. That was right. He would be little more than a pawn at her disposal. A pawn that could be used against her, but it was better that she wasn't entirely alone, if she had indeed escaped.

Tholdri relaxed his stance. "You're taking this better than I expected."

"Lyssandra asked me to stay away."

He smirked. "For some reason, I didn't think you capable of listening."

I turned my head as something shifted in the periphery. "Geist is coming. He must have already met with Steifan."

Tholdri's heart beat a little faster at the mention of the other vampire. Interesting.

We waited until Geist appeared. He slowed as he came closer, climbing the hill atop which we stood with an easy gait. But when he reached us, his words belied his seeming sense of ease. "We have an issue." He glanced behind him, almost as if he feared being followed, though such a feat should have been impossible to any but another ancient. He moved closer to Tholdri. "The hunters are not the only ones being lured to the city."

"Who else?" I asked.

"Vampires *and* witches. Traveling separately, though both seem aware of each other."

I moved closer without thinking. "How close?"

He eyed me steadily. "I imagine they are just as far as the hunters. Eiric has timed whatever he plans to utter perfection."

The hunters would near the city within two nights, and would likely search for Lyssandra the following day. I looked up at the sliver of moon. Tomorrow night, there would be a scant slice, and the next, no hint of it. Rituals were often tied to the moon, and it seemed this one was no different. "He will have Lyssandra perform the ritual two nights from now."

"But Markus claims she has escaped," Geist countered. "He's riding toward the city as we speak."

Shaking his head, Tholdri raked his fingers through his hair. "There's no time then to convince the hunters to stay away. I know we cannot allow Eiric to locate us, but how can we just stay back when Lyss might need our help?"

"We cannot." I gazed toward the city. She had asked me to stay away, but she was running out of time. "Tomorrow, you'll speak with the hunters, then we will meet here again. If the hunters cannot be stopped, we will go to the city, but we'll keep our distance from Lyssandra."

"And if Eiric captures one of us?" Tholdri asked.

"Just don't let him take you alive. Alive, you become a tool to use against Lyssandra."

His brow furrowed as he nodded. I knew Tholdri would do whatever it took.

And so would I.

CHAPTER EIGHTEEN

Lyssandra

The smell of bread woke me, coming long before the sun had the chance to warm my face. Cael was gone, but I knew he rested nearby. I still wasn't entirely sure I could trust him, but I could at least trust that he wouldn't go far.

I lay on the rooftop until the light stung my eyes, and I could hear the sounds of people milling about below. Asher could not track me during full daylight, but that was no reason to be lax about covering up my scent. Xavier might already be able to track me through Eiric, but maybe Cerridwen could track me too. I wouldn't put it past her to put a demon on a leash for such purposes.

After scanning the streets below, I pulled up my hood and lifted my sword. Being without its sheath was an issue. I had to keep it in hand, hidden in the folds of my cloak. I awkwardly lowered myself from the roof, wondering why my sword had been silent since I'd escaped the temple. Perhaps I should have thanked it for its help.

I inhaled the scent of baking bread again, making my stomach ache and my mouth water. I needed to eat, but I had no coin.

Thievery it was, though I disliked the notion.

I picked my way through the streets, avoiding a few curious glances. I neared market stalls setting up for the day and hesitated. I could steal a loaf of bread or a few apples, but the shopkeepers would be on the lookout for thieves, and sleight-of-hand was not a skill I possessed. I might be better off looking elsewhere.

I was about to move on, when I overheard a conversation between two shopkeepers. They made no effort to lower their words, which echoed down the nearest alley I'd been skulking through.

"Torn up like a wild animal got to him," one was saying.

A moment of stunned silence from the other. "A wild animal? In the city?"

It could have been anything. Vampire, ghoul, or even just a crazed human, but my curiosity was enough to still my feet.

"Not far from the temple. They found him in the night. Thing must have crawled through his window."

I leaned my back against the wall, clutching my sword in both hands beneath my cloak. The coincidence was too great. At least one of the demons had escaped the temple. It might have even followed my scent out of the hidden entrance.

I wanted to listen for what was said next, but a

familiar sensation tugged at my senses. *Markus.* He was somewhere near.

Asher couldn't be with him—it was daylight and I would sense a vampire even if it was night—but Tholdri and Steifan might be, and I couldn't risk Xavier or Cerridwen searching for me and finding them instead.

Focusing my attention on the feel of our bond, I roughly pinpointed his location, then ran in the other direction. I darted down every alleyway I could, my breath already laboring. Perhaps if I could make his path complex enough, it might take him time to locate me.

I kept running, catching the occasional person off guard as I took another turn and veered right in front of them, my sword flashing from within my cloak. I still only had a vague understanding of the city. I knew where the gates were, the temple, and the crypt where I'd come up, but little else. And Markus had already been here for days. He might know something I didn't.

I veered down another street, then paused to catch my breath, my boots clapping across hardened dirt as I staggered against the nearest wall. Huffing and sweating, I reached out my senses once again for Markus' location.

Closer now? How had he cut me off? My body protested as I turned to start running again, and there he was, looking both ways down the nearest intersection. He spotted me before I could move.

"Stop right there." He marched toward me.

I lifted my free hand, backing away. "You need to stay away. Xavier and Cerridwen will be searching for me."

"Let them." He looked over me grimly as he neared. "If you die, I die, remember? I have little to lose."

A bead of sweat dripped down my brow. I probably looked awful in my stained clothing with my hair a mess, my body panicked and hungry. "Eiric could threaten you to make me do whatever he wants."

He stopped in front of me, looking me up and down again, clearly noticing my hidden sword. His unremarkable clothing was neat and clean, somehow, even after the travel he'd endured to reach the city. "Do not flatter me. My life is not worth that much to you."

My jaw dropped. "I wouldn't just let him kill you."

"If Eiric was going to kill either me, or Tholdri, and you could only save one, who would you choose?"

I stared at him. "That's a ridiculous question."

"It's a practical one. You would choose Tholdri, and I would not blame you. I am the least valuable member of our little party, at least in your eyes. Therefore, I am the best to help you. Now tell me, what has happened?"

I usually did not respond well to someone displaying such utter authority, but . . . he was right. And I was too tired and hungry to argue. If I didn't regain some energy soon, I would start taking it from Markus. He had the right to help me if he so chose.

I looked both ways down the street, then gestured for him to follow me down the nearest alley. Huddled together in the shade, I told him everything.

By the time I finished, his jaw was clenched so tightly I thought his teeth might crack. "Asher mentioned Isolde's presence. Are these demons a danger to her?"

"They're a danger to everyone, especially if they really have come out into the city. I'm not sure how long they can stay in this realm, but even if it's a short time, they can do a lot of damage before they go."

"And how many are there?" His tone was utter business. A hunter asking about his prey, nothing more.

"I don't know. It depends on if they continue escaping." I had already explained to him that *escaping* meant killing the girls they resided inside.

His jaw twitched. "We need to get Isolde out regardless. She is in danger if anyone realizes who she really is."

I anchored my sword's tip on the ground as I leaned against the wall beside him. "Not exactly our most pressing issue."

"Yes. The grimoire. Do you need it?"

My shoulder slipped from the wall and I nearly fell. When I recovered, I asked. "What are you talking about?"

"Drucida gave it to us before we left. She thought you might need it."

My stomach did a nervous flip. Drucida had determined that the grimoire held half of the ritual, which meant Eiric needed it. I had worried that he would return to the fortress to search, but now . . . it had been in the city all this time?

I turned to grip his arm. "No. It *must* stay hidden. Do not speak of it again." Markus looked down at my hand on his arm. After a moment, I released him.

He visibly relaxed once I was no longer touching him. "She said you found it in one of the Blackmire cottages. Does Cael know of it? Is he here with you?"

He had witnessed Cael's betrayal himself. What must he think now? "He is. He will be with me come nightfall. As far as I know, he has no idea I found it."

I shook my head. Cael didn't know, and Eiric might not know either. He may have still returned to the fortress. He had been away much. He might have even returned to Castle Helius for a more thorough search of my grandfather's things.

Markus let out a long breath. "Well, it is hidden. I will not tell you where if you prefer it. Now what would you have me do? Tholdri and the others will be awaiting word."

I didn't know what to say to him. He was giving me what I wanted, but at what cost? I couldn't convince myself that it was worth the risk. There had to be another way.

"First, I need food and a sheath for my sword." I lifted the blade from within my cloak, my head drooped in resignation.

He glanced at the blade. "Simple enough, though we don't have time to commission a proper sheath. Whatever we find is not likely to fit perfectly."

"I just need it to be good enough."

He nodded. "And after that?"

"Then we wait for Eiric to come. And we kill him, or we die trying. Either way, his ritual will not be performed."

"And what do you think he wants with the hunters?" he asked. "What role are they to play?"

My hand flexed around my sword's hilt. "I wish I could tell you."

He watched me for a long moment. I thought he might actually have something meaningful to say, but then he shook his head. "Let's find you something to eat. Your weakness is taxing."

I wanted to say something scathing like, *I should have let you die with your master*, but I didn't. It just didn't seem right, now that his fate was tied to mine.

And my fate for once, I realized, was simply my own.

I WAITED in the shade while Markus searched for a new sheath for my sword. He had a bit of coin, but not enough for anything worthwhile. Whatever he found would have to do. My wrist was already getting sore from hiding my sword in my cloak all day. It would draw too much attention to walk about with a naked blade. Attention from the city guard, who were allegedly in the priestesses' pockets.

I stepped further into the shade as the sun shifted. I had a nagging, itching feeling between my shoulder blades like someone was watching me, but no one looked my way. My sword was yet to warn me of a single thing. It was yet to speak again at all.

Maybe it sensed the uncomfortable ball of magic in my gut. It had grown and swelled over time, ever since the bracelet was removed. I took a deep breath, and let it out slowly. My grandfather had been right. My bond with Asher had helped, probably far more than he could have imagined. I had never experienced this uncomfortable weight while I was still bonded to him. If I'd had it as a child . . . I just couldn't remember.

Still feeling like I was being watched, I glanced the other way down the street. People milled about, nothing out of the ordinary. I had heard a few more whispers of a man killed in his home by some sort of animal, but nothing new. No other bodies had been discovered.

My skin prickled and I whipped my gaze in another direction. A man had gone into the shop Markus was in. Had there been something *off* about him, or was it just my imagination?

Sweat trickled down my brow. I took another steadying breath, which cut off abruptly as I felt my sword awaken.

What's happening? I thought. *Why do I feel this way?*

The memory hit me so abruptly I staggered. Then I couldn't feel my body at all. I was in another place, watching through the eye of my sword. It was night. A few lanterns lit the room.

My grandfather's face looked down at me. I could barely see shelves of books to one side, and a window to the other. My sword was on the desk in his study. His hair was dark, the crimson color muted by brown stain. This was before his hair had gone white, and the dye was no longer needed.

Cael stood at his shoulder. He looked a few years younger than his twin, so this was after he'd become a vampire. His hair was its usual vibrant crimson. There was no need to stain it, because he would never be seen. He had entirely given up his life to protect his family. To protect *me*.

"Has it spoken to you?" Cael asked, his voice normal and cultured, no hint of the monster within.

My grandfather shook his head slightly. "It awaits a new master."

"Alicia?"

He frowned at the mention of my mother's name. "No. It does not awaken for her. She is powerful, but she does not have blood magic."

"It must be why Eiric's minions have stayed away. He's waiting for a new heir to our curse."

My grandfather turned his back on the blade. "I can feel my granddaughter's magic, but only time will tell what her gifts will be. I do hope she is like her mother."

Cael continued looking down at the blade. "Sorcha's line was strong. You chose well."

"Did I?" My grandfather's voice held countless sleepless nights. A lifetime of worry. "Or should I have let our line die with us?"

Cael turned toward him. "If you had, there would be no one left to stop Eiric."

"You mean no one left to release him."

Cael stepped closer, placing his hand on my grandfather's shoulder. "He will need to be freed eventually, if only to finally end him. He has stirred all the young vampires. Even within his tomb, he has too much power. It has only grown over the years. What will happen when his control becomes too great?"

My grandfather stepped out of Cael's reach. "Sorcha was not supposed to die. She was supposed to be alive to protect our daughter. Alicia hates hiding. I have ruined her life."

"She loves her daughter," Cael soothed. "And her husband. It is enough. We will all protect Lyssandra."

"She is just a baby. So small. So innocent. I hate to think of the life I have created for her."

Cael looked at the sword again. "Her father has no

magic. She may grow to be a hunter, and nothing more. The sword may reject her as well."

My grandfather turned again, showing me—the sword —his face. Tears glistened in his eyes. "But if she has blood magic—" He swiped a palm across his face and shook his head. "It is what we need. We need someone to perform the ritual. But if she has it . . . I don't want her to die because of it."

Cael placed his hand once more on my grandfather's shoulder. "We will watch over her. And if she needs help, we will find a way."

My grandfather nodded, but his expression was grim.

"Lyssandra!"

I jolted back to the present, bracing myself against Markus' hands on my arms, shaking me.

I blinked at him, nearly releasing my sword's hilt in my surprise.

He stared into my eyes. "Are you back? What happened?"

I opened my mouth to speak, but I wasn't sure what to say. Cael. My grandfather . . . At least now I knew what happened to my grandmother. She was dead. And she had been a powerful witch, but not a blood witch. My mother had magic on both sides of her family line, but I only had magic from her. Still, it would have been a toss up which gifts I received.

Markus still tightly gripped my arms. I could sense his urge to continue shaking me. "Lyssandra, what happened?"

I shook my head. "Nothing. It was just a memory." I

focused on his worried expression. "Did you find a sheath?"

He finally released me, then bent down to fetch the new sheath where he had dropped it beside me. We were in between two homes now. He must have dragged me aside when he found me.

With trembling hands, I took the sheath from him, observing it. It was a little short, but it would suffice. I slid my sword into it.

Markus stared at its open eye. "I rushed back out here when I couldn't feel you anymore. I thought something had happened."

"It was just a memory," I repeated. "My sword had something to show me."

"Will it help you in our task?"

"No." I started walking, needing to be away from the din of the crowd. I wiped my sweaty palms on my cloak as I went, thinking over the memory. Then I stopped so abruptly, Markus nearly ran into me.

He reached out to steady me. "What is it?"

I turned toward him. "The memory. My sword showed me a conversation between my grandfather and Cael. At first I thought my sword was simply telling me why I was chosen, but they mentioned something else. They spoke of needing a blood witch to cast a ritual."

His eyes searched my face. "And Cael has said nothing of this?"

I shook my head slightly. Just as he had said nothing of my grandmother. My misgivings about him swelled once more to the surface. "He will find me tonight. It's time for him to talk."

"And if Eiric finds us too?"

I shook my head, there was nothing I could do about that.

Reading as much in my expression, he sighed. "We'll find a place to wait. You can tell me more about it then."

He was the last person I wanted to talk to. I wanted Asher, Tholdri, anyone else.

But I could not have them. I had become what my grandfather feared. I had become a danger to everyone around me—including myself.

CHAPTER NINETEEN

Asher

I hesitated, torn between what I'd agreed to do, and what I *wanted* to do. In one direction was the hunter camp. I had scouted their location as soon as I woke for the night. In the other, the city, where Lyssandra might actually be within reach. And the third, the location I had agreed to, was the hilltop where Tholdri and the other hunters would be waiting. We would learn how those at the hunter camp had reacted to their claims. In the short time I'd listened, none had spoken of the encounter.

I heard Geist's steps behind me.

"What of the witches and vampires?" I asked without turning.

"The witches are near," he said. "They are aware of the hunters, and are avoiding them. And the vampires, they simply wait for Eiric's command."

"Did any of them sense you?"

SARA C. ROETHLE

"Not that I'm aware of." He stepped up by my side.

I was still not entirely pleased with his presence, but he had protected Steifan and Tholdri that night at the fortress. And with what we faced now, he was a valuable asset.

"You cannot go to the city," he said, reading my thoughts, though I knew my expression gave nothing away.

"For now. It will be another night before the hunters arrive. I believe that is when Eiric will enact his plan."

"What do you think became of Cael?"

I turned toward him. "Does it matter?"

"If he is with her, he will protect her."

My anger flared. "He *betrayed* her. He left her to fight alone at the fortress."

He gave me a slight smile. "You know it is not as simple as that. We cannot comprehend his full reasoning."

His tone made me suspect Geist knew something I did not. Even I could acknowledge that Cael had done what he thought was needed, but I could not forgive him for taking her away from me. And perhaps that was a fault. She had always wanted free of the bond, and now she was. She might come to see it as a gift, in time.

Geist looked toward the city. "Where do you think he is? Eiric, I mean."

"Searching for the grimoire, or for something else. Who can say? He may have returned to the city. He may be stalking Lyssandra, even now."

"He won't kill her."

"That doesn't make it any easier."

"No, it does not."

BLOOD OF ANCIENTS

I finally started walking. I had not stopped to have a heart to heart with the vampire that was meant to be Lyssandra's master.

Geist matched my pace. "Cael *will* die for her, if that is what it takes."

My desire to run toward the city was instinctual—difficult to fight. And Geist seemed to know it, remaining close to my side. "How can you be sure?"

"Because he already died for her once. He died for her, and her mother, and his brother. You know as well as I that it could have been no easy choice for him. Every choice he has made, it has been for his brother, and for her."

'You knew him before," I said, stating the obvious. He had known Lyssandra's grandfather, so he must have known Cael as well.

"As I have already admitted to Tholdri, I was the one who turned him."

I was not surprised by the admission. Or I was, but only that he had decided to tell me. If he had truly been Cedrik's friend, of course he would be the one they would ask. "Did you not fear he would become a monster too powerful to control?"

He shrugged as we continued walking. "Of course I did, but so was Eiric. Even sealed away, he was too dangerous. I thought it worth the risk. I never thought Cedrik's granddaughter would be the one to face Eiric. I always believed it would be Cael. But Cedrik had plans he shared with no one else. Many secrets died with him."

"You do not believe Cael knows everything?"

He shrugged again. "Perhaps not. But neither do we."

197

"And what else do you know?"

He was quiet for a moment. "I do not know if it is my tale to tell."

It was my turn to be silent. If he did not want to speak, I would not waste my energy in forcing him.

He sighed. "Have you ever thought back to the night you claimed Lyssandra? Why it was you and not I who turned her?"

I stopped walking again, my skin prickling with irritation. "What is your point?"

He gave me that infuriating smile. "The attack on her was planned. Cael would not have allowed her to die. So why did he not call off his ghouls? And why did he let *you* take her?"

His words gave me pause. There was only one explanation. "He was watching us. He gleaned my intentions, and did not interfere."

"Precisely. He was supposed to bring her to me, but he never arrived."

"But why?"

Geist shrugged. "That is something you will have to ask him yourself." Watching me, he turned slowly on his heel and resumed his casual pace.

I followed, not pressing him further. While I was curious, I truly did not care what Cael's motivations were, as long as he would still watch over her. I spotted Tholdri crouched on the nearby hilltop, Steifan and their horses out of sight. I was close enough that I did not miss Geist's smile as he looked up at him.

"Lyssandra would not approve of the way you're looking at him," I said lowly.

"Because I am a man?" Geist asked with an eyebrow raised.

I shook my head slightly. "Because you are a vampire, and she would want better for her dearest friend."

His brow lifted further. "But she chose a vampire." He laughed. "Though I suppose *chose* is too strong a word."

I ignored his attempt at levity. "That won't stop her from wanting better for him."

His expression sobered. "And do *you* want better for her?"

"Every day of my existence." I started walking up the hill.

He quickly caught up, then outpaced me, ignoring my warning, as I had expected. I would not say out loud that I wanted better for Tholdri too. No living human should be tied to a creature of death, myself included.

But I was too selfish to have ever considered my own guidance.

Shaking my head, I listened as Tholdri spoke with Geist. The hunters were not swayed. Yet another expected outcome. They believed Tholdri had simply been trying to save his friend. They'd debated letting him go, but had no orders against his name. And hunters always followed the orders of their Potentate. Even if he was a mind-addled stand-in like Gregor Syvise.

"I take it you heard?" Tholdri asked as I reached them. I spotted Steifan approaching with their horses from the other side of the hill.

"Did Steifan attempt to reason with them?" I asked. "Perhaps as the current Potentate's son—"

Tholdri shook his head. "They see him only as Lyss'

lackey. They believe she is in the temple, and that is where they will attack."

"They will not get past the wards," Geist said.

"I do not think they need to." I looked again in the direction of the city.

"So what will we do?" Tholdri asked.

I breathed deeply, scenting the night air. "If they are to go to the temple, then that is where everything will take place. We will go there, and we will be ready."

"But ready for what?" Steifan asked, nearing Tholdri's back.

I didn't answer. If only I knew.

CHAPTER TWENTY

Lyssandra

We waited on the same rooftop I slept on the night before. My magic was a second heartbeat, but lower in my gut, making me uneasy. I wished there was more moonlight, though the city was ablaze with torches after the man's death the night before. Or perhaps more had died. The light did seem excessive for just one death.

Markus stood somewhere behind me. He had been silent most of the afternoon while we ate the provisions he'd acquired. I knew he'd had the coin for more, but leave it to Markus to supply only simple bread and cured meat.

"Why do you feel so different now? It makes my skin itch."

I glanced back at him. We were high enough above the torches that I could barely make out his features. "I told you about the bracelet. This is the longest I've gone without it. And without the bond."

He rubbed his hands up and down his arms. "I suppose I didn't expect it to progress this quickly."

"Neither did I."

He stepped closer. He was honestly the last company I wanted, but I was glad now that he was with me. I didn't want to face Cael alone. "Can you manage it?"

I knew what he was asking, and I had no idea. "This is all still new to me. Perhaps if I'd been able to feel everything inside me as it was growing all these years, it might not be so overwhelming. But Asher unknowingly protected me." My gut squirmed again, and a bead of sweat trickled down my forehead despite the chill evening air.

"And if we survive, will you become a human servant again?"

I blinked at him, thrown off by the unexpected question. "I hadn't really thought about it."

"If the bond protected you from madness, it might be the only way."

"I still have the bracelet. I can cut off my magic if needed."

This close, I could see his expression, but it was entirely unreadable. "Would you not rather have the strength of a servant and enough magic to still be powerful? With the bracelet, you are nothing."

I frowned at his words. "Why do you—" Then I realized the reason he cared. He could either be servant to a human, or servant to a witch and human servant who might live for centuries, as long as no one killed me or my master.

I wondered which he preferred, but did not have the heart to ask. I had the option of no longer being a servant. He did not, unless . . .

"Cael and Cerridwen broke my bond with Asher without killing either of us," I said. "Perhaps with time, I could figure out how to free you."

He lowered his chin. "I will not waste my time on fleeting hope."

"But you would waste your time questioning my decisions?"

He stepped closer. "If you live, your decision will come. It will be one way, or the other. It seems practical to prepare myself."

I turned away. "Well I don't know."

I wanted to be with Asher, but choosing to be bonded with him for all eternity was another matter. My grandfather had altered my blood. It should be as it was before. I would retain my free will, and my magic would be dampened, but—

"Do you think it an easy choice?" I asked. "Deciding to bond myself to another being for eternity?"

"You love him."

His words were like a punch to the gut. He was right. But I was young. Would that love fade over the years? Just the thought of being with someone for so very long was mind-boggling.

"I do," I admitted, finally looking back at him. "But is love enough?"

He only stared at me. I could not give him an answer

tonight, and neither answer would truly be what he wanted.

"Cael is near," I said, then turned in the direction my senses were leading me.

And there he was, at the other edge of the roof, little more than a cluster of shadows.

When he made no move to approach, I sighed and walked toward him. I wasn't even sure where to begin. Perhaps the most obvious route was best.

I stopped before him. His otherworldly energy was stronger tonight. Was he nervous, or simply afraid that Eiric would come?

I looked up into his eyes. Unwise, now that I was no longer a servant, but I found that I at least trusted him enough to not bespell me. "What is the ritual my grandfather wanted me to cast?"

The only hint that he heard me was a slight widening of his eyes. After a moment, he asked, "What do you mean?"

"The ritual," I repeated. "It has been the plan for me since my birth, has it not? My mother was not a blood witch, but maybe I was. That's why you needed me. Why I was born."

"You were born because your mother wanted a child."

I stepped closer, getting angry now. "You and my grandfather needed a blood witch, someone stronger than either of you." I spread my arms. "Well here I am. Now what is the ritual?"

His cheeks hollowed out, or maybe it was just a trick of the scant light, or of his shadows contracting around him, stronger now that he was agitated. "It doesn't matter now. The text is lost to us. How do you know all of this?"

"My sword showed me. Now tell me the truth. All of it."

Now I was sure his face was going hollow. If he lost too much control, we might have an issue. I didn't want to use my magic on him. I wasn't even sure if I could.

"Tell me the truth," I repeated. "I saw a vision of you speaking with my grandfather. I know there was a plan for me—a ritual. And yet, you have spoken nothing of it."

"Because it is too dangerous," he hissed, recoiling. "Even if we had the text, I would never ask it of you."

I lifted my chin and stepped closer again. "But my grandfather would have. And I believe he expected you to follow through with it. *That's* why he wanted me to find you."

"He wanted you to live long enough to sacrifice *every-thing*," he muttered, barely loud enough for me to hear. "He had you bonded to a vampire. He needed to hide you from Eiric until you were ready—until your magic could grow with age. Why do you think I knew how to break the bond?" He loomed over me. "It was always the plan. Once you were strong enough. Once you were *ready*."

I stepped back like he'd slapped me. I could sense Markus closer now, wanting against his will to protect me.

I lifted a hand to keep him back. I knew my grandfather had been practical, but being treated like a tool still stung. "Ready for what?"

"Lavandriel created a ritual before she died," Cael explained, his voice strained. "I don't know if she was too old to cast it, or if she simply died before she could, but she wanted to rid the land of Eiric's creations. She felt it was her duty."

"She wanted to kill vampires?"

With his admission, all the fight seemed to have gone out of him. His shadows died down, barely visible. He hugged his arms tightly around himself and nodded. "Before she died, Lavandriel's daughter recorded her rituals in two separate grimoires to be handed down through the generations. They were too dangerous to keep together, and this specific ritual was in the two tomes. Your grandfather kept one, and we left the other hidden at the fortress where no one but our kin could find it."

He was talking about the grimoire under his sister's bed. The grimoire that was already within the city, but he didn't know about it. And the other . . . Eiric had the other. He'd taken it after he murdered my grandfather.

"What is the ritual?"

He looked away. "It would take power, great power. You would never have enough within yourself—you would need to steal it from others. Witches, vampires, any powerful beings would do."

I waited for him to tell me more, and when he did not, I touched his arm. He flinched, and I lowered my hand.

"The ritual would destroy every vampire," he continued. "It would create a powerful, magical form of sunlight. It would fill every home, every crevice, every dark little hole that a vampire might hide in. It would turn night into complete and total day, harming no mortals, but killing every vampire. There would be no escape."

My breath caught in my throat. The ritual for light. I had seen it in the grimoire, but hadn't realized what it meant.

Markus stepped forward. "But if she cast that while she was a servant, it would kill her too. If it killed Asher, she would have died."

Cael shook his head slightly. "No. The bond was always meant to be broken. She would need her full magic for the ritual." His hollow eyes met mine. "Cedrik forbade me to tell you until it was time."

I had assumed the ring and Cerridwen's chant were needed to suppress the bond so that Cael might then break it, but that wasn't the case. Cael could have broken it all along. Because he was also a vampire, his necromancy was more powerful than Cerridwen's. "My grandfather is dead," I stated. "Why did you keep this from me until now? Do you fear your own death?"

The look he gave me was cold, but I could sense it was to hide strong emotions. "I saw what was in your heart long before you were willing to admit it. I kept it from you because I would never ask you to kill the person you love. I have seen much loss, and I would never destroy you in such a way. Your grandfather was practical to a fault. He kept his distance from you. He did not let himself get too attached, just in case, but I—"

He extended a hand, as if searching for the right words. Then with a trembling breath, he let it fall. "I have watched over you from the start. Everywhere you have gone, I have always made sure you were safe. When your uncle died—" He hesitated as my eyes whipped up to his face. "I was too late to save him, but I am the reason

Karpov let you live. He sensed my presence when I arrived, and he feared me."

"But he almost killed me another night," I accused.

"I would not have let that happen. If it came to it, I would have interfered, and I would have healed you, but you were not supposed to see me unless it was the only option."

I shook my head over and over again. Every time I thought a lie had unraveled everything, there was another handful of lies waiting to damage me further. Everything I had done as a hunter was a lie. I had never even risked my life.

But that wasn't the most important part. There was a more pressing issue, one I had not taken the time to fully consider.

"The night I became Asher's servant," I began slowly. "I had assumed you arrived too late, and he had already taken me, but that wasn't the case, was it? You controlled the ghouls who attacked me, and you would have been near to make sure I didn't die. You would have been near to take me to Geist."

He turned away again, allowing me only to see the harsh line of his tense jaw. He had told me as much before —that I was meant for Geist—but I didn't question him further. I was too busy being devastated by the news that I had killed my own parents.

"Tell me the truth," I demanded. "What point is there in keeping me from it now?"

His shoulders hunched, and slowly, his jaw relaxed. "I was there. I watched you with Asher all night. I heard every word you said to him."

"*And*," I pressed.

"And after the ghouls had done their work, I was going to take you to Geist. We had agreed upon a location to meet. With my blood and my power, I would make sure you stayed alive, but unconscious. You were to never see either of us. You were to think it all a horrible twist of fate, because when the time came, you would need to trust your grandfather. And you would need to trust *me*." He looked at me again. "But then I sensed Asher returning. I needed to call off the ghouls, but instead I waited to see what he would do. And the look on his face . . . " He shook his head. "He destroyed the ghouls, but I should have called them off sooner. You were too close to death for healing. I almost took you then, but—" His gaze was distant, reliving the memory. "I knew he would do what it would take to save you. I took a risk, and I followed him to make sure it would work. If it did not, the only choice would be for you to become my servant instead."

I wished Markus wasn't with us. I wished for no one else to hear this tale. "Why? Why did you do it?"

He turned his face further away from me. "I thought, if you were to be bound to a master, why shouldn't it be to someone who had been absolutely devastated by the potential of your death? Someone who would clearly protect you, if he could. I knew he was an ancient. I knew he would keep you alive, far better than I ever could."

My heart thundered in my chest, and my magic reacted, tugging at my gut. Strong emotions made it worse. I needed to calm down, but—

"And what did my grandfather think of your choice?" I asked lowly.

"He was furious, especially when I would not tell him who your new master was, nor why I let him take you. He did not know Asher, and he trusted Geist. But it was done, and he still had what he wanted. We moved on."

I shook my head. It really had been a twist of fate for Asher to find me that night, and for Cael to let him take me on a whim. "But what about the ritual?"

He let me see his face again, his expression the most pained I had ever seen it. "I did not expect you to fall in love with him, Lyssandra. I expected him to love you, yes, but not for you to love him in return. The ritual is meant to kill all vampires. Even me. Even Geist."

"But why would Geist agree?" Markus asked.

"He was never told. Only Cedrik and I knew of the true plan." Cael looked down at me again. "And when I could see that you loved him, I knew there had to be another way. I could break your bond. I could help you be strong. And we would find another way. We *will* find another way."

My mind raced. I knew I still had so many unanswered questions, but for the life of me, I couldn't think of them. There was only one thing I could think of.

"The grimoires, they were copied from Lavandriel's original tome?"

My question seemed to surprise him. He straightened. "Yes. The original was lost long ago. We believe it was burned with Lavandriel upon her death."

I shook my head. "It wasn't burned. Someone has cared for it all these centuries."

"Who?" he asked breathlessly.

"Cerridwen. And she tried to give it to me. She tried to

give me the key to Eiric's destruction, just as she kept from him the complete form of his desired ritual. He doesn't need both grimoires. He only needs to look under my bed within the temple."

I was a fool. I should have found a way to bring it with me. Xavier had thought Cerridwen was no longer working against Eiric, but he was wrong. She had simply fooled everyone, even me.

"She gave it to you?" Cael gasped. "It cannot be true. It must be a fake."

"But why give me a fake?" It made no sense. Of course, it also made no sense that she had given it to me with so little explanation.

"What is the ritual Eiric wants you to cast?" Markus asked.

I shook my head, because I wasn't entirely sure. The rituals I had read were complex—it was difficult to tell what they might do. "I know he believes I can alter his blood for him to walk in the light, but I think it's more than that. He made it sound like he would become unstoppable."

"But why would Lavandriel write such a ritual in her grimoire? She wanted to stop him."

I thought over the memories my sword had given me, then shook my head. "I don't know. Maybe he convinced her to write it. He was trying to make her cast it before he was sealed away, but she refused. Whatever it was, it disgusted her."

"The power needed," Cael interrupted. "She had both rituals, but the power was the issue. She would have needed to steal it from others using her blood magic."

213

"Why write them then?" I asked, then shook my head before he could answer. "There's still something we're missing, but regardless, we need that book."

Cael lowered his chin. "I will get it for you."

"It's too dangerous. Eiric might be back at the temple."

"It is worth the risk, Lyssandra. I will go. *Now*."

He was gone before I could argue. My breath caught in my throat as I stared at the space he had occupied.

I sensed Markus moving closer. "This doesn't feel right."

I shook my head. I had made a mistake in telling Cael about the grimoire. I wasn't sure why, but I knew it to be so. Before I could think further on it, my sword awoke, and I fell to my knees.

CHAPTER TWENTY-ONE

The memory was the most realistic one yet. I was once again seeing through the eye of my sword, but even more, I could almost *feel* where we were. Soft light shone through a nearby window, cutting a line halfway across the table where we rested. Both Lavandriel and Cerridwen were with us this time, so it must have been before Eiric was sealed away. The eye in the sword rolled toward them where they stood, facing each other.

Lavandriel looked just as I remembered her. Crimson hair, the same vibrant shade as mine, fell nearly to her waist. Our features were similar, but not identical. My mouth was a little wider, and her eyes more tapered at the edges. She wore a cream-colored dress, contrasting dramatically with the hair.

She extended a small pendant on a golden chain toward Cerridwen, who unlike Lavandriel, looked tired and worn. Purple marks marred the skin beneath her eyes, and her hair was limp and oily. Perhaps I was wrong —maybe this was after they sealed Eiric away.

Cerridwen took the necklace with a small, sad smile. A yellow crystal caught the sun, surrounded by intricate, swirling veins of gold.

"The shadows should not be a problem for you again," Lavandriel said.

Cerridwen put on the necklace, then tucked it into the high neck of her black dress. "Thank you, friend. I'd much rather wear a necklace than wield a sword." She glanced at the sword on the table. "With Xavier gone, I thought hope was lost for me."

"He's not gone," Lavandriel said softly. "He still lives, like Eiric."

Cerridwen turned away. "Can such a state be called living? It's like he's asleep. And the witches want to seal him away in that crypt."

"If you find a cure for Eiric, you can bring Xavier back too. You have the power to do so." It was clear by Lavandriel's expression that she didn't believe either thing would come to pass.

"None of your rituals will work?" Cerridwen asked.

"I have called upon sources I should never touch for knowledge, trying to put together the pieces. He wanted me to help him walk in the light again, but the cost—" Her breath sighed out of her. "I cannot use my blood magic in such a way. I cannot steal power from others. It would destroy me."

Her back still turned toward her friend, Cerridwen bowed her head. "Would it have been so bad to steal power from the monsters he has created? He would have controlled them for you. It would have been but a small risk."

Lavandriel's mouth formed a grim line as she stared at her friend's back. "You witnessed Eiric's corruption. You would wish the same upon me so that he might walk in the sun?"

Cerridwen gritted her teeth, but Lavandriel couldn't see it. "Of course not. But I must keep trying. I will find a cure."

Lavandriel moved closer, placing a hand on her friend's shoulder. "I know you will, but I hope you will also live your life."

"I sacrificed my life to save him, and now he is lost to me. What life is there for me to live, except one where I bring him back?"

Lavandriel's expression was unreadable, and I wondered if even then, she was working on her ritual to shift night to day. I wondered if she was already planning on killing her half-brother, along with every vampire he had created. Maybe that was the true reason she would not allow him to walk in the light, because she intended to use the light to kill him.

"You will do what you think is right," Lavandriel said finally. "But my friend, I want a life. I want children, *family*."

Cerridwen finally turned to face her. I wasn't sure if I could only tell since I'd gotten to know Cerridwen in recent times, but to me, her smile was clearly fake. "And you will. I wish it for you." She touched the necklace through the fabric of her dress. "And thank you. You have given me at least a small ray of hope."

I CAME BACK to the present with a gasp. It was lucky that Markus stood behind me, tightly gripping my shoulder, else I might have toppled off the roof.

"It was like before," he said. "I couldn't sense you. If I wasn't standing right next to you, I would have guessed you were gone."

My breath hitched as I tried to inhale. My sword had gone dormant again. It had shown me what it wanted, but why that particular scene? It didn't answer our questions about the rituals. "I saw Cerridwen and Lavandriel. I believe it was their last encounter before they parted ways. They spoke of Xavier. He grew weak with Eiric sealed away, and that's why he ended up trapped in the crypt until Amarithe found him and breathed life into him."

Markus still gripped my shoulder. "Did you learn anything important?"

I started to shake my head, but stopped. "Lavandriel's grimoire. If she was still writing it when they parted ways, how did Cerridwen come to have it? It remained with her children long enough for them to create the separate tomes. Cerridwen would have needed to come for it many years later, but why?"

"Are you sure it was Lavandriel's grimoire she gave you?" Markus asked.

He released my shoulder as I turned to face him. "No, I'm not." Why had I thought I could ever outwit Cerridwen? She was ancient. She'd been playing this game for a *very* long time. I met his waiting gaze. "I think we might have sent Cael into a trap. Cerridwen wanted to give me something I'd want to come back for."

He frowned. "Do you think they will have the strength to catch him?"

I shook my head. I just wasn't sure. "If Eiric has returned, then yes. But perhaps Cerridwen could trap him herself. She still has the ring." I thought about it. "And she must still have the necklace Lavandriel made for her."

At his confused expression, I explained what I had seen. Cerridwen was haunted by shadows that had come through when she brought Eiric back from the dead. If no one had ever banished them all, it would stand to reason that she was still wearing the necklace. And without it, they might come for her again.

But that didn't help Cael.

"What do you want to do?" Markus asked.

I looked toward the small slice of moon visible amongst the glittering stars. The night was young, and there was absolutely nothing I could do. "I want you to bring me to the other half of the grimoire. The rituals within may not be complete, but I read the tome Cerridwen gave me. I will be able to tell if they match, and perhaps I can remember enough."

"And what of Cael?"

I shook my head. "We will wait, and hope he returns. Perhaps there is no trap. Perhaps we worry over nothing."

Markus didn't reply, probably because we both knew we had plenty to worry about. And I thought I was right. Cael was walking into a trap, and there was no way to stop him. He would already be at the temple, and it would be up to him to escape.

I wrapped my arms tightly around myself. Markus and my sword were both silent, but I wasn't alone. My magic was like a cauldron in my chest. All day it had gently steamed, and now it was beginning to boil. Strong emotions made it worse. I couldn't help but wonder if it was the reason Eiric was yet to come for me. If he was simply waiting for my breaking point, where he could use me to my fullest potential.

CHAPTER TWENTY-TWO

The leftover bread felt like ash in my stomach. Daylight had come, and Cael had not returned. Something had happened. It would not have taken him long to fetch the grimoire if he had remained unseen. Markus waited until the sun rose to fetch the partial grimoire, not wanting to risk that Eiric might be watching. Every moment he was gone had me squirming uncomfortably, worried that something had happened to him, though I should feel it if it had.

I tugged the hood of my cloak lower to shade my face from the sun overhead. It was late enough in the year to chill the air, yet sweat dripped down my brow. My skin itched with restless energy. I knew even far away, Markus could probably feel it, and would be worried if I moved from the roof. We had debated me waiting somewhere indoors, but I didn't like the idea of getting trapped. At least on the roof, I would stand *some* chance of leaping down into the crowd for a quick escape.

I finished off the bread, then dusted crumbs from my

fingers. My legs ached from the crouch I'd held since sunrise. There had been more whispers. More deaths. Either the same demon, or more, bursting out from those poor girls. I wondered if Gwenvere's death had triggered the remaining demons to escape. Hopefully a demon encounter was not what had become of Cael. Eiric wanted him alive. A demon would not.

My eyes searched the crowd, for what, I wasn't sure. All I knew was that I was tired of waiting. I had expected Eiric to come for me, or at least Cerridwen, but neither had shown their faces. So what were they waiting for?

My eyes caught on a familiar face in the crowd, but not one I expected. I stared for a moment, not quite believing it could be who I thought, then I lowered myself from the roof without thinking. Once I was on the ground, feeling shaky and sick, I ran toward the familiar face, pushing my way through the crowd.

"Ian!" I called when I was near.

He'd been about to walk into a shop, but turned at the sound of his name. Seeing me, his eyes flew wide. He pushed his shaggy black hair out of his face as he jogged toward me.

We met in the shade of a shop's eave. I gripped his arms, looking him over. He seemed unharmed. "What are you doing here?"

He shook his head in disbelief, staring wide-eyed at me like I was a ghost.

I had to admit, I felt like one.

"How are you here?" he gasped. "And free?"

"For now." I lowered my voice, pulling him further from the crowd since we were catching some odd glances.

We squeezed into a narrow alley, pushing closer together than either of us was likely comfortable with. Since he was barely taller than me, I looked directly into his eyes. "Now why are *you* here?"

His expression fell. "I suppose you wouldn't have heard. Eiric returned to the fortress the night after the battle, before we could restore the wards."

My heart sank to my boots. The grimoire. He must have been looking for it, but Asher and the others would have already departed. Eiric might have missed them by mere hours.

"He came around midnight with a flock of vampires," Ian continued. "They killed the guards on duty. We were already so weakened, they had no issue coming in. An alarm was sounded." He hung his head. "But I must admit, most of us hid in our homes. We were not prepared for another fight."

My stomach twisted uncomfortably. Hadn't Eiric terrorized them enough? If I had been there with my magic I would have—

I cut off my own thoughts as my magic prickled across my skin.

Ian gasped. "What was that?" He looked me up and down. "Why do you feel so different?"

I couldn't seem to take a full breath. My body felt tense and oddly limp at the same time. "You would have heard what happened with Asher."

He nodded. "Yes, the bond is gone." He squinted. "Mostly. I still see a hint of his colors mingling with yours."

My heart skipped a beat. "You do?"

He nodded. "It's faint, but there. It happens sometimes when a pair is deeply bonded."

I wanted to know what he meant, but there were more pressing matters at hand. "Tell me what happened at the fortress when Eiric returned."

"Ah, yes." He seemed oddly breathless now too, like my surge of magic had affected him. "He came with the other vampires. He made a big scene of it. Those who fought them died, but it seemed they only wanted one thing."

The grimoire. He had to be talking about the grimoire. But he wouldn't have found it.

"Ophelia," Ian finished.

My mind crashed to a halt. *What?*

"He took Ophelia. He made sure we saw it."

I turned as a shadow crossed the alley, then realized it was only Markus, looking furious at me for leaving the roof. Though his expression softened slightly with understanding when he realized I was with Ian. He nodded at me, then turned his back, keeping guard. I wanted to ask about the grimoire, but it was wise of him to not mention it in front of Ian. The fewer people who knew about it, the better.

Leave it to Markus to not be a pain in the ass when you'd least expect it.

I turned back toward Ian. "Why would he want Ophelia?"

He glanced at Markus' back as he answered, "I don't know, but he took her. He said he was bringing her here to be a prisoner alongside you. And we couldn't just *let* him, you know? We had to come."

My magic surged again at a new emotion—hope. "Drucida, is she here?"

His expression fell. "No, she was gravely injured when Eiric returned. She tried to fight him. We could only spare a small group of us to come here. I don't even know what we hope to accomplish, but we couldn't just let him take Ophelia. He needs to be stopped."

I couldn't agree more. I didn't want to see any of them harmed, but a small group of witch allies was better than no witch allies. "Who else is with you? Merri? The summoner?" I had forgotten the summoner's name, but she was the one I really wanted to know about.

He frowned. "No. Merri and Liliana stayed behind to protect the fortress. It was Liliana's shadows that finally chased the vampires away, but that was after Eiric had left with Ophelia. Have you seen her?"

The crying. Isolde had mentioned hearing someone crying, locked in a room. Ophelia had been in the temple with me the whole time, and I hadn't known. "No, but I think I know where she is being kept." I gripped his arm. "You mustn't go there. I have no doubt that it's a trap."

Magic sparked between us where my hand gripped his arm. I thought I'd never be able to fully sense the magic of others, but I did then. I could feel what was flowing through his veins, so similar to the magic I had once stolen from Ophelia.

My heart pounded. That was the key—what my grandfather had planned for me. To steal the magic—the *life force*—of others. To become a monster to defeat Eiric.

I knew he wasn't beyond such thinking. He had let Cael do the same. And now that was what Eiric wanted too, for me to steal power to perform his ritual. If it would have been necessary for Lavandriel, it was surely necessary for me.

Ian was staring at me like I'd grown a second head, but he didn't move. Maybe he was *afraid* to move.

I licked my dry lips, thinking things over. Isolde claimed the hunters were being lured to Ivangard, and now Eiric had lured witches here too. He had no other reason for taking Ophelia publicly, and certainly no other reason for leaving any of the witches within the fortress alive. They were only alive because he still wanted to use them. He wanted *me* to use them.

Ian watched my shifting expression. Or maybe he was watching my energy, something only he and Ophelia could see. "You've thought of something." His voice was a hoarse croak. I knew what I was feeling from him, but I wondered just what he was feeling from me.

"Yes." I glanced at Markus' back. We'd need to move quickly. If the witches had arrived, and the hunters were near, Eiric's plan was almost ready. I turned my attention back to Ian, finally releasing his arm. "Where are the other witches? You need to warn them."

He slumped with relief. "They are camped well outside the city. I came ahead to scout. I've heard about deaths here. I'm assuming they are more of Eiric's victims."

I shook my head, almost reluctant to release the feel of his magic. Something within me *wanted* it. Maybe *that* was the true reason blood witches went mad. Why they stole power from others. It was simply too alluring. "No, Eiric didn't kill them. I'll tell you more, but we should get moving. Can you take a message to the witches' camp?"

He nodded, though his eyes darted with indecision. "I can, but what will you do?"

I glanced at Markus again, knowing he would argue against my new plan. I would not steal magic the way Eiric wanted, but I had to do *something*. I had to gain enough power to destroy him. "I'm going to hunt demons." If I could steal magic from mortals, then why not demons? Maybe no one had to die for me to claim the power I needed to defeat Eiric. Perhaps it was a mad plan, but it was the only one I had.

Ian nodded a little too quickly. Markus glanced back at me, clearly wondering what I was thinking.

Eiric had left the remaining witches alive for a reason, just as he had lured the hunters here for a reason. They were all walking on borrowed time, and so was I.

Are you ready to go hunting? I aimed my thought at my sword.

It sent a shiver up my spine in response.

I would not turn night to day to stop Eiric, but maybe I didn't need to. Maybe I just needed enough power to obliterate him in one fell swoop. I knew he would come for me soon.

And I would be ready.

Markus took one last look out at the street, then moved back to retreat down the alley with us. Ian led the way, and once he was far enough ahead, Markus leaned in near my shoulder. "The grimoire is gone."

IT WASN'T difficult to find the location of the most recent death. People loved to talk. We had been pointed to a small stand of older homes, not far from the temple. It made me nervous being so close, but if we wanted to find a demon, we needed a place to start. And now it was more important than ever. If Eiric had the other half of the grimoire, he would be ready to enact his plan. Ian had gone to warn the witches, which was for the best. I didn't want him to see what I would do next.

Markus stood at my shoulder as we observed the small home. "He might not have it. Someone else may have taken it."

I resisted the urge to sigh. "Was it a possibility for someone to simply happen upon it?"

"It was at the bottom of a dry well."

No wonder it had taken him so long to search for it. "Eiric may not have seen you hide it, but he has vampires under his command. Once he realized the grimoire was not at the fortress, he probably had them combing the city. It was only a matter of time."

"We should have kept it with us."

I shook my head. "If his minions didn't find it, he would have doubled his efforts to find *you*. It worked out for the best."

"You talk as if you know him well."

"I don't need to know him well. All I need to know is that he will stop at nothing to meet his own ends. The rest is common sense."

Markus' jaw clenched in irritation, but instead of arguing with me, he looked at the small home. "What if it has already fled?"

I glanced at him. I had to admit, even with our dire circumstances and his irritation, he was looking better since we'd been reunited. Steifan had explained to me once that separation from me was difficult for Markus, though he would certainly never admit it. "Then we will have to come up with a different plan."

"I'm not even sure I understand the *current* plan."

I turned back toward the home. My sword was silent, so the demon wasn't likely near. Or perhaps it just meant me no harm. The other demon had recognized my sword's ability and wanted me to free it. I would gladly free the next, after I attempted to steal its magic.

"I'm not sure if it will work," I admitted. "But we must try. Without the grimoire, and without Cael—" My throat tightened. As strained as our relationship was, I did not want him to be dead. *Truly* dead. "I must be strong enough to destroy Eiric on my own when he comes for me. It is the only way."

"But without the grimoire—"

"I don't need it," I snapped. "I only need power. I must kill him quickly, before he can cloud my thoughts or threaten anyone I care about."

Markus went silent, but this close, I could sense his discomfort.

"I don't see anyone," I stepped into the street. "I think we are safe to investigate."

He didn't reply, but he followed as I walked toward the small home. The entire street was eerily quiet. I wondered if the victim's neighbors had chosen to go elsewhere, fearing the same fate. It wasn't a bad idea. Only fools played with demons.

And here I was, hoping to join the game.

I touched the door. There were deep gouges in the wood, but it wasn't how the demon had entered. The window further down the wall was shattered. There was something frantic about the demon's assault on the house, with the gouges and shattered glass. Almost like it *needed* to feed. Perhaps it was necessary for the creatures to kill if they wanted to remain in this realm without their hosts.

I tried the door. It opened without issue. It had probably been locked the night before, but someone would have carried the body out by now.

I stepped inside with Markus shadowing me. It was almost a relief to not see a body for once, but the blood, torn bedding, and broken furniture still painted a gruesome scene. The victim had struggled.

"What do you hope to find?" Markus asked lowly.

I turned to watch him studying a small painting on the wall. The home was older, but not without its comforts. The victim had probably lived a nice, safe life, and would have continued doing so if not for Gwenvere's scheme.

"A trail to follow the demon," I explained. "They can go out in daylight, but I don't think they like it. It's probably hiding somewhere dark until nightfall."

He glanced at me, his expression unreadable. "One of the adjacent homes?"

"Maybe. Or perhaps it even returned to the temple."

"We cannot hunt it *there*."

"I know. But there have been multiple deaths in the city. I don't think it went back to the temple. There may even be several demons roaming the streets. We only need to find one."

I walked to the broken window, thinking the demon had likely retreated the way it had come. Sure enough, thick, black fluid dripped down some remaining shards of glass.

Markus joined me, narrowing his eyes at the fluid. "Is that—"

"Demon blood, yes." I hadn't been sure until that moment if they could bleed. The one I'd banished hadn't, but that may have been a result of my sword. A normal weapon could have different effects. I reached my fingertips toward the fluid.

Markus snatched my wrist. "Don't touch it," he hissed.

I simply stared at him. "If I want to steal their magic, I have to touch it."

He maintained his hold on my wrist. "What makes you think there is even magic to steal? Maybe they're just monsters."

"They granted the priestesses and acolytes that blue fire. They have magic. More than any witch."

He finally released my wrist, though he continued to glower.

I touched the blood. It was thick and tacky, like tar. I rubbed it between my fingertips, not sure what I hoped to conclude. I could feel no magic in it, but there was . . . something.

"Your sword is glowing." Markus stepped back, his gaze on my scabbard.

I wiped the blood on my already stained and dirty cloak, then drew my sword. It glowed a pale white, the eye open and staring not at me, but at the blood on the glass.

Give me the blood. I will find the demon.

I nearly dropped my sword, once again startled to hear its words so clearly. *Why didn't you speak before?* I thought.

Your magic. You are only now learning to truly listen. The blood. Wipe it on my blade.

Ignoring Markus' glare, I did as the sword asked, taking more blood from the windowsill. The black fluid smeared across the blade, then soaked into it.

Power flared within the sword, similar to what I felt from it when demons were near. It did not speak again, but it didn't have to. I had a clear image of where I needed to go. I might track killers through the blood of their victims, but my sword would put me to shame. I could feel its will within my mind, compelling me to follow it. I was a hunter with a hound.

I led the way back out of the house, holding my sword openly before me. It was lucky that no one had wanted to stick around for the next death. Anyone who saw me would summon the city guard.

My sword led me across the street, then further from the temple. I was forced to lower it when I heard voices ahead, but even concealed within my cloak, I could still feel its silent pull. My feet moved forward without me willing them to do so.

I turned a corner, stepping out of the shade of the closely spaced homes. A pair of older men stopped talking, watching me warily as I passed. One opened his mouth to speak, then Markus stepped into sight and he shut it. I didn't have to look back to know what sort of expression Markus was giving them.

We moved on, my sword leading us down several

more streets before stopping in front of an abandoned shack with no door. I looked down at my boots, spotting a small dark stain in the dirt. I knelt, touching the stain. More black demon blood.

I glanced back at Markus as I straightened, giving him a nod. We were close enough now that I could sense the demon within, hiding from the sun. I stepped into the building, scanning every corner.

There were a few shards of broken furniture, some scraps of fabric, and little else. The demon huddled in the far corner, a massive black stain in the shadows. Its shining scales looked dull without any light to reflect from them.

It was hard to tell in the dimness, but I thought it was staring at me with its solid black eyes. And yet, it didn't move. I withdrew my sword from the folds of my cloak, illuminating the demon with its glow.

The creature hissed softly. It was grotesque with its too long limbs, its large maw partially open to reveal razor sharp teeth and the flick of a reptilian tongue.

Demon blade, its words slithered through my mind. *Free me, witch.* Mixed emotions of fear and weariness entered my consciousness along with the words.

Markus had drawn his sword close to my back, but I didn't think he could hear the words. He was waiting for me to do whatever I planned.

You're trapped here, I thought, unsure if the demon could actually hear my thoughts in the same manner.

Summoned. Trapped. Just as the demon in your blade. If I do not feed, I hurt. Free me.

I inhaled sharply. *The demon in my blade?*

Free me, it thought again, finally uncurling its long limbs. *It hurts*. It stood, but couldn't straighten completely with the low roof of the shack overhead.

It took a staggering step toward me, showing none of the frightening speed I'd seen before. I was right. They were weakening the longer they remained without their hosts. Or maybe it was just because the demon was in pain, which was an odd thing to consider—demons hurting just like mortals.

I lifted my sword. If the creature rushed me and I was forced to banish it, I wouldn't have the blood I needed. And bleeding on it myself seemed out of the question—I could not leave myself so vulnerable to the demon's long teeth and talons.

Thinking of Markus' unenchanted blade, I stepped aside. "I need you to wound it," I muttered.

He didn't question me, he simply lifted his sword.

"Free me," the demon hissed out loud, its words misshapen by its teeth and narrow tongue.

I kept my sword out just in case. If Markus got into trouble, I would banish the demon and look for another. "Gladly. I just need a bit of your blood first."

The creature hissed and rushed toward us, talons outstretched. Markus met it with his blade, the steel sparking where it clashed with the black talons. Markus huffed in disbelief, then spun to meet the demon's next attack.

I stepped back, wishing I had asked Markus to fetch me a dagger, or that I had even taken a piece of broken glass. Anything to draw blood on the demon. I could sense its magic, so close, but I could not steal it.

Markus parried another attack, then grunted as the demon slashed him across the arm. Blood sprayed, soaking his sleeve and splattering the ground.

I gritted my teeth. He was a strong fighter, but the massive demon was no ordinary foe. This wasn't going to work.

My sword shone brighter as I darted forward, recapturing the demon's attention. It turned on me with another loud hiss, but didn't attack, its eyes transfixed on my glowing blade. It made a high, keening noise in the back of its throat.

Send me home, it pleaded, reverting to mental communication as it huffed heavily, its thin chest expanding to show the outline of its ribs.

Markus had stepped back, lowering his sword to put pressure on his wounded arm.

I will send you home, I thought. *I will send all of you back, but I need your magic.*

So did they. And we cracked their bones and shredded their hearts. Greedy. Greedy witches.

The words stiffened my spine, because the demon was right. I was no better than Gwenvere and all the others. But . . . I would do what I must to protect those I loved.

My sword glowed brighter, and the demon made its horrible keening noise again. It cowered from my blade's unearthly glow.

I stepped toward it. My sword was too heavy for me to wield one handed, but I managed as I extended my other hand toward Markus. "I need another blade."

His eyes wide, he took the dagger from his belt, fumbling with his blood-slickened grip.

I took the bloody dagger in hand, then stepped closer to the demon. It was huddling in on itself again, weak, even though it had only fed the night before.

I was the first, it said. *First to be released, but not the last. We will make the witches pay for what they have done to us.*

The witch who summoned you is dead, I thought. I moved even closer. It seemed unable to attack with my blade shining so bright. It could not tear its beady black eyes away from the light.

Knowing it wouldn't be long before some unsuspecting passerby heard the commotion and happened upon us, I took a chance and lunged toward the demon, sinking the dagger into its chest.

It shrieked, flailing wildly. Its talons raked across my thigh, bringing instant blinding pain. With my attention on the demon and my glowing sword, I could no longer see Markus. I did the only thing I could think to do. I reached out for a connection to the demon's blood, much like what I did when I used blood to track.

I willed that connection into place, searching for the magic in the demon's blood. I called to it, and its black blood flowed faster, soaking into the hard-packed earth. It shrieked, the call echoed by shouts outside. We had gathered a crowd, but I could not focus on that now.

Bring me to the blood, my sword commanded.

"Lyssandra!" Markus shouted, his voice coming from somewhere behind me. He was probably blocking the door.

I watched the demon warily as it fell to the ground, shrieking as its blood poured out of it, far more than the small wound should have allowed. I fell to my knees and stabbed my sword into the hard earth in the center of the growing pool of blood.

It soaked it up, turning the white glow of the blade into a murky gray aura. The blackness reached the hilt, then flowed up into my hand. I gasped as my skin lit like the moon, my veins streaks of angry black marring the pure light. My blade soaked up the blood until not a hint of it was left, pouring the dark magic into my body.

I took a ragged breath, then staggered to my feet, pulling my blade free from the earth. The demon had fallen onto its side, writhing and keening. I stood over it with my sword.

Free me, it cried weakly. *Release me from this horrid realm.*

My sword came down, and the light went out.

CHAPTER TWENTY-THREE

Tholdri

Much had happened since we'd left the city. The people were being hunted, torn apart in their beds. And I did not think they were falling victim to vampires. Whatever killed them sounded more like a wild animal, but if it was, someone should have seen something. No, whatever killed those people had enough intelligence to remain unseen.

It had been Steifan's idea to investigate one of the homes. The deaths should not be our concern, but if they had anything to do with Eiric, we needed to know about it. We had no way to prepare for whatever he planned, so any scrap of information was worth gaining.

Steifan reached the door first, but stood to one side with his back against the wall, listening. He would be a fine hunter some day if the Helius Order survived. And if *he* survived. I hoped he had more of a chance than the rest of us. I would gladly go down fighting at Lyss' side, but I did not want the same fate for Steifan. I would prevent it if I could.

When neither of us heard or sensed anything, we nodded to each other. I went into the home while Steifan kept watch outside.

The sun was low enough that there wasn't much light coming through the broken window, but what I could see was enough. Blood on the bed, everything shredded. It looked like an animal attack—or maybe ghouls—just as the guards we'd spoken to had claimed.

I stepped toward the bed, inhaling deeply. The scent of blood had faded as it dried, but if the killers were ghouls . . . their odor tended to linger. And yet, I smelled nothing.

It didn't mean it *wasn't* ghouls, but I thought it unlikely.

I observed the broken window next. There was blood on the glass . . . or was it? I touched the tacky substance, and it stained my fingers black. Spotting Steifan outside, I beckoned him over.

"Now what does that look like to you?"

Brows furrowed, he observed the strange substance. His expression stretched the scar spanning one side of his face. I was grateful to Geist for giving him blood to heal, but he would still wear the scar he'd gained at the fortress battle for the rest of his life. "Is that tar?"

"It could be, but I doubt it. I think it's the blood of whatever killed the man who lived here."

Steifan gave me a worried look. He didn't have to tell me what he was thinking. A strange new creature killing people in Ivangard was too big of a coincidence. This had something to do with Eiric. Neither of us had missed how close the home was to the temple, and one other victim had dwelled even closer.

We both whipped our gazes toward a loud *thunk* in one of the neighboring homes. Those able to vacate the area had done so in hopes that the guard would catch whatever was killing people so they could return home in safety.

"Something tells me that isn't someone returning home for their belongings," Steifan whispered.

"No," I agreed. "We could never be so lucky."

With a final glance at the black blood, I left the window and exited through the door, reaching for my sword as we both approached the neighboring home. There was only silence now, but there was no doubt that we'd heard something within.

I gestured for Steifan to watch my back as we approached the next door. Maybe it was ghouls after all, hiding in the next home, waiting for night to fall. I reached the door and listened.

Ghouls didn't bleed black. Their blood was rotten and dark, but not black as pitch. Whatever might be lurking inside was something I had never faced. I would be an idiot if I got killed before Eiric's plan could be revealed, but I couldn't just *not* look.

I drew my sword, opened the fortunately unlocked door, and stepped inside. The main room was empty, the wooden furniture unmarred, but there were two open doors branching off in either direction. Making sure

Steifan was still watching my back, I chose one at random and stepped inside, sword held out before me.

The room was dark enough that I almost missed it. I *would* have missed it if the darkness in one corner by the bed hadn't shifted slightly. Once I noticed the movement, I noticed the light, but labored breathing, and the broken bedroom window.

I crept closer, catching the reflection of beady black eyes. I nearly staggered back as my mind made sense of the rest of it. The creature was huge, but all curled up on itself. Long teeth prevented its maw from closing fully. It watched me, its breath growing louder.

Suddenly those long limbs uncurled and it launched itself at me, faster than I had expected. I slashed it with my sword, shouting for Steifan. The creature hissed as I sliced through its arm, but its reach was too great. It sliced my chest with its talons.

I gritted my teeth against the sharp pain and readied my sword for the next attack, but the creature wavered. It was weak—possibly injured.

Home, a terrible, keening voice cut through my mind.

I flinched like it had struck me again. I knew Lyssandra could sometimes hear things from her sword, but I hadn't considered how strange it might feel for something to speak without speaking.

Steifan had entered the doorway, sword drawn, but he didn't seem to know what to do. Footsteps sounded behind him—it must be the guard coming to investigate the commotion.

I didn't see who else entered the room as the creature lunged for me again. I lifted my sword too slowly, distracted by someone ordering Steifan to move. It slashed at me again, catching the flesh near my throat, then fell away abruptly, shrieking like it had been the one injured and not me.

I held a hand over the second wound near my collarbone as a blinding light approached. Just a hair closer and I would have been dead. My heart thundered, increasing the blood flow I couldn't see with the light blinding me.

Once the glowing orb was close enough and my eyes adjusted, I realized it was Lyssandra's glowing sword. She didn't seem to notice me with her attention entirely on the creature. Her pants were torn and stained with blood, but she didn't seem wounded. She held out her free hand, then clenched it into a fist. The creature shrieked loudly as black blood spewed from the small wound I'd caused it. It fell to the ground, writhing and screeching.

Lyss wrapped both hands around her sword, I thought to end the creature, but instead she stabbed the blade into the floorboards. The black blood soaked upward into the blade, like a rag sopping up spilled ink, and now . . . Lyssandra was glowing. Her skin glowed like the moon, but it was cut through with black, pulsing veins. She looked at me, and I saw nothing of the friend who had been by my side my entire life.

That look stole the rest of my strength. I could not reason with her. All I could do was watch.

Once the blood was absorbed, she effortlessly freed her sword from the flooring with one hand, then parted the creature's head from its body. The whole thing turned into a cloud of black smoke, then was gone.

I clutched my bleeding chest, panting heavily,

wondering if I had somehow fallen into a nightmare. It took me a moment to realize Markus had also entered the room, and was standing back beside Steifan. His clothes were bloody too, his shirt sleeve in long tatters, but he also appeared uninjured.

Lyssandra looked at my bleeding chest, then raised her eyes to my face. "Where are Asher and Geist?"

I stared at her for a moment, too shocked to answer. Her skin was losing its glow now. She seemed to be turning back to normal, except for her expression.

When she only stared back, I finally found my words. "We're to meet them at the gates at nightfall."

She nodded. "Good. They can heal your wounds. I have much to do before the sun sets. Eiric found the other half of the grimoire."

I reached for her as she stepped back. "Lyssandra."

Her expression crumbled, just for a moment showing me that she was still there. She hadn't been consumed by her magic like I'd feared. "No. I have to do this, Tholdri. Something has happened to Cael, and soon Eiric will come for me. I must be prepared to defeat him on my own." She took another step back.

Markus moved past Steifan toward the door.

I looked at him, desperate for an explanation.

"If you want to help, go to the witches," he said. "Ian has gone to warn them of Eiric's plans."

Lyssandra walked toward him, her naked blade still in hand. It had stopped glowing, but even I could sense the power emanating from it.

I wanted to say a hundred different things. I wanted to

grab Lyssandra and shake some sense into her. But in the end, I let her go. Markus followed her without another word.

Steifan turned his attention to me, his expression urging me to do something, but I shook my head. This wasn't the plan. We needed to remain free and able to help Lyssandra when the time came. We knew that whatever Eiric planned would happen at the temple. Both the witches and the hunters were being lured there for a reason. So that was where we would be when the time came.

Glancing once more toward the space the demon had occupied, I leaned my sword against the wall and started removing my scabbard. It would be a while before Geist or Asher could heal me, so I needed to bandage the wounds as best I could.

I could only hope that there was no venom or poison involved, but I imagined if there was, Lyssandra would have said something.

I hoped.

Giving up, Steifan moved to help me. "What was that?" he whispered, though Lyssandra and Markus were gone. "What was that creature, and what did she do to it?"

I shook my head, wincing as I peeled my shirt away from the fresh wounds. "Her sword glows for demons, so that answers one question. As for the other . . . " I shook my head again. *Trust.* I had to trust her.

But could I? Desperation could make us all fools, and she was contending with forces I could hardly fathom.

Steifan balled my shirt so he could push the clean part

against my bleeding wounds. I inhaled sharply at the fresh pain. I was already feeling lightheaded. We needed to reach the meeting location before I could lose consciousness. We needed to find Asher and Geist, not only for healing, but in hopes that they might know what in the light was going on with Lyssandra.

CHAPTER TWENTY-FOUR

Markus

"Lyssandra, stop!"

My words had no effect on her. She charged down the alleyway like a woman possessed, and maybe she was. I should have stopped her after the first demon. I should have known, seeing her blade drink up demon blood like a happy kitten, that this was not a path we should tread.

But as always, she was only concerned with herself. She would not stop to consider how absorbing demon magic would also affect me, her unwilling human servant.

She was far worse than any vampire. She had witnessed Tholdri bleeding out from gaping chest wounds, and had barely batted an eye.

I clenched my jaw and followed after her, ready to draw my sword in an instant to *protect* her. I knew my thoughts weren't entirely true. I didn't hate her as much as I wanted to. I could feel what was inside of her, and it wasn't evil. It was a roaring mixture of power and *fear*.

But fear was the enemy. It would get us both killed. Any hunter worth his—or *her* training—knew that.

She had already turned down another alley when I caught up with her. She didn't care about the startled glances as she passed unsuspecting people in the streets. Just as she hadn't cared about the gawking crowd outside that first shack, after she had slain the first demon. I grabbed her arm, spinning her toward me.

She lifted her sword from the folds of her cloak reflexively, then lowered it. "What is it? We don't have much time."

I maintained my grip on her arm lest she run off again. "You cannot defeat Eiric if you can't even think straight."

"My thoughts are fine," she snapped.

I stared her down. She knew what it was to be a human servant—she knew even better than I. One moment, she was gaping at me with her insides laid bare, and the next, her mind and heart shut me out like a steel trap.

"Hiding your emotions from me is pointless," I said.

She tugged her arm free from my grip. "You're welcome to go after Steifan and Tholdri."

"And if Eiric can track me through my bond to you?"

Her lips sealed into a grim line. It wasn't an idea I had pondered previously, but here, now, with her magic leaking all over me . . . We were more connected than either of us liked to admit.

"If he could track you, he would have done so already.

You may be my servant, but we do not share blood. You do not share *his* blood."

"I'm on your side, Lyssandra," I said more softly, a tone more fit for reasoning with a madwoman. "We all are."

She frowned. "Then do as I say. My sword senses another demon nearby."

"And will you continue collecting them until nightfall? When will it be enough?"

With the first demon, our wounds had instantly healed. With the second, one her sword had been able to sense without blood but with power alone, her magic had grown so full that it spilled over into me. I could feel it thrumming in my chest. I was no expert, but feeling just a fraction of what was inside her led me to believe she might be able to defeat Eiric.

If she could hold on to her sanity long enough to do so.

Sweat dripped down her brow, glistening on her pallid skin. "Their power won't remain inside me forever. I will only have one opportunity to use it. If it is not enough, there will be no going back to collect more."

"But won't Eiric sense it? What if he doesn't come?"

There was a flash of something in her eyes I didn't like. "His blood is my blood. If he does not come for me, I will hunt him." Her magic flared, making me squirm.

And I had never been a man accustomed to *squirming*.

"Will that be all?" she asked.

No, it wasn't, but I did not know what else to say. I was in this, bound to her, for better or worse.

When I offered no further arguments, she turned

away, intent on finding the next demon. That we'd already found two and were on our way to the next let me know that more had likely burst forth from their hosts. We had no way of knowing what was going on in the temple, but I could only hope Isolde was safe.

She was smart, resourceful, and a finer hunter than most men I'd known. But she could only do so much. I had tried to face that first demon, and without Lyssandra, I would have failed. She was the only thing they feared. She might become the only thing Eiric feared. The only thing that could destroy him.

But when she did, what would be left?

Asher

I FELT odd when I woke for the night. My skin felt too tight across my bones, a sensation almost like magic tingling through my veins.

I smelled the blood before we found Steifan and Tholdri outside the gates, not far from a large farmhouse with a candle burning in the nearest window. Tholdri held his arms across his chest, a cloak tightly wrapped around him. He sat leaning against a small tree, the only support to keep him from slumping over while Steifan stood at his side, ready to protect him.

And protection might become a necessity soon. I had witnessed the vampires moving closer to the city, likely preying upon those dwelling outside the city walls. But not the witches. According to Geist, their camp had not moved.

Geist knelt beside Tholdri, opening a vein in his wrist without question. Resting his free hand on Tholdri's golden locks, he helped the other man to drink.

My throat tight, I looked at Steifan for an explanation.

He didn't quite meet my eyes, which wouldn't have been unusual if he hadn't trusted me enough to do so on other occasions. That he avoided them now made me all the more anxious to go to the temple.

"Demons," he explained, gesturing down toward Tholdri. "And . . . Lyss. She's hunting them and doing something with their blood. She didn't seem herself."

I forced my thoughts to still. Was that why I felt so strange? But that couldn't be right. There was no bond left between us. I could no longer feel what she was feeling. "What sort of demons?"

Tholdri winced, wiping the blood from his mouth as Geist leaned back. "Big horrible ones with long teeth and talons that slice through flesh like water." He panted, then gritted his teeth. His wounds would be healing now from Geist's blood, but it would not be pleasant. "Oh, and they can speak into your mind."

Remaining crouched near Tholdri, Geist looked back at me. "Have you any idea what this might mean?"

I looked toward the city, as if I could see her. Would she go to the temple tonight? "It means time is short. Let us go."

If Lyssandra would face Eiric tonight, I would be there. I had waited long enough. I had told her once that if she were to fall, I would fall with her. Not just in madness, but in pain, death, torture—whatever was to come. And if only I died, then so be it. At least now, she need not die with me.

CHAPTER TWENTY-FIVE

Tholdri

I leaned heavily on Geist, mostly healed, but still weak with blood loss. A whole lot of good I would do if Eiric attacked Lyss tonight. I supposed I could stagger in front of him, forming a meaty shield for her before he tore me apart. It would be a shame to shred the fresh black shirt Geist had found for me, but I supposed once I was dead, I wouldn't care.

Geist's arm flexed around me, almost as if he could sense my thoughts. "The graveyard is not far. Hopefully you can rest there for a while."

We had agreed to go to the graveyard, while Asher and Steifan would wait near the front of the temple, which was exactly where the hunters would go to demand Lyssandra's head. I was glad to not see them again, but I didn't like being cast aside on the vague chance that someone might come through the secret passageway. I knew it was only because I was too weak to do much good elsewhere.

We neared the small wall circling the gravestones. "If something happens, I want you to leave me here. Your strength and speed could make all the difference."

Geist smiled down at me as he helped me sit against the wall. "You give me too much credit." To my surprise, he sat beside me, looking up at the dark night sky. The moon was entirely gone now, making the stars seem all the brighter. I had always disliked the fresh turned-earth scent of vampires, but with him near, for the first time I found it enjoyable.

"You're ancient. You may not be able to best Eiric, but you could best any of his minions."

He sighed, leaning his shoulder a little closer to mine, almost touching. "Except perhaps Cerridwen. If she still has that ring, I would not like to face her."

I looked at him, but he was still looking up at the stars, his expression peaceful. "What do you think it is?" I asked. "The ring, I mean. How was it made?"

"In the same manner as Lyssandra's sword, I imagine." He finally looked at me, his dark eyes keen on my face. "Why the sudden curiosity?"

"A demon spoke into my mind today, just as the sword speaks into Lyssandra's. It has me wondering how the sword speaks at all when it is simply steel. It has no mind."

He lifted a brow. "You were bleeding, near death, and this is what you thought about?"

"I needed something to distract me."

He looked back up toward the sky, but settled in against my shoulder a little more comfortably. I had never considered that a vampire might be comfortable with casual touch when it had nothing to do with ownership or violence, but Geist was. Or so it seemed. "I have thought much on it over the years, ever since Cedrik first showed me the sword. But he himself was unable to create magical objects. He knew others who could enchant, like Drucida, but to create true relics like the sword and the ring?" He shook his head. "I'm afraid the knowledge of such things died with Lavandriel."

"Do you think Lyss could do it?" I asked. "With magic so similar to her ancestor's, could it be possible?"

He shrugged, brushing the fabric of his coat against my shoulder. "Perhaps, but she has little knowledge of such things. I never understood why Cedrik did not teach her, except that perhaps he had little knowledge himself. He and Cael's mother abandoned them, along with their sister, early in their lives, as soon as they all displayed signs of blood magic."

I sat up a little straighter. "Does Lyssandra know?"

"Not unless Cael told her, which I doubt he did."

I shook my head, leaning back once more. My wounds were feeling worlds better, but I was still horribly weak. "So many secrets and lies. They were never fair to her."

He looked at me again. "Her life was always meant to be dangerous. It was simply how she was born. I do think Cedrik and Cael did the best they could with limited resources. And with fear of what might happen to her if her identity was revealed too soon."

I met his waiting gaze, which still felt odd to me. I was so used to looking vampires in the nose. I was also used to killing them. "So you don't know what the sword really is?"

The edges of his lips curled. "No, I do not. Do you think it important?"

"It chose her. It has remained with her. Though Eiric would have taken it away, she had it tonight. I can't help but feel there is something we're missing."

"It's all ancient history—I'm sure we're missing *much*." He had leaned a little closer, lowering his eyes to the buttons of my fresh shirt. "How are your wounds?"

My heart skipped a beat at his lingering gaze. "Mostly healed, I think. Thank you."

His lips curled a little further as he met my eyes again. "It was my pleasure."

My pulse quickened, and my mouth was suddenly dry. "You know, you're rather strange for an ancient."

"And how many ancients have you known?"

I thought about it. I had fought ancients the night Karpov died, but I hadn't really *known* them. I had mostly just studied the more notorious vampires in books. "Not many."

He chuckled, the sound seeming to snake its way around us. A slight mist had formed on the ground, the only movement in the absolute stillness of the graveyard and its surroundings. "Living so long can do odd things to anyone. Many go quite mad. Others, like Asher, actually learn from their experiences and hope for better."

I moistened my dry lips. "And you?"

He leaned close again. "Perhaps a bit of both, if I'm being honest. But unlike the others, I also enjoy a sense of whimsy."

My brows lifted. "Whimsy?"

"Yes. Whimsy, romance, indulging in fleeting fancies?"

"I stand by my former statement," I laughed. "You are strange for a vampire."

"And you are interesting and intelligent, for a hunter. I regret that we have met under such strained circumstances."

I wasn't sure what to say to that. That I regretted it too? I did, but I also did not, for under any other circumstances, I would not have had the chance to get to know him. I wasn't sure how Lyssandra tolerated romancing a being with so many years of experience and knowledge. Geist made me feel like an absolute novice.

He was still watching me, his expression unreadable.

"What are you thinking?" I asked.

"I'm thinking, that what better time for fleeting fancies, than the night we all may perish?" He leaned closer, pressing his lips against mine.

I tensed, then relaxed into the kiss. Ye gods, I was kissing a vampire. His hand went to my neck, pulling me closer, and I dared to run my fingers through his long hair. I wasn't sure if it was a bit of vampire magic, or simply the elegant man pulling me even closer, but I melted against him, despite my weakness and pain.

All I knew in that moment as my body filled with heat, was that Lyss had been holding out on me.

CHAPTER TWENTY-SIX

Lyssandra

I was walking in a dream. I had to be. My body felt weightless as I approached the temple, its lanterns at war with the dark of night. I wondered if this was how vampires felt, moving so effortlessly.

The thought of vampires made my mind waver. I had a purpose. There was a purpose to this.

A hand on my shoulder grounded me, made me more aware of my surroundings. Markus stood closer than he normally would, as if frightened I might simply slip away.

Hunters, my sword said into my mind, and I realized there was another reason Markus had grabbed me. Hunters stood outside the temple gates, conversing with the guards. They would be demanding an audience, asking for my head.

I almost had to laugh. If only they knew I was standing right behind them. I would show them. Let them try to enact their misled plan of justice.

Markus' fingers dug into my shoulder. "Not yet."

We were still out of sight, hiding in the shadows. Darkness had fallen, and still Eiric had not come. And so, I would find him. I would call the blood from his veins like I had the demons'. I would bleed him dry, until he was no more.

I waited, but only because my sword wanted me to wait too. It was not yet the time to act. I could not waste a drop of my stolen magic.

The shouting continued until finally, a priestess exited the temple and approached the gates. Would she invite the hunters inside? Was that what Eiric wanted?

I watched her speaking with the man in the lead. I recognized him, but my memories of him seemed somehow distant, like they had occurred a decade in the past rather than months. I narrowed my eyes, wishing I could hear what was being said.

Finally, the priestess stepped aside, and the hunters walked through the gates, past the confused guards. She must have granted the men a formal invitation. They were all marching to their deaths. I didn't know what Eiric wanted with them, but death was inevitable.

"What should we do?" Markus whispered, still gripping my shoulder.

"I don't sense Eiric. I'm not sure if he's in the temple."

"Could you sense him that far if he was?"

I shook my head, not in answer, but because he would want an explanation, and there was none. My instincts told me I would feel Eiric if he was near, just as I would feel Cael. The demon magic had amplified the power in my blood, and as a result, had amplified my connection to those who shared it.

"This feels like a trap."

Of course it was a trap. Eiric wanted me, the hunters, and the witches all inside the temple, but the witches had not come. Ian had reached them in time to issue his warning. They could not rescue Ophelia, at least not yet.

My skin prickled at a sudden new sensation. "Something is happening." I clenched my fists, unnerved by the new wave of power. "Cerridwen." It had to be. The magic felt like *death*. It also felt like a challenge. "It's time." I tore away from Markus, then marched toward the gates.

"Lyssandra," he hissed behind me.

The guards moved to block my way as I neared. With a wave of my hand, they were on the ground, teeth chattering as their cold blood moved too slowly through their veins. They were fools to bar my way.

After all, I already had an invitation.

I stepped through the open gates, only realizing after I was through that the invitation might not have worked since Gwenvere was dead. But apparently invitations could reach beyond the grave.

"Lyssandra!" Markus called again.

I turned to see him just outside the gates, struggling to get in. That was right. He'd never been inside.

"You'll have to go through the other entrance!"

I turned away without seeing his reaction, though I could feel his panic. He was too overwhelmed to shield it from me. And it was a dull thing compared to the death magic pounding in tune with my heart.

I flung open the temple door, dropping another pair of

guards when they tried to stop me. The rest of my journey was a blur, winding my way through long halls until finally, I neared the source of the magic. It came from a place I'd never been, a central courtyard open to the night sky. The doors were already open. Open for me, I realized.

I stepped outside, searching for the source of the magic. My sword was quiet and calm. Whatever came next, we were ready.

The first thing I noticed were the bodies. Not corpses, but living, *bleeding* bodies. The hunters were strewn across the courtyard, most in the dirt, but some draped from decorative benches like grotesque adornments. A few were already dead, and the rest were so gravely injured that they would be soon. I spotted a few blue robes amongst them. Replacements for the witches who did not arrive.

It had to be Eiric. He was here somewhere. No one else could have slaughtered them so quickly. I knew I should be feeling something, *anything*, about their pending deaths, but all I felt was power. Their blood called to me, even though I was brimming with demon magic. No matter what I gathered, it would never be enough.

At the center of the courtyard stood Cerridwen, surrounded by ghouls, and beside her, on his knees, was Asher. My heart pounded steadily, a mixture of demon and death magic keeping my emotions just below the surface. Cerridwen wore black now instead of pale blue. Once again, the time for blending in was over.

Asher looked at me, his expression urging me to run.

But I could not run. A ring glittered on Cerridwen's hand. *My ring.*

Wasn't it mine? I realized the thought had come from my sword.

"So kind of you to join us!" Cerridwen called out.

"Hello, Lyssandra," a low voice purred into my ear.

I lunged forward, leaping down a few stone steps onto the bare earth of the courtyard. I spun to see Eiric standing atop the steps, his billowing white shirt catching an unearthly breeze. For there was no true breeze in the courtyard. The wind was from Cerridwen's death magic. She had used it to hide Eiric from my senses. He held two grimoires beneath one arm.

He swept his other arm out toward the dead and dying. "Do you like your gift?" He smiled. "It's all for you, Lyssandra."

I shivered. I could feel their blood leaking into the earth. It would take only a thought for me to draw power from it. There were a few true witches amongst the priestesses, their magic calling to me more than the rest. And the hunters . . . it was a different kind of power, but power none-the-less.

I swallowed the lump in my throat and set my sights on Eiric. "How did you find the second grimoire?"

He tilted his head, still smiling. "You forget, I can control most any human. Once I realized your lover was in the city, I had everyone searching day and night." He took a step down the stairs.

I moved back, but it put me closer to the bodies. My stomach churned as their magic called to me. It wasn't right. Whatever was inside of me . . . it was evil. I tried to move away, and nearly tripped over a bleeding hunter in an attempt to keep both Eiric and Cerridwen in my sights. I didn't see Xavier anywhere, but with Eiric and Cerridwen here, I knew he'd be nearby.

Eiric stalked toward me, still smiling. "And here I thought you'd need magical blood to fuel the ritual." He gestured to the bodies, then to the grimoires beneath his other arm. "I supplied you with everything you would need, but now you've gone and procured something *better.*"

In the blink of an eye he was before me, and somehow, my sword was already out. I slashed at him, narrowly missing his throat as he darted aside.

He chuckled, giving me my space. His eyes sparkled by the light of the stars. "Perform my ritual, Lyssandra, and you and your lover may both leave here in peace. I have no need of your deaths." He splayed his free hand, his white sleeve fluttering around his fingers, showing how *harmless* he was.

I didn't glance at Asher. It would have done us no good. I had asked him to stay away, hoping Eiric could not find him, but he found him anyway. Maybe he had been able to all along. But no—that's why he had wanted me to escape. He could control humans to search for the grimoire, but they would not have the skills necessary to trap an ancient vampire. He must have come too close to the temple, and that's how Cerridwen found him.

One of the hunters groaned, then his final breath shuddered out of him. Everyone Eiric had injured had lost too much blood. Even if I wasn't going to steal their innate power, they were still going to die one by one. And for what? I already had the power I needed.

My throat went tight as I fought the urge to scream. I knew if I started screaming, I wouldn't stop. Instead I shook my head as I looked calmly at Eiric. "You're lying. If I perform your ritual, you'll kill us both."

I blinked, and suddenly he was closer. "I *will* walk in the light, Lyssandra. It is my only weakness, and once you have remedied it, you will no longer pose a threat to me."

Another lie. I was one of the only true threats to him. He would never let me live.

Reading my expression, he gestured toward Cerridwen, and I felt a wave of power.

This time I had to look as Asher grunted, but he refused to cry out. He was still on his knees, but hunched forward, blood pouring from his eyes and nose.

My magic flared within me at the sight of him. I had no control as my free hand extended, and I called heat to my blood.

Cerridwen gasped, her suddenly hot breath fogging around her. "What—" She staggered forward, clutching her throat. She'd slid the ring onto one of her fingers.

I boiled her blood, intent on eliminating the threat she posed.

"No!" Eiric hissed.

I darted out of the way as he rushed me. He spun toward me, following my movements with his eyes. "What exactly have you done, Lyssandra?"

So he didn't know. He hadn't kept an eye on me after all. He had thought me too weak and ineffectual to ever pose a threat. He had lured his victims to the temple to give me power I would never acquire on my own.

Now, he could feel the magic in my blood. He probably thought I'd stolen it from witches or vampires, like he'd intended. He never would have expected *demons*.

My lip lifted in a snarl as I turned my magic on him. I had tried heat before, but this time I tried cold. Anything to slow his too fast movements.

Ice crackled across his skin as he took a slow, painful step toward me. Rage contorted his features, now glistening with frost. I poured my magic into his blood, freezing it in place, and yet, he continued to move toward me.

"How . . . did—"

"Demon magic," I said. "You should have cared when they started bursting out of those poor girls."

His eyes widened, then stayed that way. I realized they were frozen in place. He had stopped moving.

And yet, he was still alive. I could still *feel* him.

I lifted my sword, ready to shatter him to bits, but movement caught my eye. One of the hunters was climbing to his feet, but his eyes . . . his eyes were glazed with death. As if pulled by strings, more of the men around us shambled to their feet. Only those still living remained groaning and bleeding on the ground.

I desperately swung my sword at Eiric, but one of the dead men flung himself in front of my blade. It cut into his flesh, nearly slicing him in half, but with little blood. Most of his blood was already soaking into the earth. Cerridwen's ghouls howled and the courtyard became a moving mass of bodies and monsters, blocking my path to Eiric.

I hacked through them, intent on ending him while I still could. I had used much of my borrowed magic in freezing him, enough that my thoughts and emotions were returning. If I didn't reach him, I was going to die. *Asher* was going to die.

I hacked my way to where Eiric was supposed to be, but he was gone now. One of the ghouls got close enough to sink its broken teeth into my shoulder.

I pulled away, ripping my flesh and nearly dropping my sword.

"Enough!" Cerridwen shouted. Everything went still. "Enough," she said again, closer this time. "Fetch her."

I wasn't sure who she was speaking to until Xavier shoved his way past one of the corpses. He was unharmed, but how? What I'd done to Eiric should have frozen him too, or at least caused him pain.

He shrugged apologetically as he came to stand before me.

"You're not Eiric's human servant, are you?"

He smiled sadly. "I used to be, until he grew weak in his tomb. Weak enough for the bond to be severed."

"But not severed like mine with Asher." He *was* a servant in some way. He was acting against his will.

"I'm surprised it took you this long to figure out." Cerridwen came into view, dragging Asher by the collar of his shirt as if he weren't twice her height. She had a ghoul on either side of her, ready to shield her should she once more become my target. The corpses loomed around us, awaiting orders.

Asher's face was so bloody, I could hardly see his skin, and still he stared at me. I didn't need words to know what he was thinking. He wanted me to run. To save myself. My sword shivered in my hand as a small sliver of my bond with him reignited within me. A tiny thread that I hadn't known was there. Asher's eyes widened at the sensation, but he didn't move. He gave nothing away.

"You made Xavier your servant instead," I said to Cerridwen. "He hasn't been following Eiric's will. He has been following *yours.*"

She sighed. "Well, Eiric does still speak into his mind. He is too selfish to let him go entirely."

Xavier was still looking at me apologetically. He had to obey her will—I had seen him struggling with it—but he was also able to shield from her. It must be the case, since he had visited me one morning without her knowing. She didn't have him entirely.

"Why do you want me to perform Eiric's ritual?" I asked. "Why would you want to make him even stronger?" She was still too close to Asher. Once she released him, I would use whatever magic I had left to end her.

"He does not want to simply be stronger," she explained. "Once you allow him to walk in the sun, he will have you perform a second ritual. He will have you turn night to day to kill the rest of the ancients. He knows they work against him, and will kill him if they can."

My mind raced. The ritual for light, the same one my grandfather wanted me to perform—Eiric wanted it too. Of course he did. He would destroy every single threat to him. He would never be sealed away again.

Cerridwen watched my shifting expression. "I see you

understand now."

"Why are you telling me all of this? I thought perhaps you were secretly working against Eiric. Why would you want me to make him invincible?"

She smiled coyly. "I don't. I only want you to perform the second ritual. Why do you think I gave you Lavandriel's grimoire? I had hoped you would understand what we needed to do. I thought you might join me willingly." She looked down at Asher. "But now I see that your love for this one will interfere."

"Eiric will kill you for betraying him," I blurted before she could act impulsively.

Cerridwen laughed, making me grit my teeth. "I am a necromancer, Lyssandra, and of the old blood. You have no idea the power I exert over the undead. Eiric may have had his own plans, and I have played along with them, but in the end, he answers to *me*. He has been a valuable tool. Something for you to fear. Something to motivate you to ally yourself with me, if only to destroy him. I needed you desperate—willing to do almost anything." She lifted a brow at me. "But I understand what sort of woman you are now. I know what must be done to put an end to the bloodshed."

It dawned on me then that I was right. She had both of Eiric's desired rituals all along, but she kept them hidden. She didn't want him to walk in the daylight, she only wanted me to kill him with it.

"You want to destroy Eiric?" I asked. "I thought you loved him."

Something dark and unnatural rippled in her eyes, like a serpent moving through water. I realized it was her power flaring. Just like mine, strong emotion had an effect. "I do, but he is a monster. I tried for so long to save him. I searched for a cure, but he simply couldn't rest. He inspired his creations, the vampires, to continue killing, searching for a way to free him. It took me many years to accept that he cannot truly love me. And now, I must set things right. I must undo everything Eiric has done."

I flexed my hand around my sword. "You want the same thing as my grandfather. You want me to destroy all vampires. And you have had the grimoire with the complete ritual all along. You only needed to convince me to perform it. But you know I will not."

"Not as long as Asher is still alive." She looked down at him and smiled.

My remaining magic flared. I would kill her before she could harm him.

"You would see me dead?"

The pained words drew Cerridwen's attention. I looked through the crowd of corpses to see Eiric, his clothes damp with melted frost and his skin tinged blue with cold. He staggered toward Cerridwen, not yet recovered enough to move in the blink of an eye. "You told me I would have what I lost."

She dropped Asher to face him. "What? Your humanity? That died a *long* time before you did. You do not *deserve* to walk in the light."

"You lied to me?" His voice cracked. If he weren't purely evil, I might have felt bad for him.

"You know what you are." Despite her bold words, her voice wavered. "You know how this must end."

He inhaled sharply. "Then why bring me back at all?

Why promise me my ritual, if only I were to retrieve the grimoires?"

"Because I needed your help. The grimoires were a necessary distraction—something to keep you patient while Lyssandra learned the mental skills needed for the ritual. All while the very threat of your existence motivated her to learn. She would not have done so otherwise. She knew she must not fear her magic if she hoped to beat you, and now look at her." She gestured toward me. "She is ready. She has the strength to do what is needed."

He lunged at her, and Xavier was suddenly there, shoving a dagger into his gut. Eiric barely seemed to notice. He lifted an arm to swat the other man away, but Cerridwen turned the ring on him. Eiric's arms lowered, then he fell to his knees.

He looked up at her with wide eyes. "Why, my love?" he choked. "Why?"

She stared down at him. "I tried. I tried for decades to save you, but you simply could not rest. You continued speaking into the minds of the young ones, intent only on saving yourself. I promised Lavandriel I would see our mission through. I promised her I would turn night to day, and rid the world of the plague I unknowingly created. I *must* atone for what I have done."

Tears leaked down his face, clear at first, then dark with blood as she drained his life-force away. But he stayed on his knees. He was ancient, after all, and the very first vampire. He would not die so easily.

"But I loved you," he rasped, splattering blood across his lips.

Cerridwen moved to stand over him. "Perhaps once.

But your sister loved me more." A sword appeared out of nowhere, and she lopped off his head.

I stood stunned, my own sword forgotten in my hand.

Cerridwen dropped the sword and stared down at Eiric's body as it fell over, then she turned her attention back to me. She held her eyes open wide, fighting tears, but when she spoke, her voice did not waver. "I had not expected you to steal demon magic, Lyssandra. I am impressed. There is more of Lavandriel within you than I realized. It will make things easier." She took a step toward me. "You and I are the same. We must sacrifice those we love most to set things right." Another slow step. "I know what you have seen. The death. The brutality. You know exactly what these creatures are capable of— why they must all be destroyed."

I had to moisten my mouth twice before I could speak. Eiric was dead. Well and truly dead. And *Cerridwen* had killed him. Now she expected me to do the same to Asher. "How many have died to give you what you want?" I gestured to the walking corpses, and the others now dead at our feet. I hadn't even noticed as they breathed their last breaths. They had died for nothing. Acknowledged by no one. I tightened my grip on my sword. "*You* are a greater monster than any vampire. I would do everyone a much better service in getting rid of *you*."

Xavier had stepped closer to Asher without me realizing. I pointed my sword in his direction, though I knew the warning would fall flat. The ghouls and undead would bar my way if I tried to reach Asher.

Cerridwen edged closer to Xavier as he picked up Eiric's fallen grimoires. She was being cautious, wary of my magic. Little did she know I had spent almost all that I had. "You are right, Lyssandra. I am a monster. And I will gladly let you kill me once my task is complete. You *will* perform the ritual." She crouched down and grabbed Asher, who'd been trying to crawl away from her and Xavier. "Come to the center of the courtyard with me, or your lover will die here and now."

My heart pounded in my chest. Eiric was dead. It had been her plan all along. Everything to prepare me for her ritual—the same ritual my grandfather had wanted me to cast. She had never needed me to defeat Eiric. She could have done it all along. "If I turn night into day, Asher will die regardless. You cannot use him to force me to do it."

She smiled. "Oh, we're not doing that just yet. We need to go somewhere else first. He can die here, now, and I will take you against your will. Or you can save him, and hope he that can escape me." She looked me up and down. "I don't believe you have much stolen magic left now. Would you care to test it upon a hoard of the undead?"

I looked at the walking corpses, and at the drooling, panting ghouls. I could kill many, but would it be enough? I glanced toward the center of the courtyard, wondering what would happen if I went, and that was when I noticed it—a swirling stain of darkness standing as tall as I was.

"It's a portal," she said like it should make perfect sense. "Another gift of the old blood. Now, shall we go?"

Xavier had moved closer to me. I'd been too distracted by the portal to notice him. If he managed to disarm me, it would all be over. Cerridwen was right, I'd given too much magic in my initial attacks.

"Why kill the hunters?" I asked, stalling. "And why lure

the witches here? Do I not need to absorb their magic?"

She lifted her free hand toward the portal and it grew larger. "That was Eiric's plan. I knew it would bring you here, placing you in the predicament you now face, so I let things play out, as I have always done."

The ghouls watched the portal warily, while the living dead hardly seemed to notice it. All I knew was that I could not go through it. But Asher . . . he was no longer moving. His head hung limply. It would take little from Cerridwen to kill him right before my eyes. Then she would overwhelm me with ghouls and take me through the portal anyway. She had planned everything perfectly. I would go willingly if it meant maintaining a slim chance that I could escape the ritual and save Asher.

When the portal was to her liking, Cerridwen lowered her hand. "*Come*, Lyssandra." She dropped Asher, then extended the ring above him.

I took a step in her direction. Whatever was to happen, I could not let her kill him now. If I could get her alone, she wouldn't be able to stop me from ripping out her throat. I took another slow step, then re-coiled reflexively at a familiar sound.

A crossbow bolt shot past me and wedged into Cerridwen's shoulder. She cursed, turning her attention beyond me to one of the high windows lining the courtyard. "Around me, now!"

At first I thought she was talking to me and Xavier, but then the remaining corpses and ghouls shuffled to hide her from sight. More bolts fired, staggering the corpses, but many still protected her.

I lifted my sword again, ready to hack my way through

while she was distracted, but a new portal flashed in the middle of the corpses as more bolts struck them from above.

"You will come to me, Lyssandra!" her voice called out right where the portal flared. "If you ever want to see your beloved uncle, or the hazel-eyed hunter again."

I started hacking through the corpses, desperate to reach her before she could disappear, but then the portal flared and winked out. The surrounding corpses fell in a heap.

I gasped. Xavier, Cerridwen, and the ghouls were gone.

Tears leaked down my face as I noticed Asher, curled up on his side, his eyes closed. At first I thought Cerridwen had killed him, but when I reached him, his hand gripped mine. He managed to turn his head enough to stare up at me.

My heart hammered at my throat. Nothing had gone to plan. And now Cerridwen had Cael, and Steifan? He was the only hazel-eyed hunter I might care about, but when had she taken him? It didn't make sense. I needed Asher well enough to tell me what had happened.

I pushed up my sleeve, then used my sword to slice my arm. I offered him my blood, and as he took it, Geist, Tholdri, Markus, and Isolde all hurried into the courtyard.

I put down my sword to stroke my free hand through Asher's hair as he fed. Our fight was not yet through. I could not leave Steifan, or even Cael, to their fates. But too much of the demon magic had left me. We would need another plan.

CHAPTER TWENTY-SEVEN

We burned Eiric's body, along with the other corpses. So many deaths without reason, just to give me the power Eiric and Cerridwen had both wanted to use. I was yet to tell the others of Cerridwen's actual plan. As it stood, only Markus and I knew about the ritual to turn night to day. And Asher, if he had heard our words, but he had made no mention of it.

I hoped he had not been conscious to hear them. If he didn't know now, it would remain that way. I would never do it. As much as I had hated vampires most of my life, I could not in good conscience murder them all at once. Even if Asher could somehow survive, how many others were like him? Or even like Geist. They were monsters, yes, but so were all the rest of us. At one time I had thought it was for me to choose where that line was drawn, but no longer. If I survived, justice could be someone else's problem.

My blade did not awaken to protest my thoughts. I

held it naked in my hand since it would need to be cleaned before I returned it to its ill-fitted sheath. Perhaps Xavier had left the proper one somewhere in the temple for me to find.

I sensed Asher approaching my back as the others continued piling the corpses. We were tired, but had good reason for burning them now that I had witnessed Cerridwen's control.

Asher's long fingers wrapped around my shoulders, then he leaned in near my cheek. "I'm sorry I was not strong enough." His voice was low, for my ears alone.

"It's not your fault."

And it wasn't. He'd stayed away as I'd asked. Cerridwen and a flock of Eiric's vampires had found him. The vampires abducted Steifan as a distraction, giving Cerridwen the opportunity to use the ring. They were already gone when Markus ran past toward the grave-yard, where he found Geist and Tholdri. He'd explained everything to them while they took the secret entrance into the temple.

And it was not so secret now. When more girls died, some acolytes attempted escape. Isolde had followed them, running into Marcus and the others on her way out. We learned from the remaining women and guards that Eiric had requested several come to the courtyard, and that they were not to be disturbed. Those poor women had walked right into a trap, along with the hunters.

None had survived. The magic Eiric wanted me to steal was gone, and so was the demon magic. I had nothing left to fight Cerridwen with when I went to rescue Steifan. I didn't even know *where* to go to rescue him, but I was sure Cerridwen would deliver the message when she was ready.

It was all as she planned. She knew I would steal magic one way or another, and that I would use it to weaken Eiric. I had made it possible for her to kill him with no risk to her own hide.

Just as she had planned.

I could have let it go if she only wanted Eiric dead, but I now knew she would stop at nothing to right her original wrong. She would see all vampires destroyed.

Asher went still behind me as Geist approached, his figure rimmed with smoke and yellow flame. The stench was unbearable, but I felt obligated to see it through. At least the remaining priestesses were in no hurry to kick us out.

Geist looked down at me, then bowed his head. "We failed you. I'm sorry."

"Eiric is dead. And thanks to the rest of you, Asher is not."

Asher's fingers flexed around my shoulders, but he did not speak.

Geist lifted his eyes to my face. "What will you do now?"

I felt so weak, I could hardly stand. I was glad the magic was no longer dulling my thoughts, but with that came grief. "We will find Steifan. I will not lose him."

"And Cael?" he pressed.

They had not heard Cerridwen's final words, but everyone had been caught up, to a degree. "If he can be saved, I will do it. But Cerridwen wants him for a reason. Unlike Steifan, Cael is not merely bait."

Geist nodded, then glanced back as Tholdri approached.

I was grateful they were all with me again, but I needed rest. And space. Space to align my thoughts and consider what we would do next. I did not have the capacity to answer any more questions.

Asher stepped close enough that my back pressed against his chest. I wasn't worried about him getting blood on me. We both had plenty of it to go around. Even with all that had happened, his presence relaxed me. We might only have a fraction of our bond left—something else to be explored when there was time—but he knew me well.

Geist also seemed to know what I needed. He gave me a small smile. "The two of you should retire. The rest of us can finish up here."

It was exactly what I wanted, but I hesitated. With Gwenvere dead, and most if not all with demons inside them following her to the grave, we should be safe enough within the temple. But the remaining priestesses and guards were scared. There was no telling when they might turn against us. Fear had made many of them take in demons, after all. Their decisions could not be trusted.

"We will be fine," he assured.

I slumped against Asher's chest. I'd have to take Geist's word for it.

Asher smoothed his hands down my arms, then laced his fingers with mine on one side, prepared to lead me away. It would have been a more soothing gesture if his hands weren't coated with drying blood—if my other hand wasn't gripping my sword's hilt so tightly it hurt, just to keep my body from trembling. It was difficult for me to even look at Asher's face, to consider just how close I'd come to losing him *again*.

But Eiric was dead. *Light*, I could hardly believe it. The time for separation and strategy was over. When we faced Cerridwen ...

There would be time to consider that later.

I nodded to those who remained, then let Asher lead me away.

Markus scrutinized me as we passed, but he seemed calmer now that the magic had left me. Though I was sure I would get an earful from him about it tomorrow, once the vampires were resting.

I took the lead once Asher and I were inside. It felt odd returning to the chamber where I'd been held prisoner, but it also seemed the most sensible location to rest. I knew the room and surrounding area well. I did, however, have Asher break the lock from the outside wall before we entered.

Once we were alone, I left the room dark, having had enough of fire for the evening. Even though the hunters had been here to kill me, I still regretted their deaths, and it had been difficult burning their bodies. With the demon magic out of my system, I had recognized many of them. Some had been good men, if a little misled.

I cleaned my sword first, then leaned it against a nearby chair, turning my back on Asher as I started removing my filthy, torn clothing. A bath would have been nice, but it could wait until morning. I winced as I removed my shirt, forgetting that one of the ghouls had bitten me.

I let my breath out in a huff. I was no longer a human servant. The wound needed to be cleansed before infection set in. The wound I'd used to feed Asher had been cleaner, but it should still be tended. I had used too much of my magic beforehand for either injury to be healed, and I would not take Asher's blood with him so weak.

Maybe there was time for a bath after all.

At least it was late, and most everyone with the option of being locked in a room had done so. The communal bathing chamber should be empty.

I turned toward Asher and forced a smile. He was alive, and Eiric was dead. I had not thought it possible, and without Cerridwen, it wouldn't have happened.

I wasn't sure how to feel about that, so I asked the only thing my tired mind could come up with.

"How about a bath?"

He stepped toward me, wrapping me in his arms.

I relaxed against him, realizing I didn't have to say all the other things I thought needed to be said. He already knew. For tonight, a bath and rest would be enough.

I STEPPED into the steaming water with a hiss, leaving my sword next to the edge in case I needed it. It had stayed silent since leaving the scene of the battle. I couldn't help wondering how it felt about the demon magic being gone. With all that had happened, I was starting to question its intentions.

The hot water relaxed my muscles bit by bit. One of the nicer aspects of the temple was the massive, constantly burning furnace. It heated the lower levels with pipes of forced water, which also filled the two large communal baths.

Not wanting to draw any extra attention, we had opted for darkness. Asher would see or hear anyone approaching long before they could notice us . . . unless it was Geist, but I doubted he would choose to disturb us. Like my sword, I was still unsure of what to think of him. He had come all this way to rescue me, claiming friendship with my grandfather. If it was the truth, then surely he had not known my grandfather's true plan, to eliminate all vampires. I almost felt guilty on his behalf.

Asher stepped into the water behind me, barely rippling it with his movements.

Finally alone again after so long, I felt oddly unsure of myself. I turned—to say *what*, I wasn't sure—but the words died on my tongue. Water streamed from his bare chest, the rivulets turned pink with the blood flaking from his skin. He had wet his hair without me noticing, turning it dark silver instead of white. With only a hint of the bond remaining, and so much left to be said between us, I was still drawn to him like no other.

My body throbbed with sudden need. I had once been used to being alone. I had *liked* it that way. A part of me still felt that way, but my skin begged to differ. It ached for him.

He smoothly closed the space between us, then lifted his fingertips to my cheek. I gasped as my magic flared. It was already rebuilding, spooling in my core like a ball of yarn.

"It's different now," he said. "Stronger."

"You have no idea." My throat felt raw. This was the first time we had been together with no bond and no bracelet, which I had left with my clothing.

His eyes searched my face, and I realized he was wondering if the madness was already setting in. It must have been unsettling to witness me consumed by demon magic. It had been unsettling on my end too.

He moved closer, pulling me against him, our skin slick with moisture and heat.

My magic tried to spark between us again, but then his energy washed over me, soothing me.

I relaxed against him. "The bond really is still there, at least a sliver of it. But how?" It should have been entirely destroyed. I was no longer a servant. But then I remembered what Ian had said, about bonds formed of closeness.

His hands ran down my back, then he started untangling what was left of my braid. "I felt strange when I woke tonight. I believe I was sensing the demon magic inside you."

I stiffened against him. A bond of closeness was one thing, but he wasn't even near me then. "But how?"

"I don't know. Until it happened, I did not know that a master and servant bond could be broken at all, other than by death." Finished with my hair, his hands smoothed up and down my arms, eliciting goosebumps as my magic flared, then calmed. Flared, then calmed again.

"How are you doing that?" I asked.

He moved my hair to kiss the side of my neck. "Doing what?"

"Each time my magic tries to flare, you calm it."

"It is not intentional."

While our lack of knowledge was unnerving, it was a relief to feel more like myself again, more myself than I had been in a long time. "Tomorrow I will go to Ian and the witches. I will see if any understand how Cerridwen created that . . . portal." I'd seen mentions of portals in texts during my lessons with Drucida, but according to her, they were a long-lost art.

He spoke with his mouth still near my skin, his kisses trailing lower. "I believe Cerridwen spoke the truth about her intentions. She wants to rid the land of vampires. I fear she is not the villain of this tale."

"You heard everything," I sighed.

He pulled away enough to look down at me. "About you turning night to day? Yes, I heard. Do you think it's possible?"

"My grandfather thought it was. It was his plan for me all along. To destroy all vampires."

He lifted a brow. "Some might say it is a noble cause."

"Some might say it should be no sole person's choice whether countless creatures are to perish in the blink of an eye."

"It does not change the fact that your grandfather was not a villain. Nor is Cerridwen. Not entirely."

Frowning, I moved away enough to run my hands up his chest. "She is if she is willing to torture and kill to get what she wants. To manipulate the man she once loved, all the while planning his death."

He looked down at me, his brow furrowed. "He was a monster. A *true* monster."

"He was," I agreed. "He deserved to die, but . . . I suppose it's just that the reasoning behind it seems wrong. I would have killed him because of the lives he took."

"I believe that was Cerridwen's motive as well."

I shook my head, unable to put a finger on exactly why it bothered me. With Eiric gone, everyone was safe, except for the vampires. And Steifan. But Cerridwen wasn't entirely the issue. The only true danger to the vampires now, was me.

Asher cradled my cheek, looking into my eyes. "You are not one for manipulation. You don't appreciate her tactics. That she could feign such devotion in the name of love."

My frown deepened. "I guess that's part of it. She had me entirely fooled. I knew she was afraid of him, but I also thought she still loved him."

Asher lowered his hand and pulled me close again. "She did. She still loved him very much. At least, she loved who he used to be. But death and violence wear on us all. She wants to end it."

I pressed my cheek against his chest, trying to focus just on the feel of him, and not my tangled thoughts. "Eiric is dead. It should be enough."

He kissed the top of my head, then lowered his hands under the water, down across my hips.

I gasped, and my magic flared, then was calmed. "Strange," I breathed.

"Quite." He lowered his head and our lips met.

The kiss was chaste at first, making my heart well with

emotion. I had pictured so many ways that Eiric might kill Asher. My dreams had been haunted and bloody. Even with Eiric dead, our time together felt fleeting, like he might still slip away, and I would never see him again.

I ran my fingers back through his damp hair, deepening the kiss. As heat flared inside me, my magic built, but this time, it didn't calm. It throbbed and pulsed, making me all too aware of the blood in Asher's veins, of the magic inherent to every vampire.

Asher kissed me deeply, molding our slick bodies together, and my magic pressed against my insides. My skin felt warm and cool at the same time. His hands moved down my hips again, then lower, cupping me against him.

I trailed kisses down his chest, warring with the emotion threatening to choke me. Emotion made the magic worse. I had to learn to control it, but—

"I love you, Lyssandra," Asher whispered in my ear.

I came undone.

Emotions crashed within and around me like waves. I wrapped my arms around his neck, then hopped up, circling him with my legs.

He walked us to the edge of the pool. It was almost unbearable waiting with the feeling of him hard and ready against me. He set me down gently, and I balanced on the edge with my arms still around his neck.

I could feel so much of his power now, responding to mine, like two currents coming to meet in the middle. His, the cool magic of the grave, and mine—something hot and scalding. Something violent.

The sensation was so much I felt myself struggling for

air, but I was too consumed to pull away. I moved my hands to his jaw and pulled his mouth against mine, kissing him fervently enough to draw blood from my lower lip.

Even at the small drop, my magic flared, hungry for more. Asher's hands roamed my body. It was different without the full bond between us. I couldn't sense what he was feeling, but the way he gripped me let me know that I was not the only one experiencing the frantic energy.

I cried out as he pushed against me, slowly entering me. My magic in that moment blinded me to all reason. I didn't care if someone walked in on us. I didn't care if my magic consumed me. I simply wanted *more*.

Asher slid deep enough to fill me entirely, balancing me on the edge of the pool. My skin should have been cooling as the water on the upper half of my body dried, but I felt feverish instead. He moved against me slowly, drawing out every movement, pulling tiny gasps from my lips.

My magic built with each thrust. I could sense the blood in both our veins. When Asher lowered his mouth to my neck in silent question, without thinking I groaned, "*Yes.*"

He bit me, and as my hot blood poured into his mouth, our bodies moving together as one, I filled us both with molten light. I had been so focused on using my magic for harm, I had nearly forgotten how easily it could be used to heal. Even the demon magic had healed me—had healed Markus from even graver wounds.

Asher thrust into me, drinking down my blood, and I

vaguely noticed lights dancing around us. But there were no candles. No fires. The lights were coming from *us*.

We cried out together, and with our release my magic exploded outward. I felt it searching for an outlet other than our bodies, for we already had too much.

We were left panting, still pressed together. Slowly, Asher slid me down into the water, cradling me against him. It was for the best—I wasn't sure I could stand on my own.

I laid my cheek against his shoulder, trying to catch my breath as I reached one hand toward my neck. The bite wound had already healed. The area where the ghoul had torn my flesh was smooth skin once more.

Asher whipped his gaze toward something at the other end of the room. I looked in that direction to see Geist standing there, his eyes glinting in the near darkness. I should have been nervous, but my heart beat steadily. He wasn't being voyeuristic. He had sensed my magic searching for an outlet.

"What have you done?" he asked softly, his voice carrying though he stood beyond the second pool.

"I don't know what you—" I cut myself off as something shambled into the room behind him. Something towering and grotesque, with beady black eyes. Those soulless eyes watched me—watched me like I was its salvation.

CHAPTER TWENTY-EIGHT

Asher quickly lifted me out of the pool, where I struggled into the clean clothing I'd brought down with us. Geist was beside me in a heartbeat, but the demon wasn't attacking. It simply continued watching me with those horrifying black eyes.

With vampires standing on either side of me, I lifted my sword. I had thought there were no demons left, but this one must have been hiding in the temple. Or maybe . . . maybe it had only recently escaped. With only a few narrow windows, the space was dark enough that the creature's body melded into the inky blackness behind it.

Demon Caller, it spoke into my mind. *What would you have of me?*

Command it, my sword said into my mind.

My blade drooped. I should banish the demon, send it away, but my arms felt suddenly weak.

"Lyssandra," Geist said lowly. "What are you doing?"

Asher had dressed back in his bloody clothes, having

no others. He stood near me silently, waiting for me to gauge the situation.

What do you mean, demon caller? I thought.

It took a step toward us. It wasn't shambling and panting like the others. Either it had just escaped, or it had just fed. *You called me here. Bound me here. What would you have of me?*

My heart pounded in my throat. *That's not possible.*

The demon merely stared at me.

Panicked, I spoke out loud, still pointing my sword at the demon. "Go back. I release you."

For a sickening moment, nothing happened. Then, the demon bowed its head and disappeared in a cloud of black smoke.

Geist and Asher both went still as the true dead.

Finally, Geist cleared his throat. "Lyssandra?" He was quiet for a moment, but when I didn't answer, he continued, "Did your magic summon that demon?"

I lowered my sword, unable to make myself answer him as my own answers were finally cascading together in my mind. Things I had read in the grimoire. One of the demons calling my sword a *demon sword*. Lavandriel making a necklace for Cerridwen that would somehow keep the demons away from her . . .

Asher caught me as my knees buckled, but I hardly felt him as the memory took me.

"THE SHADOWS FEAR THE SWORD," Cerridwen was saying. "But they fear you more."

Lavandriel had her back to her. She was hunched over a workbench, creating something small. "I cannot command those which I have not summoned, Cerri. But I'm making something to help you."

Cerridwen's gaze was dark as she watched her friend. I imagined the sword I was seeing out of was leaned against a wall near the doorway. "Something with another demon inside of it?"

"It's the only thing they respond to," Lavandriel sighed, then set down what she was working on. She turned toward her friend. "You know I never wanted to be involved in this type of magic."

Cerridwen's expression softened. "I know. I know I did this to myself. It does seem wrong though that they continue to haunt me with Eiric sealed away."

Lavandriel closed the space between them, gripping Cerridwen's hands. "Once you are protected, I will use the sword to send away as many as I can. The entity within it is much stronger than the shadows, and it *wants* to be here. Hunting other demons is its purpose."

Cerridwen frowned. "Why did you never tell Eiric you could summon creatures from other realms? Why didn't you tell him what the sword really was?"

"I did not tell anyone," Lavandriel lowered her head. "The others already fear our line. What would they think if they knew I could control demon blood too? I would not have my brother using that information against me."

Cerridwen hugged her. "You're right. I will take your secret to the grave. I promise."

I CAME BACK to myself with my legs sprawled across damp stone. Asher cradled me against his chest. I shouldn't have been able to sense his worry, but I felt it then.

"It's alright," I croaked. "I'm back."

I couldn't see where Geist was standing as he spoke. "You've been holding out on us, Lyssandra. What did the sword show you?"

I saw no reason to keep secrets from him. Not anymore. "Did my grandfather know that Lavandriel was a summoner? Did he know my sword has a demon inside of it?"

He came into view as he crouched in front of us. "It has a *what* inside of it?"

We all turned as Markus entered the bathing chamber, a lantern held before him. He scowled at all of us. "I tried not to come. But I found I had no choice."

I stared at him, wondering just how much he had heard. And if he now realized he owed his life to demon magic, since the sword had created our bond.

His expression told me he had heard everything. He was not just a hunter saved by witch magic. He was bound by demons.

And so was I.

CHAPTER TWENTY-NINE

With the night almost through, we relocated the vampires to one of the cellars—one *without* a secret entrance. My chamber had no curtains, and was sunny enough that Asher would have been uncomfortable, though he had proven to me many times that indirect sunlight wouldn't actually hurt him.

We hadn't spoken again about the demon. I wasn't really sure it changed anything, unless I figured out how to use the creatures against Cerridwen. Now *that* was something burning in the back of my mind, but I hadn't realized I was summoning a demon at the time. I wasn't sure if I could replicate it.

And I wasn't sure I wanted to. Just like blood magic, summoning seemed to drive the caster mad, if Matthias was any indication.

Markus walked me away from the cellar. He, Tholdri, Isolde, and I would take turns remaining near, though two ancients were hardly defenseless, even during daytime hours. I doubted Cerridwen would risk returning when she already had Steifan and Cael to lure me out, but I didn't want the remaining priestesses getting any funny ideas.

"You're not well," Markus muttered as we walked toward the dining hall.

"I'm fine."

He slowed, giving me a sidelong glance. "Your magic itches at the back of your skull."

"How could you possibly know that?"

"It itches at mine too."

We reached the dining hall, but didn't go inside. The remaining priestesses had agreed to seek out the witches from the fortress. They would be granted food and shelter in exchange for a possible alliance. As far as anyone would say, all the women with demons inside them were gone. They had either been amongst those who'd attacked the fortress, or they had perished when their demons escaped. Those who remained were afraid now that without power, their control of the city would be overturned. And maybe it should be, though I could not entirely fault them for their motives. The hunters may have come for my head, but they would have been just as glad with any of the witches'.

"I'm fine," I said again. "I used a lot of power last night. It will take time for it to rebuild."

"It's getting worse. You cannot hide it from me."

"And what would you like me to do about it?" I hissed.

His jaw clenched. He glared at me for a moment, then shook his head. "Nothing." He proceeded into the dining hall.

Regretting my tone, I followed.

It was the least lively I'd ever seen the place, even after the girls started dying. The few diners present hung their heads, barely touching the food on their plates. A few looked at us. They knew who we were now, that we were hunters, or at least that we used to be. But they also knew we were not the ones who slew their sisters, and that we had played a part in Eiric's demise. They needed protection, and for now, we were it.

"Sit down," Markus ordered. "I'll fetch us plates."

I was too tired to argue, though his tone made me bristle. I sat at a vacant table, instantly feeling far too alone with my thoughts. Just what was happening to Steifan while I sat here waiting for a meal?

Cerridwen wasn't purely evil, of that I was sure. In fact, she might be considered noble, except that she had let too many die to further her plans. She had been willing to kill hunters and priestesses to draw me back to the temple. Just as she had helped Eiric spy on me at the fortress, knowing he meant for the witches to die.

And Cael . . . Cerridwen hated all vampires. It might already be too late to save him, if such a force could even be *saved*.

Markus returned with our plates. My thoughts made me ill, but I was still ravenous. With no more magic to steal, I needed sustenance. He slid a plate before me, then sat by my side.

I looked down at the white meat in a creamy sauce sprinkled with steamed vegetables, and wondered if Steifan had even been fed since his abduction.

"We'll find him," Markus said, surprising me with his

caring tone. "We'll find him, then we'll send him some-where far away from us. He should never have come to the fortress. I knew there was no convincing Tholdri, but we should have made Steifan stay behind."

I realized he didn't care because I was hurting. He cared because he felt guilty, which was something I could relate to. I felt guilty about everyone around me who'd been pulled into an ancient vendetta all because of the blood in my veins.

I scraped my fork across my plate, but didn't eat. "You're right. Even once Cerridwen is dead, it won't ever be safe to call me a friend."

"Or me, by extension." The bitterness had returned to his tone, but I couldn't quite blame him.

I finally took a bite of my food, wanting to get the meal over with so I could escape him for a time.

"You summoned that demon out of nothing."

I gave him a sharp look, though he'd kept his voice down. "Yes, what of it?"

"Those creatures are not undead. Cerridwen would be powerless against them, especially since she doesn't know of your newfound . . . skill."

"Are you proposing I try to summon another? To drive myself even further toward madness?"

His fork remained untouched near his fingertips. "You will do what must be done, and if it sacrifices us both, then so be it."

I studied him, from his hair needing a trim, to the stubble on his cheeks, to the hollows beneath his eyes. "I'm surprised you're not encouraging me to go through with Cerridwen's ritual. To kill all vampires."

His jaw twitched. "I do not think it the worst idea, now that neither of us are tied to a vampire, but Cerridwen has caused countless deaths. She is a greater monster than those we hunt."

I agreed with him, but I was still surprised that he wasn't even considering the ritual. Not that it was his choice, but he might at least try to convince me. A few years back, I would have thought the ritual an excellent idea.

"And what happens after we kill her?" I asked. "Where do we go from there?"

"Either you will go mad, you will don the bracelet, or you will become Asher's servant once more." He met my waiting gaze. "Have you considered it? Reforming the bond?"

He knew I had, so that wasn't why he was asking. "Do you believe that our best course of action?"

"It's better than you losing your mind and taking me down with you."

"And the bracelet?" I pressed.

He turned away, not answering me.

"Markus?"

"I did not like it when you wore the bracelet. I didn't know why it was at the time, but shortly after you were taken from the fortress, I felt . . . hollow. Like a piece of me was missing." He turned back toward me. "I would not like to feel that way again."

I watched him for a long moment, then nodded. "Then it will not be an option. Either I will be able to withstand my growing magic without losing my mind, or I will become Asher's servant once more."

"You would do that simply because I asked?"

I sighed, slumping my shoulders before spearing a piece of meat with my fork. "I would. I do not like you, and I'm quite sure you don't like me, but we *are* bound together. If we cannot figure out a way to separate us, then I will view this bond as a partnership." *Just like Asher had done with me*, I added silently.

"Well," he said, finally lifting his fork. "There's always the option of Cerridwen killing us. So maybe we won't have to worry about any of it."

Shaking my head, I smiled and started eating, though the smile soon wilted. If a message did not come from Cerridwen today, I would try to use magic to track Steifan. It was probably a lost cause without his blood at my disposal, but I had to try. I forced my meal down because I needed to be strong, and I prayed to whatever deity might listen that Steifan could hold on just a little while longer.

I PARTED ways with Markus as I went to check on Tholdri. None of us had slept yet, and we would need to take shifts. Since I felt oddly energized, I would watch over the vampires so the others could get some sleep.

I found Tholdri leaning against the wall near the cellar, arms crossed. He stood casually, as if aware of nothing, though I knew he'd noticed my approach.

Once I reached him, he finally deigned to look me up and down. "Have you summoned any more demons since we last spoke?"

I scowled, *not* deigning to answer.

He smiled, though it didn't quite reach his eyes. "Sorry, Geist told me what happened. Did you know ancient vampires don't fall fully asleep as soon as the sun rises?" His tone said he was only joking. He knew I was well aware of that fact.

I leaned my shoulders against the wall beside him, pinning my sword. It had gone silent again after granting me the memory of Cerridwen and Lavandriel. Oddly, I didn't think the occurrence was entirely intentional on my sword's part. It had almost seemed like I stepped into the memory myself.

Comfortable silence stretched on until Tholdri asked, "Do you think she'll hurt him?"

"I don't know," I answered honestly. "Hopefully not. If he's not alive when I find her, she won't have him to use against me. She won't be able to force me to perform her ritual."

"And what ritual does she want you to perform? Geist doesn't seem to know."

I gave him a curious look. "And have you and Geist become fast friends?" Light, he was *blushing*. I'd never seen Tholdri blush before. I pushed away from the wall to face him. "What exactly happened while we were apart?"

He finally cracked a grin. "So Markus didn't tell you?"

I gripped his arm. "Tell me what, Tholdri?"

"When he found us outside of the graveyard, we were . . . sharing an embrace."

Despite all that had happened, I couldn't help but match his grin. "Prepare to pay for all the teasing you gave me over Asher."

"I never teased you!"

I crossed my arms. "You most certainly did."

He tried to scowl, but it soon turned into a smile. "Asher attempted to warn Geist away from me on your behalf."

I shook my head. "Of course he did. He would assume I wouldn't want you tied to a vampire."

"Was he right?"

Perhaps he would have been once, but I'd had a rough few months. I patted his shoulder. "Tholdri, I'm just glad you're alive. As long as you're alive, I'm happy." I gave him a sidelong glance. "You do intend to stay alive, right?"

"I have no plans of becoming one of the undead, if that's what you mean."

"And if you fall in love?"

He blinked at me, stunned by my bluntness. "You know, the old Lyss would have never asked such a question."

"The old Lyss has almost died too many times."

He smirked. "I suppose that's true. And in answer to your question, I will face that moral dilemma should such an issue arise. Now, tell me why you are avoiding discussing Cerridwen's ritual. What does she want you to do?"

I patted his shoulder again, then left my hand there as I leaned against him, ignoring his question. "I can stand watch if you want to get some rest."

He leaned into me, and curse it all, it was nice to have him back, solid and real and warm beside me. I loved Asher, but my friendship with Tholdri was irreplaceable.

"No," he sighed, giving in. "I think I'll just stay here

with you for a while." He wrapped his arm around my waist and pulled me close. "I love you, Lyss."

"I love you too, Tholdri. Thank you for coming to rescue me."

"Always."

The silence stretched between us once again, only it felt a little less heavy than before.

CHAPTER THIRTY

Markus and Isolde relieved us a few hours later, freeing me to return to my chamber. I would not rest there—I wanted to be at the temple's ground level should anything happen—but I wanted to take one last look for the grimoire. It hadn't been there when I was with Asher, but maybe it had fallen behind the bed. Even without stolen magic, something within the pages might help me against Cerridwen. It was worth checking.

I entered the chamber, already knowing what I would find. Cerridwen had taken Steifan and Cael somewhere else before I returned to the temple. She had been prepared to leave—preferably with me as her hostage—directly from the courtyard. She wouldn't have left the grimoire, and she had taken the two copies Eiric had acquired.

But then, why had she let me look at it in the first place? In hopes that I would find the ritual to change day to night and take matters into my own hands? Did she really think I would come to her side willingly? I shook my head as I glanced around the empty room.

If it weren't for Asher, maybe I would have. If I didn't care about one particular vampire, maybe I would have been willing to burn them all.

I knelt on the floor, first looking under the bed before doing a quick scan of the other furniture.

Nothing.

With a sigh, I stood, then sat atop the bed. I was ready for sleep, if it would come, but I didn't like resting without any semblance of a plan. Steifan was depending on me. I couldn't just blindly go wherever Cerridwen might lead me.

My magic tickled my throat along with my frustration, each increasing the other. With a growl, I snatched the pillow from the bed and flung it across the room. It hit the armoire with a less than satisfying impact, then fell to the floor with a piece of paper fluttering after it.

Brows lifted, I was across the room in a flash, clutching the parchment in my hands.

I hope this letter finds you well. Really, I hope this letter finds you at all. I can only shut her out for short periods of time, and I couldn't risk devising a better plan for its delivery. I thought perhaps you might find it while searching for the original grimoire—which we have, so do not waste your time.

If you're reading this, it means Cerridwen failed to convince or capture you, and she has now threatened your fellow hunter to lure you in. I warn you, do not come unprepared. She will force you to perform the ritual, and the one you love will perish. When you come, I will have no choice but to fight against you. Please, this time, do not hesitate to kill me. Save those you love, and rid the land of the rest of us.

I may have never known such love, but I know it's worth fighting for.

-X

I lowered the letter to my lap, fighting tears. I did not regret Eiric's death, and I would not regret Cerridwen's. But Xavier . . . I wished I could save him. I wished he could experience the love that surrounded me. I had thought myself unlucky to be born as I was, but at least I had not been submitted to a half-life such as his.

A knock on the door drew my attention. I stuffed Xavier's letter under the bedding as I stood, wary of who might come to find me when I had just seen the other hunters. Not quite paranoid enough to draw my sword, I crept across the room and opened the door, keeping myself back enough in case an attack came.

I was confused at first to see two priestesses in blue

robes, then they stepped aside to reveal Drucida. Her dark curls had been cut short, and her gold-flecked eyes were a bit hollow, but it was her.

I stared at her, stunned. "Ian said you were gravely injured and could not come."

She lifted her chin, the gesture softened by her smile. "I am healed enough. I saw you in a vision, and knew I must come. I left shortly after the others, but only arrived last night." She glanced at the two priestesses. "Thank you for delivering me, but Lyssandra and I must speak in private."

The two women, their eyes a bit wide, each bobbed their head then hurried off.

Recovering from my shock enough to invite her into my chamber, I stepped back. "How did you know to come here? Did Ian find you?"

She stepped past me into the room, looking around. Her traveling cloak was vibrant purple. Not the wisest choice for stealth in the countryside, but Drucida was powerful enough to protect herself from predators and would-be bandits. "I was already at the camp with the other witches when he arrived, warning us to stay away. So of course, we packed up camp and traveled through the night. Unfortunately, some of our horses were weary, and we could not travel quickly enough. The priestesses you sent found us once the city was in view."

I offered her a chair, but she sat on the bed instead, close to where I'd hidden the letter. For some reason, I didn't want her to see it. Not because I didn't trust her, but because I felt that Xavier's words were meant for me alone.

I pulled up a chair to sit across from her. "Ophelia is safe. She's resting now."

Drucida nodded. "The priestesses told me. They also told me Eiric is dead." She lifted a brow, clearly wanting details.

I told her everything that happened the night before, including the part where I had stolen demon magic. I didn't like admitting it, but if she might help me devise a plan against Cerridwen, she needed to know what I was capable of.

Once I was finished, it was her turn to be silenced by absolute shock. She blinked a few times, then licked her lips, considering her words. "Well, Lyssandra, I'm not even sure where to start. At least the vision I had makes sense now. The rational part of me would like to advise you to go forward with the plan to destroy all vampires."

I stiffened at her words. "And what about the rest of you?"

"The rest of me only cares about paying Cerridwen back for all she has done. I will help you kill her, even if it takes demon magic to do it."

"You didn't happen to bring Liliana with you?" I asked hopefully.

Her brows lifted. "The summoner? Do you hope she can summon shadows for you to siphon their magic?"

I winced. "No. The shadows are lesser demons. The things I banished were far more powerful."

"Then you would like to send her shadows after Cerridwen?"

I sighed, slumping down in my seat. "There's still one thing I haven't told you. Something that happened after the battle. *Something* that might be the key to defeating Cerridwen." I didn't want to face it, but if I could use demons to save Steifan, then I might have to.

Drucida watched me intently, waiting for me to continue.

Not quite making eye contact, I told her about the demon I had summoned, and what I now believed about my sword, the ring, and even the necklace Lavandriel had made for Cerridwen.

Her eyes bulged the further I got into my explanation, until finally I finished, and she was left shaking her head. But she now understood why I had brought up Liliana. "You want to ask her if the summoning will make you go mad?"

I nodded.

She sighed. "Liliana and Merri stayed behind with Charles to protect the fortress."

My shoulders slumped. Merri, a necromancer, could have also proven useful.

We both turned at a knock on the door.

I hurried to open it, ready to reach for my sword, though it wasn't warning me. I opened the door to find the same two priestesses as before. Their eyes were even wider now, and their faces ashen.

One held out a sealed envelope. "We were headed down the stairs when a fellow sister found us. Some of the guards went to bar up the cellar entrance the girls were fleeing through, and they found this nailed to the door."

I took the envelope, already knowing who it was from, but not knowing why it had been left in such a place. I looked down at it. "Why is it covered in dirt?"

The priestess swallowed loudly. "Well you see, according to our sister, the guards were drawn to a loud banging sound. It seemed to go on forever until they finally found it." She swallowed again, her eyes going wider.

Drucida moved to stand at my shoulder as one priestess looked to the other, then the one who'd handed me the letter explained, "There was a walking corpse, just pounding away at the door, as if it wanted our attention. According to the guards, it barely had any flesh left to it. They cut it down, then, brave men that they are, they investigated further."

I gripped the letter tight enough to bend the envelope without thinking, remembering the horror of the fresh walking corpses the night before.

The priestess took a shaky breath. "The entire grave-yard has been emptied. The headstones are ruined. It's only so much turned earth now."

I fisted my free hand at my side. "They're all gone? You're sure of it."

The women looked at each other again, then one answered, "We didn't see it, but yes, those who did are sure."

Cerridwen must have taken them, raising them from their graves just as she had raised the freshly fallen. She could have used a portal to bring them wherever she was hiding. I looked at Drucida. "I imagine you didn't come here thinking you'd have to face an army of corpses."

Her skin was just as ashen as the priestesses'. "I suppose it's better than an army of vampires?"

I winced. "She's a necromancer. She probably has those too."

"Light, Lyssandra." Her shoulders slumped. "Knowing you has most certainly been interesting."

That was one way of putting it, though probably not the most *apt* description. "It doesn't change things," I decided. "Either way, I'll go in with the intention of leaving nothing, living or undead, remaining in my wake."

"But go in *where*?" Drucida asked.

I lifted the letter in my hand. "Let's find out, shall we?"

I opened the letter. There was dirt smudged on the envelope, presumably from the fingers of the corpse that had carried it. I let the envelope fall to the floor. My heart beat steadily, counting down the moments until my fate was sealed. Once I knew Cerridwen's demands, I would have to act.

I read the words a second time with Drucida looking over my shoulder. I should have known Cerridwen would be cautious. After all, that's what she'd been doing for centuries—only taking the most calculated of risks.

"Portals?" Drucida asked. "She truly has such power?"

I lowered the letter. "I told you. That is how she left the courtyard."

She stepped around me, frowning. "Yes, but I thought you must have been mistaken, that it was simply a glamour."

I shook my head. "I've broken through her glamours before. I know what they feel like."

She looked out the nearest window. The sun was still high. We had time to plan, but it might do us no good.

Not after reading the letter. "She could take you anywhere."

"That is my fear." I walked up beside her, following her gaze out the window.

Come nightfall, someone would die. *Many* someones, if Cerridwen had her way. The letter had detailed her terms. I would leave the temple, alone, and travel beyond the city gates. She would open a portal for me, but *only* if I was alone, and I alone could walk through it. If I missed the portal, Steifan would die.

I had assumed she would give me a specific location to meet her, where I could come with a plan, and *friends*. But if she would not tell me where Steifan was, I had no choice but to stick to her terms, or try to find him myself. I doubted she'd wait around for me to do the latter.

"What will you do?" Drucida asked, still gazing outside.

"I have to go. I have to kill her myself."

"And if she makes you perform the ritual?"

"I will not do it. I will give my life to save Steifan, but I will not give the lives of others. It is the best I can offer."

She turned toward me. "I had worried the blood magic would have consumed you by now. I felt you last night— felt your power. And my first thought was that you had lost yourself."

Remembering how I felt with the demon magic inside of me, I lowered my gaze to the floor. "I almost did, I think."

Drucida gently gripped my arm. "She won't expect you to summon demons after stepping through her portal. I believe that is how you must defeat her."

I agreed, though it scared me almost as much as losing Steifan.

"If they are not too far," she continued, "Markus can track you. We'll try to come, though we will need fresh horses."

I met her waiting gaze. *Strong.* She was always so strong. "If she took him through a portal, there is no saying where he may be. They could be on an island, or the other side of the continent for that matter."

She gave my arm a reassuring squeeze, then lowered her hand. "I only know of portals in theory, but they take *tremendous* power. Historically speaking, it has only ever been managed with a strong group of casters all focused on the same goal."

I pursed my lips, not following her point.

"I don't think she can summon them as easily as you believe," she explained. "A true portal can go anywhere. What she can more likely create is a small . . . tear. A tear in the fabric of time to jump through. It is probable that she cannot go far, nor travel often."

"The corpses," I realized. "That's why she wants them."

Drucida waited for me to explain.

I tried to think of any other option, but only one thing made sense. She did not need to threaten me with the undead. She had Steifan and Cael. And she had her magic, Xavier, and her ghouls to threaten them with. "If you try to come for me, you will have to fight your way through the undead and whatever young vampires are still under her thrall. She will use them to keep anyone from interfering. She has ordered me to come alone, but she knows my allies will inevitably follow."

Drucida's expression darkened as she lowered her chin. "We will do what we must."

"I know." And so would Asher, Geist, and the other hunters. If they were to face an army to reach me, I needed to act quickly.

But what if I was wrong? What if she had some other trap in store for them? "This is all just in theory. Her portal may take me somewhere too far for any of you to follow."

She bowed her head. "Yes. If I am wrong, then you will be on your own."

I wanted to wilt in upon myself at the thought, but my sword was itching at my back. It was impatient to go into battle. I supposed I wouldn't be going fully alone. I would have my *demon* sword watching my back. The thought gave me chills.

Drucida studied my expression. "What are you thinking, Lyssandra?"

My sword sent another shiver of anticipation down my spine. "I'm thinking I'm going to need a very big favor."

She nodded. She would do what I needed her to do. The sooner I left, the more time I would have to end things before anyone else was in danger.

"One last question," I said.

"Isn't there always?" She smirked.

"What was your vision? What made you come here?"

"I saw you surrounded by shadows, but glowing like the moon. There was someone dead or unconscious at your feet, but I couldn't tell who it was." Her gaze went distant, as if she were seeing the scene once again before her.

"I wish I wouldn't have asked," I muttered.

Her eyes refocused, then landed on me. "That is usually the case with such things." She straightened her slumped shoulders, then lifted her chin. "Let us go. If I'm to delay hunters and vampires, I would rather do so during daylight."

CHAPTER THIRTY-ONE

I departed well before nightfall. I needed to be through the portal before Asher could track me by scent. I hated doing it. I hated betraying his trust, but there was no other way. I could not risk that he might delay me, and Steifan would end up dead. I knew Cerridwen would do it. She would prove her threat, and then she would take someone else to use against me. She had to die before that could happen, and before Asher could face an army of undead just to reach me.

I borrowed Drucida's horse to make the journey. She would prevent the others from following me once she knew I was gone—at least until I could escape through the portal. Having no other clothing, I wore tan pants, a loose white shirt, and a fresh blue cloak from my acolyte wardrobe. Though with only my sword and my magic at my disposal, I felt absolutely naked.

There was a different feel to the city as I rode through, catching whispers here and there. Not about me, but about whatever had happened at the temple the previous night. No one could say for sure, but they'd heard noises, and had seen a great flashing light. And there had been no hiding the smoke from the burning corpses.

I pulled my cloak further up, making sure my hair was covered. Since I would look like an acolyte, I wasn't sure if the guards would give me trouble at the gates, but let them try. My magic was a living, breathing thing—all barriers lifted. I felt confident that I could drop anyone in my way without even a trickle of blood being drawn. I could use their blood against them with no wounds, just as Drucida and the other witches had feared. I had become exactly what they knew I would. It was the reason they hadn't wanted to teach me, and they were right. No one should have such power.

The best I could do was use it to end Cerridwen's long life, even if she had to die at the tip of a demon's claw.

I neared the gates, and the men standing guard. Unexpectedly, one simply shook his head. "Another one." He looked up at the man minding the pulley. "Let 'er out, Auggy!" He looked at me again. "I hope with all ye fleein', we won't have any more murders. I always knew there was somethin' off about that temple."

Having nothing to say to him, I bowed my head, then rode through the open gate. It wasn't like they were wrong about the temple. Gwenvere had caused the deaths that had the city locked up and afraid. And with the demons all out and either banished or weakened enough to wither away—hopefully—the deaths would end.

I rode through the gate, not sparing the guards a second glance. The sun was setting. I had to find the portal before the vampires could awaken. *Or* before

Markus could get past Drucida. Stopping him was the favor I had asked of her. He would be the first to notice my departure, and he would attempt to find me.

I could not blame him. His life depended on my own, but Steifan's life depended on all of us. I would do what Cerridwen had requested, and once I was close enough, I would summon demons to kill her . . . if I could. While my magic was like a bloated thing within me, it was the emotions I had felt for Asher that made me lose control the previous night. I would need to summon such feelings again, if I could.

I rode away from the city, scanning the horizon beyond the homes and expansive farmland. I had missed this view before, riding in the carriage with Xavier. It was lovely—the greens all darker shades than what I was used to in the South. The distant sea had a different feel to it here. *Colder.* I would have loved to explore the terrain under different circumstances.

Now, once I found the portal, I might not see it again. Cerridwen was the final ending, and she would not go down without a fight, if the empty graveyard was any indication.

Following my instincts, I sent my horse into a gallop toward that distant sea. Cerridwen could probably sense me. She would be watching, waiting for me to leave the city and my allies behind.

When a dark portal flashed before me, I rode through.

I DISMOUNTED at the foot of a lone, dark tower. The crumbling black path looking down from a great height hinted that few traveled this way. And how could they? The path behind my horse's hooves dropped off into nothing. Far in the distance, I could see the ocean. But was it anywhere near Ivangard?

Holding my horse's reins, I stepped closer to the edge, my eyes searching for something familiar. But all I could see were hills dotted with more black rock, and the sun disappearing where the ocean met the sky.

I turned my attention to the crumbling tower. If not for the gentle glow of firelight emanating from a few narrow windows, I would have thought it abandoned, especially since my sword had no warnings for me.

Of course, Cerridwen meant me no *physical* harm since my life was no longer tied to a vampire. Emotional harm was another thing entirely, but my sword didn't care about *that*.

I patted my horse's neck, then stepped away. I didn't want to anchor her reins in the event of her being the only survivor. She could eventually make it down the steep cliffside on her own, but not with a rider. She could not help me flee, even if I wanted to.

Movement caught my eye at the tower's entrance. The ancient door—the wood stained nearly black with age—had opened, and two walking corpses were staggering out. The only flesh left to them came in withered scraps, their clothing just shreds of white. They looked like they should crumble at a single touch, yet they both gripped swords, the blades held steady in the air. Though they had no eyes to see me with, they seemed to be looking right at me.

My horse stomped its hooves, uneasy, but not yet willing to descend the dangerous cliffside.

I drew my sword as I approached the skeletons. I had faced far worse monsters in my time. I saw movement in one of the high windows, but didn't dare take my eyes off the skeletons.

"They only wish to take your sword, Lyssandra," Cerridwen called down to me.

I dared a glance upward. She leaned out one of the windows, rimmed by firelight, dark hair streaming in the coastal wind. If only I had brought a bow, I would have tried to kill her then and there.

Dusk was waning, but I could still see her smug smile. "I have you trapped here, Lyssandra. If you like, I can kill Steifan now, and we can fight our way through the rest."

"You need my cooperation," I growled at her, still gripping my sword.

Her smile didn't waver. "Trust me, Lyssandra, I do not. The ritual *will* be performed. You can make it as easy, or as *painful*, as you wish. I speak to you now for courtesy alone."

I debated my options. Could I risk summoning demons now to send after her? It might surprise her enough for it to work, but I'd be risking Steifan. So no, it would have to wait. I needed him in my sights first.

Cerridwen had pulled in through the window while I had my internal debate, but she returned a moment later with someone cursing and grunting ahead of her.

She leaned Steifan out the window, holding him in

place with a dagger to his throat.

"Don't—" She put pressure on the blade to cut off his words. One of his eyes was badly bruised, and blood had dried down the edge of his face, coating his scar. There was no fear in his expression, only rage at his capture.

If he actually survived this, he would never forgive himself for being used as a hostage again.

My anger echoed his, and my magic flared.

I could see enough of Cerridwen's face behind Steifan to notice her eyes widening.

She has expended a great deal of her power, my sword said into my mind. *She is weak, but . . . I sense something else within. Something familiar.*

Steifan struggled, and Cerridwen tossed him back inside, ordering someone, or *something* to take hold of him. She might have used much of her magic, but she still had the strength and speed of her bloodline, the Sidhe.

"Leave your sword and come to me, Lyssandra," Cerridwen's voice floated out the window. "Come to me now, or I will start cutting off his fingers one by one."

My magic snaked through me, blossoming in my chest. My hand flexed around the hilt of my sword, then I dropped it in the dirt.

I told myself I didn't need it. It was just another demon at my disposal, and I could always summon more.

The skeletons followed me with their eyeless sockets as I walked past them, making my skin crawl. There was no scent of rot—they were too old for that. It was a small blessing, because I knew there had to be more of them inside. She hadn't emptied an entire graveyard for no reason.

The smell of stone and mildew overwhelmed me as I walked into the ruined castle. My magic was already making me sweat, pooling within me as if it knew it would soon need to be ready. I walked straight for a crumbling spiral staircase, knowing that was where I would need to go. Candles lined the edges of the steps, melting onto the gray stone. I reached out with my senses as I ascended, knowing Cael would have to be here somewhere. Cerridwen wouldn't have just killed him. There was a reason she had allowed him to find me, only to recapture him.

I continued up the stairs, sweat dripping down my brow. I could feel cold air coming from somewhere above, damp from the sea. Just as I reached a narrow hall at the top of the stairs, a rickety wooden door swung inward, inviting me inside. I walked toward it without thinking, sending more candles flickering around my boots.

The room was larger than I had pictured with just seeing Cerridwen hanging her head out the window. Living shadows darkened every corner, surrounding a nimbus of candlelight atop a round table near the center. The first thing I saw beyond the candles was Xavier with a knife to Steifan's throat. Xavier briefly met my eyes, then his gaze shifted to the darkest corner. I realized someone was sitting there in what I could only call a throne, though the carved wood had seen better days. As I tried to study the figure, the shadows lifted, providing a dramatic effect.

Cerridwen stood beside the throne, only revealing herself to me just then. But I wasn't looking at Cerridwen, I was looking at the ancient woman holding her chin high atop her ancient seat. Wild white hair streamed around her, reaching well past the waist of her shapeless blue dress. Despite her sagging skin and the dust collecting on her dress and hair, her eyes were sharp, seeing everything.

"I welcome you here, blood of my blood."

Something tugged at my magic. It wanted to go toward the woman. It only took me a moment to realize why. Like attracts like. "It's not possible," I gasped

Cerridwen smirked. "She will not die until the task is done. You will lend her your power, Lyssandra. Together, the two of you will be strong enough."

More shadows moved, revealing Cael in a heap at her feet. He braced himself on his elbows, barely able to lift his head enough to show me his beaten and bloody face. I immediately looked toward Cerridwen's fingers, seeing the ring glinting there, just visible at the edge of her billowing black sleeve.

She smiled again. "If you need more power, you will take it from him." She nudged Cael with her boot.

The room went eerily quiet, other than Steifan's labored breathing. "Lyssandra—"

Xavier cut him off with more pressure on the blade.

Cerridwen took a step toward me. "You can join us willingly, Lyssandra. You know it is the right thing to do. Together, we can rid the world of the monsters. We can make things how they always should have been."

I glared at her. "The only monster I see here is you."

The woman in the chair, Lavandriel, if my wild thoughts were to be believed, chuckled. "You're right. She is quite a bit like me, or at least the woman I used to be."

Her voice was stronger than expected. It seemed wrong that her voice should remain so steadfast after she had been kept alive in such a delicate condition all these years. Her body was centuries old, as was her mind. Both had continued to age. Just how long had she been trapped here?

I felt another tugging at my magic, and Lavandriel smiled. "I can't imagine what Eiric must have thought the first time he saw you. He probably thought he was seeing a ghost. Our magic is almost identical."

The shadows shifted again, and I realized something. They were not one of Cerridwen's glamours, nor the type of shadows that always loomed around Cael. They were demons, controlled by Lavandriel. She could control them, just like Liliana and Matthias.

Lavandriel watched my thoughts play out across my face. "You have encountered the shadows before. Do they speak to you?"

The shadows hadn't, but the demons had. "Some of them," I answered honestly. "Including the one you trapped in my sword."

She lifted a white brow. "So you figured it out. I'm impressed. My brother never did. Even he knew it's best to never play with demons."

"And yet here you are," I said. "A summoner, and seemingly sane."

"Not all summoners must go mad, Lyssandra." She gave me a meaningful look.

It was true then, she was just like Matthias. She didn't need Cerridwen. She could kill us all in the blink of an eye. "If you can summon demons, why have you aged? I met another summoner who was centuries old. Perhaps you do not really control them."

"You owe her no explanation," Cerridwen interrupted. "She is simply—"

Lavandriel lifted one wisened hand to cut her off. "Her life has never truly been hers, Cerri. The least we can do is help her understand. There can be a life for her after this. A *true* life."

Cerridwen looked like she tasted something sour, but she explained, "Lavandriel does control the demons, but she does not take their magic inside her, gaining their immortality. She would not be sane now if she did."

"Yes," Lavandriel agreed. "Nor have I used my blood magic as a weapon. It's the use of it that drives you mad. I can help you with that, once all of this is over."

"I don't want your help. I only came to fetch Steifan and Cael. Allow me to leave with them, and you may both live."

Lavandriel laughed, the sound startling me with its fullness. It echoed through the stone room, sending more shadows slithering around us, avoiding the candles at the center of the room. "I wish I could give you a choice, but it must be done. We must set things right, once and for all." She eyed me steadily. "Your master is a monster, just like all the rest. You would have come to realize that in time."

I flexed my hands, wishing for my sword. "Are you aware of how many innocents Cerridwen has killed with her actions? Far more than any vampire."

Cerridwen's eyes flared. "They are nothing compared to the countless lives that will be saved in the future."

"And it's for *you* to judge which lives are more valuable?" I snarled. "You are worse than Eiric. Far worse. And just as mad." I noticed a gold chain around her neck, and remembered the necklace. She'd actually put herself in a room with the same type of demons that wanted to kill her. Too bad I'd never make it close enough to tear it from her neck.

"Enough of this." Cerridwen couldn't quite meet my eyes, probably because she knew I was right. In her quest to atone for her initial wrong, she had become what she hated. She nudged Cael again with her boot, extending the ring toward him. "It is time. Go to your niece. *Bleed* for her."

Steifan struggled again, slicing his neck further on Xavier's blade. Xavier grunted, trying to keep a hold on him without killing him.

"If he dies, I have no reason to contain myself," I hissed at Cerridwen.

She extended a hand toward Steifan, and he stilled, watching a glamour only he could see. The sight of his slack face made me ill, but it was better this way. I would not let him kill himself to free me from needing to save him.

Cerridwen nudged Cael again. "Go. Crawl to her. Complete your mission."

He lifted his head enough to glare at her. "My life is hers, but I will not make her do this."

"You have no choice." She kicked him hard enough to send him sliding across the room into a patch of shadows. They swarmed around him, but did not attack.

I reached out, trying to sense them while Cerridwen

was distracted with Cael. If Lavandriel was controlling them, maybe I could too.

Lavandriel tsked at me. "That will not work. I summoned them here. They are under my control. Call it extra assurance."

I glared at her, but inside, I was thinking of all that had happened. I could not blame Cerridwen alone, for at the heart of matters was Lavandriel. This had always been her plan, to stay alive long enough until one of her line was born with her same magic. She wasn't strong enough to cast the ritual on her own, but with both of us, and the magic of demons . . . She believed it would work. That was the reason I was here.

I thought of the witches dying at the fortress, and the hunters and priestesses last night. I wrapped myself in righteous anger, then with one eye on Lavandriel, I reached out for her shadows.

Their movements stilled, then the darkness grew at my command.

Lavandriel's lip lifted in a snarl. "This is not a game you want to play, young one."

My anger built, and my power flared, calling to the shadows.

Cerridwen fetched Cael, dragging him near Steifan and Xavier. She watched us both warily. "Lavandriel—"

"Hush," Lavandriel hissed, just as her power flared over me, prickling my skin. She broke my control on her shadows, then sent them swirling around me.

Sharp pain stole my breath. I could barely see beyond their darkness as they covered me in a thousand tiny cuts, shredding my clothing. She called them off just as abruptly, leaving me panting and bleeding all over the floor.

Blood leaked from my forehead around the corner of my eye as I smiled at her. I no longer had any stolen demon magic, but blood helped. I flung my bleeding hand toward Cerridwen, and pictured the sun. She wanted me to turn night to day, so I would make her own personal sun explode from within her.

She fell to her knees, shrieking, but her screams cut off halfway through as the moisture dried from her throat. The sky flashed with lightning outside the nearest window, but the room grew brighter than it should. It flashed again, and half the tower wall was missing, having crumbled away long ago. The sound of the ocean was louder, right outside the tower walls. And far beyond the open space, I could see the distant city.

It was a glamour. Drucida had been right, Cerridwen didn't have the power to take me far. Glamours were her strongest gift. She only had to make me *think* I was far away. Which meant I was right about the undead. If Markus was already searching for me—

My thoughts cut off as Lavandriel's magic slammed into me, bringing me to my knees with searing pain—worse than what Gwenvere had done.

I swallowed that pain, hoping it was another illusion, and with the last of my strength I surged to my feet and dove for Cerridwen, wrapping bloody fingers around the chain of her amulet. I tugged at the chain, breaking it, then everything went dark.

The shrieking of demons drowned out the sound of the ocean, followed by Cerridwen's screams.

CHAPTER THIRTY-TWO

Asher

I tore a walking corpse's head from its body, but there was immediately another to take its place. The hills writhed with undead, and amongst them, the vampires that had waited outside the city. Eiric's death had changed nothing. He was simply a pawn. Cerridwen was the true power all along.

Tholdri thrust his sword into a vampire's chest beside me, then he tore the blade free to lop off another's head. They were all younglings, probably just innocents Eiric had turned shortly before his demise.

Cerridwen had laid her plan well. In order for Markus to track Lyssandra, we had to keep him alive, which was proving difficult with every walking corpse trying to kill him.

Ice sparkled across a portion of the battlefield. *Drucida.*

I decapitated another corpse, tossing its head aside. This could not stand. Cerridwen would never let us reach Lyssandra in time. She would never perform the ritual. She would sooner die. If it were between that fate and my own demise, I knew which one I'd choose, but I had no control over her. I had never had any control. She had left me resting in the cellar to sacrifice herself once again.

It could not stand. I looked at Tholdri with more shambling corpses walking toward us. Our eyes met. Beyond him I could see Geist, stemming the flow from another direction. Already knowing my thoughts, Tholdri nodded. There were only so many places Lyssandra could be. Markus felt she was close, but if they would not allow him to get to her . . . I looked to where he stood amongst several of the witches, helpless to do anything but accept their protection. It was time.

With a final nod from Tholdri, I fled the battle. I could move faster without the rest of them. Guilt snaked through me, but I pushed it away. If I didn't do something, we would all die regardless.

And so I ran, letting the piece of me that was still within Lyssandra guide me. Still within *us*, somewhere, somehow. I had to trust that I would be able to find her. I had to trust that I would get there in time.

Lyssandra

SOMEONE WAS SHIELDING me with their body, and I knew through instinct alone that it was Cael. His blood poured over me as the shadow demons shredded his flesh. They had gone into a frenzy once the necklace was free from Cerridwen's neck. Her screams let me know we were only catching the edge of their assault.

I blindly searched the floor with blood-slicked fingers, wrapping my hand around the amulet when I found it. The pressure on top of me lessened as the demons pulled back from us. I had a brief moment where I could see, then bright light blinded me.

"Lavandriel has your sword," Cael hissed.

"Let me up." Though I wasn't sure if I could stand. My entire body felt like an open wound.

Cael rolled off of me. I used my remaining strength to sit up, lifting a trembling bloody hand to shield my eyes from the unearthly light.

Lavandriel looked like an ancient goddess, wielding the glowing sword toward the shadows swarming a lump on the floor. My eyes searched desperately for Steifan, finding him leaning against the crumbled wall, stars glittering beyond him. Xavier must have dragged him away from the shadows before collapsing himself. Now he was on the floor, unmoving. Could it mean . . .

Lavandriel stood in a pool of Cerridwen's blood with my sword. I should have attacked her, but I couldn't stand. But if Cerridwen was dead—

The bloody lump took a ragged breath. Her hair shifted away from her face, revealing a mass of cuts by the glow of my sword. All the candles had gone out, and there was no moon, so the sword was a sole beacon in the darkness.

As I watched, Cerridwen's face began to heal. She squinted past the light of the sword toward Lavandriel. "You would think they would have given up after all these years."

Lavandriel's bony shoulders slumped. "You brought the dead back to life. You tore the fabric between realms. They will never stop until we put things right."

Cerridwen nodded, then slowly sat up.

I clutched the amulet in my hand. Steifan staggered back as Xavier took a loud, ragged breath.

Still on the floor, Cael slid one bloody hand over mine and squeezed. "Take my strength," he whispered. "Take all of it and end this."

I gripped his hand, but I knew he didn't have much to give. Cerridwen had kept him weak, draining his life away with the ring the entire time she had him.

Xavier sat up. He would grab Steifan again and we would be right back where we started.

My heart pounded, sending more blood trickling down my face and body. I felt my uncle's hand in mine and realized despite his monstrous side, he was family. Far better family than my grandfather had ever been. I looked at Steifan across the room as another bolt of lightning flashed, lighting up his features.

He wasn't afraid. He was willing to die to save me. And I was willing to lose myself to save him.

My emotions overwhelmed me. Not anger, not fear, but love. It called to my magic just as much as anything else. I opened myself to it, and put out a call of my own.

Lavandriel lifted her sword and came toward me as she realized what I was doing, but she would be too late.

I didn't need stolen magic to summon demons. All I needed to do was accept what I was. What I had always truly been.

I was Lavandriel's descendent. And if I had to go mad to beat her, so be it.

CHAPTER THIRTY-THREE

Asher

I staggered in the sand as I reached the dark shoreline. The angry sea was deafeningly loud, but that wasn't what stopped me. It felt like . . . Lyssandra, but something else. I had the thought that I had consumed her blood the previous night, allowing her magic to affect me. But it was not like the first time. I had never felt anything like this before.

As if on cue, thunder and lightning gave way to rain, the sky opening above me. I hardly noticed the rain drenching my skin. I had felt her magic before, but not like this. This . . . this was enough to consume her. Enough to consume us both, and all the world with us.

Lyssandra

A ROARING GALE cut through the room from the crumbled wall, pelting us with swirling rain. My hair whipped around me as I got to my feet, facing Lavandriel with the amulet still in my hand. Xavier had grabbed Steifan again, but only to tug him away from the center of the room where I faced Lavandriel and Cerridwen.

More wind whipped around us, and not just from the storm. Most of the wind was coming from Lavandriel, and from me.

"Do not do this, Lyssandra!" Lavandriel called over the howling gale. She still held my sword, glowing like the moon. It was her creation, after all. She had put a demon inside of it. It answered to her just as easily as it answered to me. She had summoned demons, but now so had I.

I extended my arms. We were about to see if I could summon another. Magic flowed through me, removing my mind from my body, almost like I was watching everything from above. Distantly I heard more of the tower wall crumbling. The stones shook beneath my feet.

With a growl, Cerridwen charged toward me, but Cael lunged to his feet and intercepted her. Cael's shadows swarmed around them. He threw her to the ground hard enough to shatter her bones.

Gritting her bloody teeth, she lifted the ring, but Cael was on top of her before she could use it. He ripped off her finger and the ring went tumbling out into the rain. Ghouls howled somewhere outside, whether they were controlled by Cael or Cerridwen, I could not say.

I lost sight of them as searing pain cut through my body, bringing my attention back to Lavandriel. She still held the sword, but it was her open hand pointed in my direction nearly bringing me to my knees.

Barely able to breathe, I welcomed the pain. I welcomed the emotions it would call up within me. I could try to boil Lavandriel's blood, but it was magic she had mastered centuries ago. Instead, I had to give myself over to her greatest fear. I sent my power outward, calling to anything that would listen.

Unable to withstand the onslaught, I fell to my knees. Cael had stopped moving, lost to one of Cerridwen's glamours. Steifan was trying to pull away from Xavier, but the much stronger man held him back.

We were losing. If Lavandriel bested me, Cael and Steifan would die. There was no doubt in my mind that she would find a way to use my magic to carry out her plan. In her own way, she was just as mad as her brother had been.

Every last drop of magic within me surged outward, leaving me immobile. For a heartbeat, nothing happened, then the wind abruptly stopped, and all went dark.

Witch, you summon me?

I gasped, my blood suddenly turned to ice. A figure rimmed by an unearthly glow appeared before me, but I could hardly make sense of it. It was all long limbs and sharp teeth like the other demons, but somehow worse. Its power crawled across my skin. Power so great it made my bones hurt.

Suddenly it shifted, reforming into a tall handsome man with short black hair. His eyes were like sapphires centered in his perfectly symmetrical face. His black

SARA C. ROETHLE

clothing flowed from one thing to another, as if he couldn't quite settle on an option.

Is this form easier for you to comprehend? he asked into my mind.

Lavandriel held out her glowing sword, backing away from the demon, her eyes wide and unblinking. "What have you done, Lyssandra?"

The man—*the demon*—smiled, showing perfect white teeth. "Two witches for the cost of one." For a moment his form shifted into something out of my worst nightmare, then back to the man standing between us. His blue eyes met mine. *Summoner, what do you offer me?* His words slithered through my mind, his voice monstrous and unearthly once more.

What do you want? I thought back.

He smiled, and I knew I had said the wrong thing.

Lavandriel spun, holding up the glowing sword as ghouls crowded their way through the doorway, growling and spitting. The creatures flocked to Cerridwen, protecting her as she cradled her bloody hand and kept my uncle under her thrall.

Lavandriel turned her attention back to me, keeping the glowing sword between her and the demon. "You must send him away, Lyssandra. You do not understand what you have done. You did not summon him through your will, you simply opened a path. He cannot be controlled."

The demon disappeared in a cloud of darkness, then reappeared behind Lavandriel, close enough that her back touched his chest. He reached an arm around her, surprising me by stroking her cheek. "Long have I watched you summoning lesser beings. You could have been powerful enough to do anything. You could have been immortal. Truly immortal. Not trapped in this withering shell."

Rain mingled with cold sweat dripping down my brow. Just the demon's presence felt *wrong*. I realized then that there was a reason others only summoned shadows. Gwenvere had lured greater beings, and they couldn't be contained. Their very existence could drive someone mad, or worse.

Lavandriel's throat bobbed, but she otherwise held herself perfectly still. "Lyssandra—" Her words cut off as his hand wrapped around her throat from behind. She wasn't even fighting him.

Cerridwen had edged toward the crumbled wall with her ghouls. She was going to run. Even with her dearest friend in danger, she was going to run to save her own skin. Her wide eyes were locked on the demon as she backed toward the edge.

The demon watched me while he gripped Lavandriel's throat. *I think this one will be payment enough.* Black smoke enveloped him once more, and he was gone. Inky darkness flowed into Lavandriel's nostrils.

Cerridwen took her cue and leapt out through the crumbling wall. Still gripping Steifan with a hand clamped over his mouth, Xavier hesitated, his eyes on me. A pained expression crossed his face and I knew Cerridwen was calling to him.

"Go," I said to him. "I will hunt you down and reclaim Steifan later." I couldn't believe I was saying it, but he was safer with them than he was with whatever was happening to Lavandriel.

He nodded, then dove out into the night.

Cael reminded me of his presence by gripping my shoulders. "We need to go."

But my feet were rooted to the spot. My sword stopped glowing, then fell from Lavandriel's grasp, clattering to the stones at her feet. She swayed, then snapped rigidly upright.

A cruel smile swept across her face, barely visible in the darkness.

Cael tugged at my shoulder, but I shook my head. I couldn't just let a demon have Lavandriel's body, especially not with the magic she possessed.

The demon inside Lavandriel tilted her head. "What will you do now, little huntress? Will you steal my magic too?"

I opened my mouth to ask how he knew, then shut it. It didn't matter. Lavandriel had to die. I extended the amulet toward Cael. It would do me no good against a greater demon.

He took it, resigned to whatever fate I chose for us.

I flexed my hands, glancing at the sword on the ground. I needed to deal with the demon, then I would find Steifan. Realizing my intent, the demon's smile broadened. He stepped the toe of his boot over my sword's hilt, then used his foot to send it sliding in my direction.

I didn't look down as I stopped it with my boot, then I crouched to pick it up. It started glowing again as soon as it was in my hand. *He is a ruler of demonkind. Proceed with caution.*

I gripped the rain-slick hilt tightly as thunder boomed, shaking the tower. My throat tight, I nodded at my sword's words.

"What would you have me do?" Cael said at my back.

"We must make sure Lavandriel does not leave here alive, demon or no."

I didn't wait for his answer. The demon ran Lavandriel's tongue across her teeth, then gave me a wink.

I lifted my sword and charged.

CHAPTER THIRTY-FOUR

Asher

The distant tower shook and swayed, threatening to fall into the sea. If Lyssandra was still inside, she would be crushed. She was no longer a servant—she could not sustain such injuries.

I made to run toward the tower, but caught sight of several figures fleeing in the rain. Without thinking, I was upon them in seconds.

Cerridwen staggered back, huddling amongst her ghouls. Her hand still bled where the ring would have been on her finger, and a thrill of dark delight coursed through me. Her ghouls numbered only four—they would not be an issue. Cerridwen had used me against Lyssandra too many times, but never again.

She saw her death in my eyes and staggered back further, nearly colliding with Xavier as he caught up to her, dragging Steifan along. At first I thought the other man was dead, but then I heard the faint thrum of his breath and heartbeat through the pattering rain.

Cerridwen lifted her hands, watching me with dark eyes. She was still a necromancer, and capable of strong glamours, but no glamour came. She must have used too much magic summoning the dead from their graves to fight her battles.

"Kill him," she ordered.

The ghouls rushed toward me, biting and snarling, their rotten skin iridescent in the rain dampened night.

I easily snapped the neck of the first one that reached me, tossing it aside. The next almost caught my arm with its teeth before I twisted its neck hard enough that its rotten skin tore. The other two fell just as easily.

Cerridwen had retreated further. I could already see that she meant to flee when Xavier tossed Steifan into the sand and charged toward me. She would sacrifice her human servant to save herself, and that too could not stand. I tossed him aside like a doll, charging toward Cerridwen.

She cried out as I grabbed her. Her wet, dark hair slapped against my skin as she struggled to protect herself. "Lyssandra is inside with a demon! You must be swift if you hope to save her!"

"What demon?" I snarled, spinning her into Xavier's path as he charged me again.

Xavier darted aside just before he would have collided with her. "A greater demon. We know nothing more except that Lavandriel fears him."

My thoughts halted at her name. She spoke as if she was still living.

Watching Xavier, I balled my fist in Cerridwen's hair and tugged her head to one side, baring her neck. I lowered my fangs toward her flesh, keeping my eyes on her human servant. "How do I save her?"

I could feel Cerridwen trying to control me with her magic, but she was far too weak, and she no longer had the ring. She had been too bold summoning an army of undead and using a portal to steal Lyssandra. Her arrogance would be her undoing.

Xavier only watched me with a strange smile on his face now that Cerridwen was no longer ordering him to attack me. "You don't," he said. "She saves herself."

Cerridwen pleaded for her life, offering to rescue Lyssandra, but I knew it was a lie. She had fled to save herself, just as she had always done. I gave Xavier a final nod, then I tore out Cerridwen's throat.

Lyssandra

I SWEPT my glowing sword in a slice that would have cut the demon in half, but he made Lavandriel's body disappear in darkness, only to reform near the crumbled wall. He laughed with Lavandriel's voice. He was toying with me, nothing more. He knew I could not beat him.

Cael was a blur as he dove toward the demon, but he simply disappeared again, reforming right behind me.

I spun with my sword, ending with it pointed at his throat, but he merely smiled. "You only live, witch, because you opened the path for me, and you will do so for others. You will be our anchor, and we will pay back those who would trap us and use our power."

"They're already dead," I snarled. I thrust my sword against his throat, but he was gone.

Using the weapon would not work. I had to try something else. I had to try magic. But when I spun to watch him reform again, the magic I reached for was a mere spark. I had used too much in summoning him.

I can help you, my sword said into my mind. *Open yourself to me.*

Cael tried to grab the demon from behind, but Lavandriel's body spun, batting him aside like an insect. He crashed into the ruined wall, and his lower body fell out into the rain. His fingernails scratched across ruined stone, barely catching himself.

What will you do? I thought, still holding my sword between myself and the demon.

I will lend you my strength.

Lavandriel tilted her head, wet white hair draping her thin frame. "Have you tired yourself already? Very well, let us be gone from here. You will need your strength for what is to come." He reached one thin, frail hand toward me.

I gritted my teeth. If he wanted to take me, I could not fight him. The only thing I could do was trust the demon in my sword. My only hope was that I could trust the demon I *knew*. I let down my shields, beckoning to the magic in my sword.

Realizing what I was doing, the demon in Lavandriel's body lunged toward me. Having pulled himself up, Cael intercepted him, yanking Lavandriel's arm back hard enough that I heard the shoulder bone pop out of its socket. The demon tried to swat him away again, but Cael held on, reaching for Lavandriel's throat. At his full strength, he could have ended her in a heartbeat, but not now. The demon disappeared in another wash of darkness, then that darkness swarmed around Cael. He cried out in agony, lifting the amulet I had given him toward the darkness. The yellow stone embedded in gold glowed brightly, chasing back his attacker.

Then the demon reformed in Lavandriel's body. He ripped the amulet from Cael's fingers and crushed it in one bony hand. When the hand opened, the amulet was gone. Sneering, he reached down toward Cael.

Tears stung my eyes. *I will give you everything I have,* I thought to my sword. *Just help me now.*

Abruptly, the light in my sword went out. *All* light went out, abandoning me in rain-streaked darkness. The demon in my sword flowed into me, leaving behind one prison for another.

Magic lit up my veins enough to make my skin glow with murky light. My sword was not only a demon, I remembered, but a demon hunter. And now that hunter was inside me.

The demon in Lavandriel abruptly straightened, forgetting Cael. Lavandriel's body stood perfectly still, eyes dancing over my glowing form. Finally, the demon smiled. "What have you done, witch?"

It was my turn to smile. I spread my arms wide, knowing just what to do, like my sword's magic was meant for me all along.

The demon in Lavandriel's body, visible only by the

glow of my magic, swallowed itself up in darkness, then reformed again at my back. He already had his hands reaching for my throat as I turned, and I let him. I let him grab me, whether he was intent on choking me, or breaking my neck, it did not matter. As soon as his hands touched me, I hit him with every ounce of raw magic I had.

A cloud of darkness exploded out of Lavandriel. She fell to the floor, just as the darkness became a man once more.

Unfortunately, he seemed unharmed. He tilted his head, looking not quite at me, but *through* me. "I was wondering where you had gone."

I realized the demon in my sword knew him personally, but I had no time to consider it. I hit him with another blast of light, the force making the entire tower sway dangerously. It could crumble at any moment.

The demon cried out in rage as he dissipated, then reformed near Cael. Shadows swarmed from the demon's hands, wrapping around Cael's arms to yank him to his feet. Cael gasped in pain, and I realized that when the demon last attacked him, he'd pierced his side with a broken board. It stuck out of him awkwardly, steadily dripping blood.

Watching my face, the demon used more shadows to grip the board, shoving it deeper up through Cael's chest.

Cael's body went rigid, and panic shot through me. Even a creature like my uncle could not live without his heart.

"The blood!" Cael gasped, more of it splattering from his lips. "Use it!"

He was right. Demon magic alone would not suffice. It wasn't stolen demon magic that let me summon and control such beings. It was blood magic.

Seeing no other choice, I called to the power in Cael's blood, mingling it with my own. Using the presence of my sword within me, I absorbed my uncle's power. Necromancy, vampirism, demon and blood magic all became one.

"No!" the demon shouted in Lavandriel's voice, dropping Cael.

I held my arms at my sides, palms out, and I hit him with everything I had.

He cried out in rage, turning into nothing but a writhing mass of shadows, but as soon as the attack relented, he reformed, staggering once more to his feet. His form blinked in and out of existence, then shifted again, becoming the monster I had initially seen when he first came through. It growled, then took a slow step toward me.

Cael tried to sit up between us, but the floor was slick with his blood. "Light," he gasped. "It is a creature of shadow, just like the others. It fears light."

Even with so much magic overwhelming me, panic still rippled through my body. I took a step back as the demon drew near. "I don't know the ritual," I breathed.

I created it, my sword said somewhere in the back of my mind. *I created the ritual for Lavandriel.* And with its words came a certain knowing. I could do it. I could create sunlight right in this tower but—

My eyes locked with Cael's.

Leaning his back against the crumbling wall, he gave

me a sad smile. "My life is yours," he rasped, splattering blood across his lips. "It always has been."

The demon lunged, and with the last of his strength, Cael surged to his feet and threw himself in front of it.

I slammed my eyes shut, chanting the ritual without needing to think, because my sword fed me every word. Light exploded out of me, tearing through Cael and the demon—light so powerful it burned my skin. I tried to call it back, to rein it in before it could go too far, but it consumed me.

I squinted my eyes against it as the light consumed both the demon and my uncle in a fiery flash. I cried out at my last sight of my uncle, unwillingly feeding my emotions into the ritual.

I fell to my knees, my thoughts a frantic torrent. The demon was gone. And my uncle—

I needed to rein it in. I had to stop the light before it could go further.

Something gripped my hand, and I realized it was Lavandriel when her magic joined with mine. I had freed her from the demon, and now she would still use me to fulfill her mission.

She directed the magic, making it lighter and easier to bear. She spooled it around us, preparing to send it outward. To truly turn night into day.

Tears streamed down my face. My uncle was gone. I did not know what had become of Steifan, and Lavandriel was about to kill Asher. I felt it as the magic fully built, ready to be released.

"Get your filthy claws off my friend!" someone cried out behind us.

I heard a loud clang, then Lavandriel fell away. The moment she lost her grip on me, the magic became all-consuming once more. I was no longer a body with breath and a heartbeat. I was pure molten light.

Someone gripped my arms from behind, hissing as I burned him. Then Steifan's strained voice reached my ears. "I'm here with you, Lyss. For better or worse, I'm here with you."

Agony raked through me. My uncle was dead. He had died so I could defeat the demon. But he would not want this. He wanted me to have a life with the person I loved.

My light amplified with every thought, my emotions feeding into it even as I warred to draw it back in.

I could smell Steifan's flesh burning, but he stayed close to my ear. "If you will burn, then I will burn with you."

My eyes flew wide at his words. *No.* No, I would not let him burn.

My chest swelled with breath, and I tried to call the magic back into me. It filled me up to the point of unbearable pain, and there was too much left to pull in. I couldn't make sense of it. I had to make it stop. I had to release it.

Steifan wrapped his arms around me, pulling me against him though his body trembled with pain. He was killing himself to hold on to me, to make sure I wasn't alone.

That final thought was enough to bring me back to myself. I inhaled a ragged breath and spooled the rest of the magic back in. The light went out like a candle abruptly extinguished, leaving us in darkness.

There was a loud ringing in my ears, then suddenly

everything went eerily quiet. My vision and hearing came back in stages. First, the pattering rain. Second, the dark night sky, and more crumbling stone as the tower began to fall.

Steifan panted loudly, his arms still wrapped around me from behind.

I gripped his hand, and I wept.

Lavandriel revived at my feet with a gasp, then flopped over, coughing. Blood stained her white hair where Steifan had knocked her unconscious. "You fool!" she rasped. "We were so close! I only wanted to rid the world of monsters!"

Trembling, I pulled away from Steifan, then knelt beside her to reclaim my lifeless sword. The tower rumbled again, threatening to bury us all.

Lightning lit up Lavandriel's face as she blinked the water out of her eyes. "It's not too late. We can still fulfill our purpose." She met my gaze as another flash of lighting struck, followed too close by deafening thunder that shook the stones around us. "This is what your grandfather wanted. This was his plan for you, Lyssandra. You were born to slay monsters. To slay *all* monsters."

I smiled down at her. She wanted to kill Asher, and Geist. To her, they were nothing more than monsters. They were creatures who could not love, just as her brother could not love. Just as she would have thought my uncle could not love.

But she was wrong. The light save us all, she was wrong.

The tower swayed again, but I couldn't bring myself to care. "My grandfather saw to it that I was trained to kill.

And for most of my life, I have killed monsters. As you say, it was my purpose."

"Yes," she gasped, her neck straining. "You will do great things, Lyssandra. You will carry out justice for all who have suffered. It's not too late."

I looked at the sword in my hand, its demonic presence still lurking within me. I wasn't a hunter. I was a witch, and a summoner, and now, I was host to a demon for however long it chose to stay. I smiled and looked down at Lavandriel. "I think I would rather protect those I love. I'll leave the justice to someone else."

I thrust the sword downward, piercing her ancient heart. The tower swayed, and stone crumbled. I looked up into the rain as the downfall swallowed me whole.

CHAPTER THIRTY-FIVE

My body was cold, unbearably cold. I seemed to float above the ground. I could no longer feel the pain in my body, crushed by falling stone. It had buried me alive. And Steifan . . . I didn't know what had become of him. He had been closer to the ruined wall. Maybe he had made it out.

Distantly, I could smell the salt of the ocean and the scent of fresh rain, but a more relevant smell overwhelmed my senses. I smelled the turned-earth scent of vampire, with an undercurrent of vanilla and sage.

More strange still, I felt *safe*. I hadn't felt so safe since the last time Asher held me.

My mind struggled to make sense of things, but my body was too far gone. Or was it? I wasn't dead yet, at the very least. I groaned as sudden nausea lanced through my stomach.

"Don't move," a male voice soothed. "You've endured much."

My pulse fluttered, too weak to hammer with panic. My breath rasped in my throat. "Asher?"

"Shh."

He laid me gently on the damp sand. My body was so cold that the sand beneath me felt warm. Blood trickled into my mouth. I realized he had already given me some when he found me.

"Will she live?" Steifan's voice. I wanted to cry out in relief, but I could not.

Magic somewhere inside me responded to Asher's blood, and I realized it was the demon from my sword. It had come here willingly to hunt after Cerridwen's actions let other demons into the realm. Now that it was a part of my consciousness, I finally knew its purpose. It hadn't wanted to kill Lavandriel, but it hadn't fought me either. It had hunted with me many times, and it knew I would help fulfill its purpose.

My eyes fluttered open. It had stopped raining, but thick clouds still blotted out the stars. Asher crouched next to me, his bleeding wrist still extended.

Coming back to myself, I weakly pushed his wrist away, then closed my eyes again.

His fingers stroked my cheek. "Forgive me, my love. But there is one last thing you must see to before you rest."

I groaned. I wanted to rest. I wanted to shut out the horrors I had endured. My uncle—I could not think of it now. "What will you give me in return?"

He pushed my wet hair out of my face. "A day or eternity, whichever you want is yours." His fingers laced with mine, waiting.

Finally, I nodded.

He helped me sit up, and I opened my eyes. I expected to see Steifan, but it was Xavier who lay at my feet. He was so quiet and still, I hadn't noticed him.

"Is he—"

"Not dead yet," Asher explained. "But Cerridwen is gone. His time is short. He wishes to speak with you."

My heart suddenly pounding, I tried to crawl toward Xavier, but ultimately Asher had to lift me to sit me closer. He sat so I could lean against him while I looked down at the dying man.

Xavier's eyes were open, his expression pained. "I thought—" he coughed. "I thought this was what I wanted." He inhaled sharply, then let out a ragged breath. "But you have shown me there is so much more that I want in this life."

Tears stung the back of my eyes as a knot formed in my throat. At one time, Eiric kept him alive, then Cerridwen, but he could not survive without a master. I might have been able to claim him with my sword's magic, but he wouldn't want that. He wouldn't want to be a servant once more.

I pushed his wet hair away from his face. "I'm sorry."

He managed a pained smile. "I'm glad at least that you were the one to live. Even if it means that all vampires will live too." He winced. "Except for the ones you will surely kill."

I smiled because that's what he wanted, and I continued to stroke his hair.

"Will you stay with me?" Xavier whispered.

"Of course." I rested my hand on his cheek.

Asher stiffened behind me as he saw what I did. My hand was faintly glowing, not with my magic, but the magic of my sword.

Its words pulsed against my mind. *Will you hunt no longer?*

I froze at its words. I thought about it, *truly* thought about it, and wasn't sure how to answer. Lavandriel had been right, in part. A hunter was simply what I was. What I had spent my life training to become. But I didn't want to kill anymore. I didn't want to spend my life seeking death. I took a deep breath, then let it out. *I will hunt no longer.*

Then I shall choose another.

Just as Xavier took what should have been his last breath, my sword's magic flowed into him. He did not wake—he was too weak—but he did not die.

He did not die, because he had a new master. Or would it be a partner? Only time would tell.

I wasn't sure if I had done him any favors, but anything was better than Eiric. And even Eiric was better than Cerridwen.

I leaned back against Asher with a heavy sigh. "We will bring him back with us. He may need my help when he wakes."

Asher wrapped his arms around me. "Of course."

My gut clenched, because I was afraid to ask my next question. "Cael?" But I already knew the answer. He could not have survived the sunlight.

"I searched, but I saw no sign of him. Not at the tower, nor amidst the army of undead Cerridwen sent our way."

I closed my eyes, trying to focus on his words over the

372

crashing of the angry sea. I wasn't sure what would happen to the undead now that Cerridwen was gone. Hopefully they could be laid to rest.

They would be lucky, in a way. I was so very tired. And that was the last thought I had.

CHAPTER THIRTY-SIX

I hated waking to sunlight, because it meant that Asher was not with me, but Steifan sitting at the foot of my bed and Tholdri in a chair next to it were almost just as good. I sat up, wincing at a sudden sharp pain in my head that had me sinking back down against my pillows. My body was sore, but not as sore as it would have been without Asher's blood.

I observed Steifan, remembering the smell of his burning flesh the night before, but he was healed. Asher or Geist must have given him blood. His hair was burned away on one side, and someone had cut the rest for him.

Tholdri leaned forward until he was in my view. "Leave it to our Lyss to bury herself beneath an ancient tower."

"Asher told you?" I asked.

"Steifan, after some healing. Asher was in here with you until the sun rose."

An unknown panic tickled my skin until I finished reliving the previous night's events in my mind.

Cerridwen and Lavandriel were dead, and Steifan had stopped me from killing all vampires.

Almost all vampires. My thoughts quickly diverted from my uncle, because I wasn't ready to give into the pain. Not yet. "Asher told me you were attacked by undead when you tried to reach me."

"Yes." Tholdri sat back out of view with a chuckle. "I've seen many battles, but none quite like that one. Fortunately, they were mostly intent on killing Markus. Cerridwen's plan for keeping us from finding you, I imagine."

"Speaking of Markus . . . " Steifan said softly.

At his tone, I forced myself to sit up.

Steifan watched me warily, but it was Tholdri who explained, "After the battle Markus tried to go to you, but then something happened. He stopped suddenly, as if struck by lightning, then he said he couldn't feel you. We thought you were dead, Lyss."

My heart skipped a beat as I realized what he was saying. "Markus could no longer feel me because he's no longer my servant. My sword is . . . gone. It no longer binds us."

Tholdri met my gaze. "Yes, that's the conclusion we reached after Geist found you. He provided Steifan with further healing, then carried Xavier."

"I told them what happened with him," Steifan explained. "I thought it might have something to do with Markus being cut off from you, but truly, I hardly understand it."

I inhaled deeply. The sunlight cutting across the room was feeling better and better, and I suddenly longed to go outside. I explained to them as much as I could about the demon in my sword first transferring to me, then to Xavier. I imagined it going into Xavier was what had freed Markus from his bond. The only thing I left out of my explanation was what happened to Cael, but Tholdri didn't ask about it.

I slumped against my pillows. "Saving Xavier could have killed Markus, and I didn't even think twice about it. I felt Xavier's plea, and wanted to give him an opportunity at some sort of life."

Tholdri winced. "Yes, perhaps we'll not tell Markus that part. Let him simply be grateful to you instead."

I gave him a slight twitch of my brow. "Markus? Grateful? The world really has come to an end."

He leaned forward to grip my shoulder. "No, Lyss, it hasn't. That's kind of the point."

But it had been close. So close. At least for *my* world. "Cerridwen didn't want to end the world. She wanted to save it." I leaned my head back. "And I nearly unleashed a greater demon to stop her. I—" I hesitated, once more thinking of Cael.

"Yes. Well. It still worked out alright." Tholdri squeezed my shoulder, then sat back.

We all turned so abruptly at a knock on the door that I had to laugh. Once I stilled my heart, I shook my head. "I imagine we'll all be jumping at shadows for some time to come."

Tholdri snorted. "It's been a rough year."

Steifan stood to answer the door. Judging by how he moved, Geist had given him more than enough blood. He'd been buried along with me. We were both lucky to be alive.

He opened the door, revealing Drucida and Ophelia. Drucida walked in boldly without further invitation, leaving Ophelia to scurry after her. They both wore blue acolyte robes, likely because they were the only clean things available.

Drucida pulled the other vacant chair near my bed and sat, smoothing the pale blue fabric around her legs.

With a smirk, Tholdri stood and offered Ophelia the other chair.

I looked at Drucida. "I hear you froze half the undead where they stood."

"More than half," she scoffed. She extended one hand toward me, palm up.

Knowing what she wanted, I placed my hand in hers.

"Should we . . . " Steifan trailed off, looking unsure.

"You can stay," Drucida said, not bothering to glance in his direction. Instead, she gripped my hand, bowed her head, and closed her eyes.

All was silent for a long moment, and no one else looked my way except for Ophelia, who watched me through narrowed eyes. Drucida must have asked her to study my energy.

Finally, Drucida lifted her head, patted the back of my hand, then released it. "There are no other entities inside you, so that's something. But I cannot say what will happen with your magic over time. I heard about what you did. It is . . . unsettling."

I studied her expression, hoping for more information. "*Unsettling* is one word for it."

"I cannot tell you what will happen with your magic over time, Lyssandra. I would love to tell you it won't consume you. You may discuss summoning with Liliana at the fortress, if that might help."

I shook my head. "No. I will not use such magic again."

"It may not give you a choice."

I inhaled deeply. I knew this talk was coming, but I wasn't ready to think about it.

"Do you still have the bracelet?" she asked before I could think of a reply.

"It's hidden." *In my pillowcase*, I finished silently. I trusted Drucida, but I wasn't sure yet what I wanted to do with the bracelet. Now that its creator was dead, it might not even work on me.

She glanced back at Ophelia, who nodded once, and Drucida turned back toward me. "A portion of your bond with Asher remains, but it may not be enough to help you."

More information I already knew. "The magic is easier to deal with when he is near me."

She met my eyes solidly. "Then keep him near, Lyssandra. You can decide what to do after you've had some time."

My body relaxed, releasing tension I hadn't realized I'd been holding. "Thank you, Drucida."

She lifted a brow. "Did you truly expect me to demand you bind your powers here and now?"

I rolled my eyes in her direction, giving her a knowing look.

She wiggled a bit in her seat, averting her gaze. "Well, I've changed. We all have." She met my eyes again. "Truly, I'm just glad we're alive, and Eiric is dead. I can return to my home to live in peace."

"Or you could stop hiding."

She wrinkled her nose. "No, we saw how that went for the women here. The Helius Order still exists," she glanced at Steifan and Tholdri, "as well as others who hate our kind."

I looked at each of them. "So nothing has really changed, has it? Witches will still live in hiding. Vampires will still need to be hunted. Everything is as it has always been."

Tholdri smiled at me. "The world may not have changed, Lyss, but *we* have."

Drucida gripped my hand again. "All of us."

I looked at Steifan, whose cheeks reddened with a blush. "I can't say I have changed much at all."

Tholdri moved to the foot of the bed and clapped his shoulder. "Only because you were already perfect to begin with."

Steifan rolled his eyes at him, and all I could do was laugh. Steifan might not have noticed a change within himself, but I had. I'd noticed it in the look in his eyes when his life was in peril. I had seen it when he stood with me, fighting against all odds.

I sat up straighter, then lowered my bare feet from my bed, wincing as my magic coiled up within me like a snake. I might have changed, but it felt like I had simply gone back to the start, to what and who I would have been had I known my fate sooner.

And now, I had survived. Most of my enemies were dead. And my future looked murkier than ever.

Steifan tilted his head. "Does anyone hear shouting?"

We all went silent to listen, and indeed there were shouts somewhere outside, beyond the temple walls.

"Do the temple wards still hold?" I asked Drucida.

She stood, brushing imaginary dirt from her cloak. "Two of the priestesses who helped set them still remain. They should hold as long as they both live."

Light, only two. They must have been wise enough to not take demons inside of them, but having only two priestesses who could invite people into the temple would be an issue. An issue for another time, if the shouts were what I thought they were.

Tholdri watched my expression. "What are you thinking?"

"I'm thinking history is about to repeat itself for the remaining witches." I walked past him toward the armoire, intent on fresh clothing. Someone had changed me out of my bloody rags, but I wasn't about to face anyone in just a thin white nightshift. Having little use for modesty at this point, I opened the armoire, pulled on fresh breeches, then searched for a shirt.

Ophelia was the first to approach me. "What would you have us do?"

I stopped halfway through fastening my buttons to blink at her, then I looked back at Drucida.

She shrugged. "I am not in charge here, Lyssandra."

"Then who is?"

Everyone stared at me.

"Oh light," I muttered, returning to my buttons. "We're doomed."

CHAPTER THIRTY-SEVEN

Markus and Isolde joined us on our journey to the ground floor.

"We heard the shouting," Isolde explained. She had a fresh bruise on the side of her face from the battle. I wasn't surprised she had chosen to fight alongside witches and an ancient vampire. What she and Markus had wasn't romantic, but he was still her partner. She would follow him into *any* fight.

I nodded at her words, then continued onward as a few more of Drucida's witches joined us. I didn't see any of the temple guards, and I wasn't surprised. They probably no longer knew exactly what they were protecting.

Tholdri opened the main door for us as we reached it, and we all went out into the courtyard. Outside the gates the city guard waited, and amongst them was a distinguished looking man in dark blue finery. Now that we were outside, they had stopped their shouting. With most of us in pale blue, they probably thought they had the attention of actual priestesses.

Somehow in charge even though I had no desire to be, I stepped forward, waiting for the man in dark blue to speak. He had a rolled parchment in his hands, presumably a message from some high-ranking official. Perhaps even the Archduke of Ivangard.

He observed me, hesitating at the sight of my red hair. Seeming to shake it off, he unrolled his little parchment and read aloud, "Priestesses of Ivangard, by order of the Archduke, you are hereby exiled from our fair city on charges of magic use, necromancy, and harboring vampires. You have until nightfall tomorrow to leave peacefully. Failure to do so will result in swift executions for all." He hastily re-rolled his parchment, then stepped a little further back amongst his guards.

My irritation ignited a spark of magic within me, which I quickly stuffed down. Attacking any of these men would not only be foolish, but pointless. I cleared my throat. "The women of this temple are innocent. Those who committed the crimes you speak of have been dealt with."

"Our terms have been stated." The man took another step back, clearly ready to flee.

Shaking my head, I watched him go. Some of his guards glanced warily our way, then filed into line behind him.

Drucida stepped up near my shoulder. "It is always the way of things. The priestesses—even those without magic —will have to leave. Those who would head south with us are welcome."

I looked at her. "So we just give up? Just like that?

Many of the girls have family in the city. They will be forced to leave them."

Drucida gripped my shoulder. "They will not be the first, and they will surely not be the last." She turned away, then walked back into the temple.

The other witches followed after her, leaving me alone with my fellow hunters.

I looked at Markus and Isolde. "And what of you two?"

Markus rested his hand casually on his sword belt. Even though the bond had only recently been broken, he already seemed like his old self—entirely sure of what he was doing, confident in every movement. "We will return to Castle Helius to see what is left of the Order. If necessary, we will launch a coup against Gregor Syvise."

Steifan winced at his father's name.

Only then seeming to remember that Gregor was Steifan's father, Markus furrowed his brow. "He will be spared if possible. Perhaps he can be reasoned with."

Steifan straightened. "I would like to go with you. If anyone can reason with him, it's me."

Isolde shook her head, tossing her long ponytail over her shoulder. "He did not listen to you before."

Steifan stepped away from Tholdri, making it clear he could stand on his own. "He sent his hunters into a trap, and now they are dead. He will listen now, I will make sure of it."

Markus studied him for a moment, then nodded. "Very well. It is a long journey. Best if we stick together." He looked next at me. "And you? Will you return to the Order?" His small smile gave up his jest.

"Not in a million years." My magic flared at the

thought of once again being accused of my grandfather's murder. "For *many* reasons."

We all looked at Tholdri, who was yet to speak.

He blushed. For the love of the light, Tholdri was *blushing* again, and this time in front of everyone.

I lifted a brow. "I'm sure the witches would welcome your help for a time. *Others* will surely be charitable enough to stand by them." My tone made it quite clear the *others* I was talking about.

His cheeks reddened further. "Well, I do have to stick around long enough to make sure you won't go mad and kill everyone."

I wrinkled my nose at him. "Take heart. If that happens, you will surely be the first to go."

Isolde sighed loudly, shaking her head. "Children, both of you." She turned back toward the temple and headed for the door.

Markus followed after her, and with a final smile, Steifan fell into step behind them.

Soon, Tholdri and I were alone in the courtyard.

He looked up at the gleaming white walls. "Do you think the remaining priestesses will leave? They do still have the wards. They could try holding out."

I thought of the remaining women, of how many had died by Eiric's hand, and by Gwenvere's. She had feared a slow, painful death, her body withering away, trapping her inside. Her fear had doomed her, and so many others. They feared being harmed *for* their magic, instead they were harmed *by* it.

It was the latter which still weighed heavily on my

mind. "I think some of them will go with Drucida, and others will try to hide."

Tholdri put his arm around me. "It doesn't seem right, having to hide what you are."

"We all do it. Every single one of us."

"Well, that's bleak."

I smiled at him. "The trick is to find the few special people that you don't have to hide from. I find that it's more than enough."

He pulled me closer as we walked back toward the temple doors. "Have you decided what you will do about your magic?"

"Yes," I realized. "Yes, I know what I want to do."

"And will Asher be pleased with your decision?" He reached for the door.

"I think he's just happy I no longer wish to kill him."

Laughing despite the dire times ahead, we both went inside. I might spend my days henceforth hiding what I was, but not from anyone who counted.

THE REST of the day was spent spreading word to those who would need to leave, followed by helping Drucida with travel preparations. For now, any heading south would travel together, including Markus, Isolde, and Steifan. There was no sense in making the journey alone.

Food, at least, would not be an issue. The temple had a year's worth of food stocked up. It would be divided and carried away. Hopefully it would help those who had no place to go to last until they could find somewhere to call home.

I was back in my chambers, packing what little I would bring, when Xavier found me. He seemed himself, walking into my room dressed in simple breeches and a soft cream shirt. Any evidence of the previous night's injuries were gone from him.

I tossed my new travel satchel onto the bed, then turned to give him my full attention. I wasn't sure what to expect, but he hadn't shut the door behind him, so it didn't seem like a confrontation was in my near future.

I looked him up and down, seeing no weapon. The physical form of my sword had been lost in the rubble, so I wasn't sure why I expected to see it now. "I thought you were still resting."

"I've been up for a few hours." He met my eyes. "I'm not sure what to say."

I gnawed my lip, feeling the same way. We weren't friends. We could never truly be friends, but— "I hope what I did," I hesitated. "I hope what I did was what you would have chosen."

He didn't answer, instead stepping closer to look out the window behind me.

I turned with him, watching the vibrant sunset giving way to darkness.

The sky was nearly black by the time he spoke again. "It is strange not feeling her anymore. And not feeling Eiric. They had both been with me so long."

"They both *controlled* you, you mean."

He turned toward me. "You *know* what I mean. Do you

not miss your bond with your master? Does not a part of you regret the loss of it?"

"He was never my master."

"You know what I mean," he repeated.

I wrapped my arms more tightly around myself, because I *did* know what he meant. The bond had been heavy on my mind since I awoke. Even with part of it still there, I did miss it. I missed that unbreakable connection. And I wasn't sure how to feel about that.

"You can be honest, Lyssandra. With me of all people, you can be honest."

The first stars twinkled into view as I considered my next words. I was unsure of how to explain myself, and even more confusing was the fact that I *wanted* to. I wanted to tell *someone*. "I do miss it," I admitted. "And that frightens me. There has been little in this life I could depend on, other than Tholdri, and more recently, Steifan. The fear of losing them is what keeps me going. I want to protect them."

"And the fear of losing Asher?"

I couldn't look at him as I answered, "It is my greatest fear of all."

"And that fear keeps you from giving yourself over fully."

"That's not true," I argued.

"Yes, it is. Trust me, Lyssandra, I have lived longer than you can fathom. I can see things others cannot. Let me help you, as you have helped me."

I watched the stars. Asher would come for me soon, and I wanted to be sure of my choice. I needed to be sure. "Every choice I have made has been made out of fear.

Either fear of loss, or fear of being known for what I truly am. I don't want to make choices from fear anymore."

"And do you fear your magic?" he asked.

"I only fear that it will make me hurt someone I love." I gnawed my lip, thinking of Cael. "But now, I also fear losing it. It is a part of me. A part of who I am. It is my only inheritance—all I have left from my mother, my grandfather, and my great uncle."

"I'm sorry." He bowed his head. "About your uncle."

"He gave up everything for me." I had not meant to release the bitter words that had been plaguing me. I winced, wishing I could take them back.

He glanced at me, clearly also surprised by the admission. "It was his choice."

I lowered my chin. This wasn't what I wanted to talk about. I wasn't ready, but . . . would I ever be truly ready? "That does not make it any easier."

He surprised me with a hand on my shoulder. "No. It doesn't."

I inhaled deeply, stuffing my tears back down. I didn't want to speak of my uncle any longer, at least not to Xavier. "I don't know what to do about the summoning. I fear if I don't learn to control it, it will happen again accidentally. I can't leave that risk out of my decision."

"Lavandriel was always afraid of that. She would never admit it, but I could see her fear. It was even worse than her fear of the blood magic, and she had seen her own half brother fall victim to their shared heritage."

"But it didn't happen," I said. "She controlled it for centuries."

"Centuries of hiding and cowering. If she hadn't been

so afraid of her power, she might not have needed to wait for you to destroy all vampires. She might have had the strength to cast the ritual herself."

I shook my head. "She didn't have it. I felt her power when she tried to control me. She was strong and skilled, but she didn't have the raw power for it. That's why she needed me."

He flashed me a smile. "My, aren't we full of ourselves?"

I rolled my eyes. "You know that is not the case. I would prefer to have less. Maybe then, it wouldn't be so overwhelming."

He pressed his hands against the windowsill, leaning forward. "If your magic was not a factor, and if no loved ones were in danger. If it was simply a choice of what you wanted—how you want to feel. What would you do?"

"It's not so simple."

"It could be. You are more free now than you have ever been. You finally have a choice. We both do."

I looked out at the night. Truly, I had always known the answer. But it seemed . . . selfish. I was used to living my life for others. And yet, I knew Xavier of all people would understand my answer. "If my magic was not a threat to anyone, I would choose to be exactly who and what I am. I would choose to hide nothing."

He laughed. "You and I are not so different."

I hesitated, but as my resolve solidified, I smiled. "And what will *you* choose to do now that you are free?"

He shrugged, stepping back from the window to face me. "I still have a demon inside of me that wants to hunt other demons freed in this realm."

391

"And will you do so?"

"I suppose I'll just see how things go. This living, *truly* living, it is new to me. It will take time."

"Well I'm glad you have the chance."

He smirked. "You know, I still find you whiny and weak."

"And I still find you annoying, pretentious, and an overall pain in my side."

We were both grinning when I sensed another presence in my doorway. I turned to see Asher standing there, and quickly realized what had taken him so long. My sword was in his hand.

Xavier leaned in near my shoulder. "Good luck, Lyssandra. I'm sure I'll be seeing you around."

"Thanks for the warning."

Chuckling, he walked past Asher and out the door.

Asher watched him go, then in the blink of an eye, he stood before me, offering me the hilt of my sword. "I thought you might want it."

Instead of taking the sword, I looked up into his silver eyes. "Why? I have no use of it."

He frowned. "I saw Drucida on my way here. Do we not intend to travel back to the fortress for a time?"

"We do." I stepped closer, nearly pushing our bodies together.

"There will be dangers faced along the way."

Maintaining eye contact, I took the sword from his grip, then set it on the table. It felt oddly . . . empty, the presence within it now within Xavier. "We can face them together, if you are willing."

He lifted a hand to cradle my cheek. "I will always be

near you. Your magic will not overwhelm you."

I laid my hand over his, pressing his fingers against my face. Just the feel of him so near was intoxicating, but safe. How ironic that after so many years of hunting, of *running*, I would finally find safety in the arms of a vampire. "I'm not worried about going mad. And I'm not worried about my dead grandfather, or the Helius Order. I'm not worried about witches or demons. My enemies are gone. I'm ready to stop running."

His eyes shifted around my face. "What would you have of me?"

I looked up into his eyes again. I could have the bond back. He would give it to me if I asked. It would mute my magic, keeping me from madness, and keeping us together. I would always be able to *feel* him.

"I don't want to run from who I am anymore. I want to trust myself enough to stay sane, but I know I am asking much from you in this. I am asking you to potentially let me fall, if that is my fate. But if you cannot," I took a deep breath, "I would be willing to accept the bond again."

He went perfectly still. I was close enough to notice that he was no longer breathing, his heart, no longer beating. "You wanted to kill me for that, once."

I smiled. "I wanted to kill you when I didn't have a choice. No one ever gave me a choice. But now, I have fought my battles, and this choice is mine alone. And yours," I amended. "But I'm not making it to please you. I'm making it because I'm ready for a new life with you, in whatever form."

His expression softened. "Lyssandra, I did this to you before out of necessity, but immortality is not a curse I would wish on anyone, least of all you. I will gladly die when you die, but I will not rob you of the opportunity to live as we were all intended. I want you to be exactly who and what you are."

"And if I go mad and try to kill you?"

He smirked. "It wouldn't be the first time."

I swallowed a sudden lump in my throat. "And if I grow old? If I wither away and die?"

He lifted both hands to cradle my chin. "I will always be with you, Lyssandra."

I wasn't sure just what to say to that. He was giving me the answers I wanted, but everything still felt so . . . unsettled. There was no way to know what would happen. But I supposed in that, nothing had changed.

"It's settled then," I decided. "We will go with the witches, for now, and we will both be exactly who and what we are."

His lips met mine, a silent promise. A life together, come what may.

Perhaps it was not the type of life my grandfather would have chosen for me.

But at least it was mine.

I WOKE while it was still dark with Asher's arm wrapped around my bare waist. I wasn't sure what has caused me to stir, but something felt off. I sat up, looking back at Asher, but he didn't move, which was odd. He did not truly sleep during the night.

I looked around the room, my eyes landing on the pile

BLOOD OF ANCIENTS

of our rumpled clothing. My sword leaned against the table right next to it, forever silent. Its eye forever closed. But the feeling I had . . .

It was a presence like my sword, beckoning me. I stood and walked toward our clothing. Asher had found Cerridwen's ring during his search for my sword. I had told him I had no use of it, and would figure out how to banish the demon within if I could.

For that's what it was, another trapped demon, just like with my sword.

I found it in Asher's coat pocket, then carried it toward the window to observe it in the moonlight. As soon as the cold light hit its red stone, the presence in my mind increased.

Hunter, it said.

I shook my head, at this point used to mental communication from demons. *I am no hunter. Not anymore.*

You are what you are. The dead will always kill, and you will always protect those who need it.

I shifted uncomfortably, not because I was standing naked in the moonlight, but because the ring's words rang true. I had no desire to hunt. But to protect? That was in my blood. I would always protect those in need. Those too weak to fight for themselves. Perhaps my magic was not my *only* inheritance.

You cannot escape what you are.

I shivered. *I don't* want *to escape what I am.*

Then a new deal will be struck. You will use me for my intended purpose. You will maintain the balance between the living and the dead.

I narrowed my eyes at the ring. *I had intended to free*

395

you, but I suppose I can use you when necessary, if that is your wish.

The ring fell silent, and I thought that would be the end of it, but then suddenly it spoke again. *You would free me?*

There was so much raw hope in its tone that all I could do was swallow the lump in my throat and nod.

And you would continue your purpose without me?

I thought about it. I didn't want to fight anymore—I didn't want to hunt things. But I knew myself well. If a vampire was hurting innocents, I would kill them. I wouldn't go looking for a fight, but if one was started, I would finish it. *Yes. I will continue being who and what I am.*

Strange girl, the ring sighed. *If you are willing, then I shall be free. I am ready.*

I glanced back at the bed, but Asher still hadn't stirred. I had a feeling the ring was keeping him asleep. I turned my attention back to the ring. *I'm not sure how.*

You are a summoner. All you must do is will me to be free.

Part of me thought I should speak with Drucida before releasing the demon in the ring, but in truth, she knew even less about such things than I did. The only person who knew more was dead.

And so I closed my eyes, and I willed the being in my ring to be free.

Almost instantly I was hit by a wave of magic. I opened my eyes just in time to watch the red stone in the ring crack in two. Murky red light leaked out, gathering into a mass before my eyes. I willed it again to be free, but instead of dissipating, it rushed toward me.

It hit me with enough magical force to knock me back.

I fell hard on the floor, losing my breath. For a moment all I could see was swirling red, then I relearned to breathe and came back to myself.

A witch willing to free a demon deserves a reward. With those parting words, the presence was gone.

I sat up, bracing myself against the stones as my heartbeat slowed. Before I could climb to my feet, Asher's hands were on me, pulling me back against him. "What happened?"

I noticed a glowing light somewhere near, and it took a moment for me to realize that it was me. I lifted a glowing hand to watch the light dance beneath my skin.

"The ring," Asher said. "I can feel its presence. What happened?"

I leaned back against him, and he obliged me by wrapping me in his arms. He held me close as new magic settled within me. *Demon magic*, but at least it wasn't the demon itself. *A gift*, it had said.

And there was more. The magic always simmering within me felt calmer, like it wasn't too much to control.

I turned so I was sitting in Asher's lap, then I tilted my head up to kiss him. "Let's go back to bed."

Letting his question drop, he lifted me effortlessly, then carried me back toward the bed. He laid me across the covers, then draped himself over me, kissing lightly down my neck. "Are you tired?"

"Not at all." In fact, I felt filled with new life. I wasn't sure exactly what the demon had given me, but I had plenty of time to figure it out.

For once in my life, I had time. I had all the time in the world.

CHAPTER THIRTY-EIGHT

The next morning Drucida and the other witches prepared to leave. Tholdri, Steifan and I would stay behind until nightfall, then we would catch up to them with Asher and Geist. Xavier had disappeared in the night. To where, was anyone's guess, though I had a feeling I would see him again eventually.

I was resting in my chamber when I heard the shouts. Not the organized shouting of guards, but something further in the city. I wouldn't have concerned myself with it, but . . . it had not been long since Drucida and the others departed. They would not have made it to the gates yet.

Shaking my head, I sat up and reached for my sword. My fingers tingled in anticipation of its presence, but of course, nothing was there. It was a simple sword once more. Without the presence inside, it would begin to age and tarnish like any other blade. I glanced at the closed eye, then buckled the scabbard behind my back and left my chamber. I felt oddly bare in just my cream-colored shirt and tan breeches, but it was no longer wise to wear pale blue in the city, and my hunter's armor had been lost long ago.

Steifan was the first to meet me on my way down. He was back in his hunter's garb, the flaming sword insignia of the Helius Order apparent across his breast. He finally looked rested, his shoulders, for once, not hunched with wariness. The scar across his face looked better with his new air of confidence, almost like it belonged there, and his freshly cropped hair made him look older.

He fell into step at my side. "Do you think the witches are having trouble escaping the city?"

"We should have expected it," I sighed. "The cityfolk likely began organizing as soon as that messenger shouted the Archduke's charges at the top of his lungs."

We hurried down the stairs where Tholdri awaited us. Though a few guards and acolytes remained to pack their things, the temple was eerily quiet.

"You know," Tholdri said, falling into step on my other side as we headed for the entrance, "rushing out there is just going to get us lumped in with everyone else."

I smirked. "Don't worry, surely there is no chance of your shining visage getting lost in the crowd. You'll get the attention you deserve."

"Not everything is about me, Lyss," he jested. "*Most* things, but not everything."

"You know," Steifan said as he hurried forward to open the door for us, "I actually did not miss the way you two make light of dire situations."

"I would think you would be used to it by now." I walked past him out the door, still smiling despite everything. Even if I was a demon summoning witch with no family left, some things would never change, and for that, I was grateful.

There were a few dutiful guards by the gates, still dressed in their pale blue livery. They had sworn oaths to protect the temple, and would see it through until everyone had escaped.

One of them, a young man with dark hair, looked my way as we approached. "I just knew they would have trouble, and Charissa is with them. Will you make sure she's alright?"

I didn't know who Charissa was, but the worried look in the guard's eyes let me know she was someone important to him. Someone he knew he would probably never see again, and yet, he still worried for her safety.

It struck me again how many lives were being torn apart because of Gwenvere, and because of Eiric and Cerridwen. None of these people had anything to do with their machinations, and yet, they were being punished. It was always the course of things, but it still rubbed me the wrong way.

"I will do what I can," I said to him, then continued onward with Steifan and Tholdri flanking me.

The shouting was louder outside the temple walls, and not far. The witches had not made it anywhere near the gates. It truly was not a surprise, but we had hoped that the Archduke's orders—banishment instead of execution —would see everyone out of the city.

It wasn't long before we reached the edge of the crowd. Tholdri tapped the nearest shoulder and asked what was going on.

An older woman clutching the collar of her threadbare coat gave him wide eyes. "A group of women tried to leave the temple. At first the city guard escorted them, but then a crowd came for their heads. The guard dispersed, and I can't blame them. Those women are murderers. They let vampires into the city!"

Of course the guard had abandoned them. It must have been the plan from the start. Shaking my head, I started pushing my way through the crowd, though I had no idea what I would do once I reached the center.

Tholdri and Steifan stayed close behind me, making sure no one tried to retaliate as I pushed them aside. I wasn't sure what would happen if they did. My magic quietly simmered inside me. It felt like it was under my control, but I knew if something happened, if someone I cared about was threatened, that control could easily be lost.

As we neared I heard Drucida's voice shouting above the rest. She had not yet loosed her magic, else there would be more screaming than shouting going on. I pushed past a portly man reeking of fish, then the witches finally came into view.

They were huddled together at the center of a small square, and a crowd was gathered all around them, many holding torches and crude weapons. I even spotted an elderly woman waving a rolling pin as menacingly as one would a battle axe. The entire scene was far too organized to have been a spontaneous riot. The guards were definitely in on it, depositing the witches where the rioters knew to be waiting. Markus and Isolde had their swords drawn, their shining weapons the only thing holding the crowd at bay.

My emotions flared at the injustice of it all, and my magic answered. I went still, gritting my teeth as I tried to breathe.

Steifan gripped my shoulder, calming me. "We are here with you, Lyss."

I knew he had no gift for sensing magic, but leave it to him to be perceptive enough to know when I needed help. I nodded, taking another deep breath, then settled the magic deep inside me. Once I had control, it was almost comfortable, and I knew it was whatever gift the demon ring had given me. I had a greater capacity for it now.

I gave Steifan a nod, then stepped forward.

A few of the rioters took my advancement as their signal to close in, but I drew my sword and faced them, warning them back.

They hesitated. They wanted blood for those who had been slain by the demons, but these people weren't fighters. Now that they had the witches, they weren't sure what to do with them. Shouting and throwing stones was one thing. Risking life and limb to bring down powerful witches was quite another.

I noticed Drucida out of the corner of my eye as she spotted me, then headed my way, leaving Ian and Ophelia with the others. Some of the shouting had gone down as the rioters waited to see if the red-haired woman wielding a greatsword was on their side, or the witches'.

"You shouldn't have come," Drucida said as she

reached me. "Someone riled these people up, but they are cowards. We would have edged our way out eventually."

"Some of them would have gotten brave enough to attack," I muttered, my eyes on Steifan and Tholdri as they joined Markus and Isolde to stand between us and the crowd. "And if anyone used magic to protect themselves, it would be chaos."

"Just as it will be chaos if you use *your* magic to protect us," she said pointedly.

At her words, my magic flared. Perhaps she was right. I had no idea what resided inside me now, just as I had no real knowledge to control it. But somehow, I wasn't worried.

Drucida narrowed her eyes at me, as if sensing that something was different, but her attention was soon drawn by the crowd.

The rolling pin lady charged forward—or else she was pushed. Either way, it was the incentive the crowd needed. Their shouts grew, and their improvised weapons raised. I moved to join the other hunters with my sword. I would try to keep my magic inside, but if swordwork failed . . . I would not let them harm my friends.

A young man lifted a smithing hammer at Markus, then froze at the sound of a horn trumpeting above the riotous shouting.

I froze right along with him, my hands tightly gripping my sword. I recognized that horn. I had heard it many times during my years at Castle Helius.

Tholdri edged toward my side, glancing around. If more hunters were here, it could only mean one thing.

They still meant to claim my head.

"You should hide," he muttered when he was near enough.

But my feet were rooted in place. If the crowd told the hunters why they were prepared to attack Drucida's group . . .

The crowd parted, making my decision for me. Roughly fifteen hunters marched in formation, and at their head was Gregor Syvise. He wore the standard armor of the Helius Order, along with a blood red sash across his shoulders to announce his temporary station.

Steifan was the first of us to move. He lowered his sword, approaching his father.

The rest of the crowd pulled further back. Even in Ivangard, the Order was well known. The crowd would not try to fight them, and they had no reason to. The Order hunted monsters. They were on the same side.

Steifan stood between us and the approaching hunters. "Father, you do not understand—"

Gregor looked remarkably similar to Steifan, only stockier and with silver at his temples. He wore the flaming sword insignia proudly, though he was not a properly trained hunter. He was a nobleman with hunter blood, a benefactor and nothing more.

He lifted his hand to cut off Steifan's words. "I know, my son. I have made a grave error. I have been shown the truth of the situation, and I have come to bring you home." He looked at Tholdri, Markus, Isolde, and even me. "To bring you *all* home."

My jaw fell open. This was a trick. It had to be a trick.

Well beyond the hunters, on a rooftop over the crowd, I spotted a flash of dark hair. A hint of a long white dress.

I blinked, then the image was gone, but recognition tugged at me.

Tholdri stepped forward. "You can't be serious. You only recently sent hunters here to *kill* Lyssandra."

Some of the men with Gregor averted their gaze, while others continued staring straight ahead. Either way, none of them were bold enough to look at me.

Gregor inclined his chin. "Yes, I believed she killed the Potentate, but I was wrong. I have found indisputable evidence of what truly happened."

I shook my head in disbelief. There was no such evidence. But then, why were they really here?

The crowd was now muttering around the hunters, unsure what to do.

Gregor straightened his shoulders. "We will escort your retinue out of the city where we may discuss things further."

"Father—" Steifan began, but the words died on his tongue. Probably because there was nothing else to say. The crowd may have been bold enough to take on a few of us, but sixteen armed men swayed the odds solidly in our favor.

Muttering to themselves, the crowd began to disburse, the boldest amongst them hanging back in the nearest alleys to watch what would happen next.

Gregor turned toward me. "Lyssandra Yonvrode, you are hereby pardoned of all crimes. I have been shown that at all costs, you have always fought on the side of the Order."

He had been *shown?* I had seen many strange things, but I couldn't help thinking this was the strangest occurrence of all.

Then I thought again of that flash of white, and I understood what had happened. I bowed my head in Gregor's direction. "We will accept your escort out of the city."

I didn't want to leave Asher and Geist behind, but I also would not lead the hunters right to them. Instead, I would see the witches out of the city, then I would figure out how to send the hunters away before they learned they were escorting a group of magic users.

Gregor smiled at my words, and the other hunters seemed to relax. They formed an escort around us, making many of the witches visibly nervous, but no one uttered a word.

I waited to bring up the rear, where Tholdri fell into step at my side. Steifan walked at the front, speaking with his father.

Tholdri shook his head, clearly as shocked as the rest of us. "Am I dreaming? This *has* to be a dream."

"It's not a dream." Though I wasn't sure how I felt about the truth. "It's a glamour."

Tholdri stopped walking, looking first at me, then at the hunters continuing onward. "You mean they're not real?" he whispered.

I sighed. "They're real, but the evidence supporting my innocence is not. I saw Ryllae watching us from a rooftop."

His jaw fell even further.

I gestured for him to start walking so we wouldn't get left behind.

Once we were moving, I lowered my voice and explained, "She must have fabricated some sort of evidence, and glamoured Gregor into believing it. She probably used her wiles on the other hunters as well."

"But why?" he asked. "Why would she do this? The last time you saw her, you killed her sister."

"Eiric killed her, actually."

"You know what I mean. You did not part on the best of terms. Why would she help you now?"

I sighed. I had wanted to think the worst of Ryllae, but I had learned that things were never so black and white. She had done what she thought was right, and when it ended up being so very wrong . . .

She was not a bad person. She wanted to atone.

"Hopefully she will stick around long enough to explain it to us."

Tholdri shook his head again, but now he was smiling. "Just when I thought no one could possibly surprise me with anything again."

"Tell me about it," I laughed.

We continued after the hunters. To what end, was anyone's guess.

IT WAS NEARLY dark by the time we managed to pry ourselves away from Gregor's profuse apologies coupled with his grand views for the future. The experience had been unbearable. Not that I didn't appreciate his plans,

408

but I knew I would not be part of them. He wanted to welcome me back to the Order, but that was not my life anymore. Hiding that I had been a human servant was hard enough. There was no way to hide the magic I could barely control. And beyond that, I had no desire to.

We finally managed to part ourselves with the excuse of helping the refugees—witches, though Gregor did not know it—set up camp. The hunter camp was not far, but at least far enough that no one would be disturbed.

Since it was pointless now for me to make my way back to the temple, I waited in the dark with Steifan and Tholdri. There were plans to be made for both of them, now that they had the option of returning to Castle Helius.

Tholdri leaned back on his palms in the dirt, peering up at the darkening sky. "I for one will not be going back anytime soon, though it is nice to have the option."

I sat beside him, trying not to worry about Asher. He and Geist should have no trouble escaping the city to find us. "I think you both already know what my answer is."

Tholdri smirked. "Yes, which means you will not be getting rid of me, as you may have hoped."

I punched his arm, then leaned forward to peer around him at Steifan. "And what about you? Will you consider your father's offer?"

Steifan gazed pensively at the tiny sliver of moon rising overhead.

"Steifan?" I pressed.

He startled, then blinked at me. "Yes?"

"You're considering going back with him," I realized, though it shouldn't have come as a surprise. Some of us were born into the Order, while others were given the opportunity to actually *want* it. While he had hunter blood, he had been amongst the latter. He could have chosen to be a nobleman, instead he ended up with me.

He didn't quite meet my eyes as he explained, "It's just that I think I can actually make a difference. With my father open to sharing the role of interim Potentate, I might actually be able to change things. We can hunt monsters, and *only* monsters. And we can leave people like Drucida alone."

I smiled. "And people like me?"

He returned my smile. "Yes, people like you, Asher, and Geist. You shouldn't have to hide."

"I'll be glad for you if you can achieve it. And I'll miss you."

His jaw fell open, as if he only then realized that his choice meant we would soon part ways. "We'll find each other again, of course, won't we?" He glanced between me and Tholdri.

Tholdri gripped his shoulder. "Don't fret. Neither of you can escape me. And Lyss? She's like bog fever. Once you catch her, she'll never truly leave you."

"Lovely," I muttered, though Steifan was smiling, so I didn't dispute his claims. I stiffened as I sensed vampires approaching, then relaxed and looked over my shoulder.

Asher and Geist stood framed by the firelight from the witches' camp. Asher smiled as I observed him, letting me know all was well, for once.

Tholdri cleared his throat. "And that is our cue to part ways until morning."

I looked at him, but his eyes were on Geist, and Steifan was already gazing in the direction of the hunters' camp.

"Until morning." I stood, ready to go to Asher.

The three of us parted ways, but only for the night. And in the morning, Steifan would leave us, but I knew it wouldn't be forever. *Some* bonds were too true to ever really be broken.

CHAPTER THIRTY-NINE

Asher and I sat in the firelight with the witches, telling stories and sharing pilfered temple wine. It was an odd feeling, being at home among so many souls, all of us different, but bonded together through bloodshed and loyalty. Ophelia and Ian had both been looking at me strangely, and I wondered if they could see what the ring had done, but neither mentioned it.

I leaned back against Asher's chest, content. The next morning, Tholdri and I would travel with the witches, and Asher and Geist would catch up to us in the night. For a time our paths would cross with the hunters' until they diverted further south to take a path around the treacherous mountains, rather than over them.

I had almost dozed off listening to Ian's tale about a girl who could turn into a wolf, when I sensed a familiar presence. With so much magic in me, it was easy for me to pinpoint exactly where she was.

I sat up, then leaned in near Asher's ear. "She's here. I'll return shortly."

His lips grazed my cheek as he turned his face to whisper, "I won't be far."

I stood, grabbing my scabbard from beside us just in case, then ventured into the darkness, following my magical senses more than my eyes.

It took me a while to find her atop a rocky outcropping near the sea. I didn't blame her for not coming near. Some of the witches might sense what she was, and the hunters weren't far off either, though she had obviously braved their ranks already.

I sat beside Ryllae without invitation, looking out toward the distant crashing waves, but keeping her in my peripheral vision. "Why did you do it?"

A soft smile curled her lips. "Whatever do you mean?"

"You planted whatever evidence Gregor found, and you used glamours to make him believe it."

"It was not so difficult."

I turned toward her. "Tell me why."

Her eyes darted my way, then her smile wilted. "I tried to go back to Silgard. I tried to do what I had promised, to go back to a life of helping others."

"*But*," I pressed, when she did not speak further.

She flashed another hint of a smile at my tone. "I could not let go of what I did to you, nor could I ignore the threat Eiric posed. It was my fault he was freed. I had to see what he was doing." She shook her head and looked down at her lap. "It was so much worse than I ever could have imagined. I shouldn't have trusted Amarithe. She had already proven to me countless times that to do so was folly."

I let out a long breath. "It wasn't your fault he was freed. It would have happened regardless."

"Still, I betrayed you. I needed to make it right."

"So you infiltrated the Helius Order, convinced them I didn't kill the Potentate, and prompted them to come here and welcome me back with open arms?"

She finally met my eyes, her small smile back in place. "Something like that."

I smiled back. "I forgive you for what you did. I have learned that sometimes, there truly is no *right* choice." I thought again of Cael—of who and *what* he was—and what he had given to protect me. To protect *everyone*. I had thought him a monster, once.

She was still looking at me, a little too intently. "Much has changed about you since we last met, Lyssandra. Your magic—"

"I know," I cut her off, not wanting to speak about it.

"And not just your magic," she pressed. "There is something else inside of you. What did you do?"

I knew I should have been guarded. Maybe she was just tricking me again, but my intuition told me otherwise. And she had recognized what my sword truly was— maybe she could tell me something about what the ring had done. I told her of the events of the previous night.

She did not seem at all surprised. "I thought it was something like that. But the ring did not simply give you power. It gave you . . . " She twirled her hand in the air, searching for the right words. "Itself. Demons are immortal. They do not die, they simply change form. It gave you what it was, so that it might fully move on."

I stared at her wide-eyed. "How can you tell?"

"Lyssandra, whatever you are now, you are *far* from human. There is a touch of immortality to you. I should know."

A lump formed in my throat. When I finally managed to speak, I simply croaked, "*What?*"

She shrugged. "Only time will tell what the effects truly are. The same will be needed to determine what your child will be."

My eyes bulged. My heart raced. "*What?*"

"So you didn't realize," she chuckled. "I'll admit, I was also surprised when I saw the truth within you today."

"That's not possible," I rasped.

"Lyssandra, you are a blood witch. Through your will alone, you can make almost anything possible. Your heart knew what it wanted, and it changed things to make the impossible possible."

My vision swam. It wasn't—It couldn't be.

Her brow furrowed as she observed me. "Oh no, I see I should have better prepared you for the news."

I swayed where I sat, then promptly lost consciousness.

The next thing I knew, Asher held me in his arms. I was pretty sure I had only been out for a few minutes, judging by the way my mind still reeled. I glanced around frantically, relaxing when I saw that Ryllae was still with us.

"I promise I didn't hurt her," she was saying. "She just got a little overwhelmed."

"I heard," Asher said softly, stroking my hair out of my face.

He had heard? He knew that I—that *we* . . .

He lightly kissed my forehead. "I love you, Lyssandra. Come what may, for eternity, I am with you."

My throat welled with emotion at thoughts of the future now being more frightening than ever. There was so much to say, but the only words I could manage were, "I love you too."

EPILOGUE

I stood atop the mountain overlooking the fortress, clutching a bouquet of snowdrops in my gloved hands. Snow swirled in the darkness, making the air almost painful, though at least this time I was dressed properly for it. The delicate flowers had frozen solid during the climb.

I had asked much of Drucida, Ian, and Ophelia in requesting they come at night, but it wouldn't have felt right without Asher and Geist present. And Tholdri—he didn't care that it was night and absolutely freezing, as long as he wasn't left out of the affair.

Asher placed a hand on my shoulder as I peered out into the swirling snow. Drucida had offered to erect a memorial in Cael's honor, but I had refused. It wasn't what he would have wanted. All he wanted—he had achieved.

There were no words to be spoken. We all knew the truth. One by one, my companions stepped toward the edge of the cliff, and I handed them each a frozen white

SARA C. ROETHLE

flower. We were all free to think our own thoughts and say goodbye however felt right. Ian and Ophelia had hardly known Cael, while Drucida and Geist perhaps knew him best of all.

And as for me . . .

I looked down at the single flower left in my hand, and I thanked my uncle for the love he had given me. With my eyes raised skyward, I tossed my flower out into the swirling wind. The other flowers joined mine, free to fall into the endless blanket of white.

Asher wrapped his arms around me, resting his palms on my belly through my thick coat. We could not say what the future would bring, but it was there, a brightly burning star in the night. We had fought for it, and we had won.

And by the light, I was going to savor every moment of it.

NOTE FROM THE AUTHOR

Dear reader,

I hope you enjoyed the final installment of A Study in Shadows! Thanks so much for reading. These characters mean the world to me, and it's been wonderful seeing how many of you feel the same way. I have many other series, some of which are listed at the end of this book if you'd like to check them out.

ALSO BY SARA C. ROETHLE

TREE OF AGES

Finn doesn't know what—or who—uprooted her from her peaceful tree form, changing her into this clumsy, disconnected human body. All she knows is she is cold and alone until Àed, a kindly old conjurer, takes her in.

By the warmth of Àed's hearth fire, vague memories from her distant past flash across her mind, sparking a restless desire to find out who she is and what powerful magic held her in thrall for over a century.

As Finn takes to the road, she and Àed accumulate a ragtag band of traveling companions. Historians, scholars, thieves in disguise, and Iseult, a mercenary of few words whose silent stare seems to pierce through all of Finn's defenses.

The dangers encountered unleash a wild magic Finn never knew she possessed, but dark forces are gathering, hunting for Finn and the memories locked away in her mind. Before it's over, she will discover which poses the greater danger: the bounty on her head, or a memory that could cost her everything.

Books in the Series:
Tree of Ages
The Melted Sea
The Blood Forest
Queen of Wands
The Oaken Throne
Dawn of Magic: Forest of Embers
Dawn of Magic: Sea of Flames
Dawn of Magic: City of Ashes

THE MOONSTONE CHRONICLES

The Empire rules with an iron fist. The Valeroot elves have barely managed to survive, but at least they're not Arthali witches like Elmerah. Her people were exiled long ago. Just a child at the time, her only choice was to flee her homeland, or remain among those who'd betrayed their own kind. She was resigned to living out her solitary life in a swamp until pirates kidnap her and throw her in with their other captives, young women destined to be sold into slavery.

With the help of an elven priestess, Elmerah teaches the pirates what happens to men who cross Arthali witches, but she's too late to avoid docking near the Capital. While her only goal is to run far from the political intrigue taking place within, she finds herself pulled mercilessly into a plot to overthrow the Empire, and to save the elven races from meeting a bloody end.

Elmerah will learn of a dark magical threat, and will have to face the thing she fears most: the duplicitous older sister she left behind, far from their home in Shadowmarsh.

THE WILL OF YGGDRASIL

The first time Maddy accidentally killed someone, she passed it off as a freak accident. The second time, a coincidence. But when she's kidnapped and taken to an underground realm where corpses reanimate on their own, she can no longer ignore her dark gift.

The first person she recognizes in this horrifying realm is her old social worker from the foster system, Sophie, but something's not right. She hasn't aged a day. And Sophie's brother, Alaric, has fangs and moves with liquid feline grace.

A normal person would run screaming into the night, but there's something about Alaric that draws Maddy in. Together, they must search for an elusive magical charm, a remnant of the gods themselves. Maddy doesn't know if she can trust Alaric with her life, but with the entire fate of humanity hanging in the balance, she has no choice.

Books in the series:

Fated

Fallen

Fury

Forged

Found

THE THIEF'S APPRENTICE

Liliana is trapped alone in the dark. Her father is dead, and London is very far away. If only she hadn't been locked up in her room, reading a book she wasn't allowed to read, she might have been able to stop her father's killer. Now he's lying dead in the next room, and there's nothing she can do to bring him back.

Arhyen is the self-declared finest thief in London. His mission was simple. Steal a journal from Fairfax Breckinridge, the greatest alchemist of the time. He hadn't expected to find Fairfax himself, with a dagger in his back. Nor had he expected the alchemist's automaton daughter, who claims to have a soul.

Suddenly entrenched in a mystery too great to fully comprehend, Arhyen and Liliana must rely on the help of a wayward detective, and a mysterious masked man, to piece together the clues laid before them. Will they uncover the true source of Liliana's soul in time, or will

London plunge into a dark age of nefarious technology, where only the scientific will survive?

Books in the series:
Clockwork Alchemist
Clocks and Daggers
Under Clock and Key

Made in United States
Troutdale, OR
01/01/2024

16597498R00268